Montana Hearts: True Country Hero

By Darlene Panzera

The Montana Hearts series
Montana Hearts: Her Weekend Wrangler
Montana Hearts: Sweet Talkin' Cowboy
Montana Hearts: True Country Hero

The Cupcake Diaries series
The Cupcake Diaries: Sweet On You
The Cupcake Diaries: Recipe for Love
The Cupcake Diaries: Taste of Romance
The Cupcake Diaries: Spoonful of Christmas
The Cupcake Diaries: Sprinkled with Kisses

Other Novels
Bet You'll Marry Me
(Originally appeared in shorter form as "The Bet" in the
back of Debbie Macomber's *Family Affair*)

Montana Hearts: True Country Hero

DARLENE PANZERA

AVONIMPULSE
An Imprint of HarperCollinsPublishers

Excerpt from Montana Hearts: Sweet Talkin' Cowboy copyright © 2015 by Darlene Panzera.
Excerpt from *You're Still the One* copyright © 2016 by Darcy Burke.
Excerpt from *The Debutante Is Mine* copyright © 2016 by Vivienne Lorret.
Excerpt from *One Dangerous Desire* copyright © 2016 by Christy Carlyle.

EPub Edition MAY 2016 ISBN: 9780062394729

Print Edition ISBN: 9780062394736

Avon, Avon Impulse, and the Avon Impulse logo are trademarks of HarperCollins Publishers.

10 9 8 7 6 5 4 3 2 1

In addition to romance, laughter, and suspense,
the Montana Hearts series celebrates families,
especially the bonds between siblings.
This book is for my brothers and their wives:
David and Karen Gant
Wayne and Carly Gant

Acknowledgments

I WANT TO thank my editors, May Chen and Gabrielle Keck, for the wonderful opportunity to write this series and for all your help along the way. I thank God for all His many blessings. And I'd like to thank my agent, Nicole Resciniti, my family, friends, critique partners, and Laurie Schnebly Campbell, who was an inspiring mentor during the creation of this particular story.

Chapter One

THE COWBOY WINKED at her. Delaney Collins lowered her camera lens and glanced around twice to make sure, but no one else behind the roping chute was looking his direction. Heat flooded her cheeks as he followed up the wink with a grin, and a multitude of wary warnings sounded off in her heart. The last thing she'd wanted was to catch the rodeo circuit star's interest. She pretended to adjust the settings, then raised the camera to her eye once again, determined to fulfill her duty and take the required photos of the handsome dark-haired devil.

Except he wouldn't stand still. He climbed off his buckskin horse, handed the reins to a nearby gatekeeper, gave a young kid in the stands a high five, and then walked straight toward her.

Delaney tightened her hold on the camera, wishing she could stay hidden behind the lens, and considered several different ways to slip away unnoticed. But she knew she couldn't avoid him forever. Not when it was her job to shadow the guy and capture the highlights from his steer-wrestling runs. Maybe he only wanted to check in to make sure she was getting the right shots?

Most cowboys like Jace Aldridge had large egos to match their championship-sized belt buckles, one reason she usually avoided these events and preferred capturing images of plants and animals. But when the lead photographer for *True Montana Magazine* called in sick before the event and they needed a fill-in, Delaney had been both honored and excited to accept the position. Perhaps after the magazine viewed her work, they'd hire her for more photo ops. Then she wouldn't have to rely solely on the profits from her share of her family's guest ranch to support herself.

She swallowed hard as the stocky, dark-haired figure, whose image continuously graced the cover of every western periodical, smiled, his eyes on her—yes, definitely *her*—as he drew near.

He stretched out his hand. "Jace Aldridge."

She stared at his chapped knuckles. Beside her, Sammy Jo gave her arm a discreet nudge, urging her to accept his handshake. After all, it would be impolite to refuse. Even if, in addition to riding rodeo, he *was* a hunter, an adversary of the animals she and her wildlife rescue group regularly sought to save.

Lifting her gaze to meet his, she replied, "Delaney Collins."

"Nice to meet you," Jace said, his rich, baritone voice smooth and . . . dangerously distracting. His hand gave hers a warm squeeze, and although he glanced toward

Sammy Jo to include her in his greeting, it was clear who held his real interest. "Are you with the press?"

Delaney glanced down at the Canon EOS 7D with its high-definition 20.2 megapixel zoom lens hanging down from the strap around her neck. "Yes. I'm taking photos for *True Montana*."

The edges of his mouth curved into another smile. "I haven't seen you around before."

"I—I'm not around much, but Sammy Jo here," she said, motioning toward her friend to divert his attention, "used to race barrels. You must know her. Sammy Jo Macpherson?"

Jace gave her friend a brief nod. "I believe we've met."

"Del's a great photographer," Sammy Jo said, bouncing the attention back to her.

Jace grinned. "I bet."

"It's the lens," Delaney said, averting her gaze, and Sammy Jo shot her a disgruntled look as if to say, *Smarten up, this guy's into you. Don't blow it!*

Except she had no desire to get involved in a relationship right now. And definitely not one *with a hunter*. She needed to focus on her two-and-a-half-year-old daughter, Meghan, and help her family's guest ranch bring in enough money to support them. Especially since her ex-husband hadn't made a child support payment for the last nine months. The money she did make she spent on lawyer fees trying to sort it all out.

Jace pulled his straw hat off his head and held the brim flat against his chest. "What are you two lovely ladies doing after—"

"Hey, Aldridge," a balding, middle-aged man with gray sideburns cut in with a shout. "Have you given any more thought to my offer to come hunt big game this fall?"

Delaney stiffened as Gavin McKinley joined them. His property lay a short distance down the trail behind her family's ranch and sometimes he crossed the line. *In more ways than one.*

"Don't have the time," Jace told him, then turned his attention back to her. "Del—"

"Delaney Collins," Gavin exclaimed, interrupting again. "Is that you?"

She'd already taken three steps back, hoping she could slink off while the others were talking, but she hadn't been fast enough. Gavin grabbed hold of her arm and spun her around. "It *is* you. I suppose you'll need to pick up some extra photography jobs now that Labor Day's approaching. Isn't Collins Country Cabins about ready to close up for the season?"

Delaney shook her head. "No. Actually, we've decided to stay open during the fall this year."

"Stay open?" Gavin's jaw dropped and he squinted at her as if he hadn't heard her right. "What for? Is your family trying to steal my business?"

"My family does not *steal*." Delaney swallowed the bitter saliva gathering at the back of her throat.

He also rented out guest cabins, not nearly as nice as her family's, but perfect for the barbarian hunters he housed, equipped, and led on backcountry expeditions.

Jace stepped between them, forcing Gavin to drop his arm away from her. "Mr. McKinley, you'll have to excuse us. I'm scheduled for a private photo shoot before it's my turn to compete and we only have twenty minutes."

To Delaney's relief, the outdoor outfitter hesitated a moment, glanced at each of them, and then stormed away in a huff.

"Good one," Sammy Jo said, smiling at Jace with approval.

Jace grinned and once again Delaney watched his gaze turn toward her. "Will I see you at the Chuck Wagon later?"

"Uh . . ." Del looked up into his dark-lashed killer green eyes, and the hope she saw within tripped up her tongue.

"It's a barbeque for today's competitors and their friends," Jace clarified, as if she didn't know what he meant. "If you don't have access, I could get you in."

"Me? No. I—I'm here with, uh, Sammy Jo," she said, heat rising into her face as she fumbled the words.

"She's included in the invitation," Jace amended, "of course."

"Of course," Delaney repeated, reminding herself, *He's a hunter, like the monster who just left*. She hesitated as the horrifying image of Gavin shooting the beautiful young doe she'd nursed back to health when she was sixteen played out once again in her mind. She'd never forgotten, nor forgiven him. "But . . . I—I'm just here to take pictures."

Sammy Jo gave her another small jab and Delaney winced. Not from pain, only from her own inadequacy at intelligent speech. If she kept talking, most likely the rodeo hero would realize she couldn't put two sentences together in his presence and leave her alone.

Except he didn't seem to be through with her yet. His grin widened into a full smile, one that consumed half his face and displayed rows of perfect white teeth that would probably make most women weak in the knees. She wasn't most women.

"All right, then," he relented. "Can I have my picture taken?"

She nodded. "Of course."

"With you?"

Just when she thought they were finally about to get back to business. "I—I don't think that's what the magazine is looking for."

Jace let out a small chuckle. "Not for the magazine," he corrected, "for me." He gave Sammy Jo a quick look and nodded toward Delaney's camera. "Would you mind?"

"Not at all," Sammy Jo said, her eyes alight with mischief. "I'm not a professional, but I can take a decent shot. C'mon, Del, get closer to him and turn around."

"I—I don't let anyone else touch my camera," Del protested, voicing the first excuse that came to mind. "It, uh, cost a lot of money."

"Are you serious?" Sammy Jo exclaimed. "Del! What's the matter with you?"

"That's okay," Jace soothed. "I understand. How about we use the camera on my cell phone?"

Sammy Jo nodded. "Perfect."

Delaney frowned as he whipped out a phone from the inside pocket of his lightweight jacket and handed it to her friend. The man probably collected photos of women from every town he pulled into along the rodeo circuit. His cell phone was probably full of them. Why would Sammy Jo want to encourage him? However, rather than cause a scene, she did as she was told. Better to get it over with so Sammy Jo wouldn't make a big deal of it, as she had an infuriating way of doing.

Taking a step closer to the man, she glanced up into his face and the intensity of his gaze stole her breath. She glanced away and turned toward the camera. His arm wrapped around her, warming her back through her light cotton short-sleeved shirt, and he rested his hand on her shoulder. With a slight tug, he pulled her even closer.

"Say cheese!" Sammy Jo instructed.

Jace's smooth, alluring voice repeated the word. Delaney didn't say anything, but counted the seconds in her head. One, two, three . . . why wasn't Sammy Jo clicking the picture?

"Just give me another few moments here," her good friend said, another mischievous grin spreading across her face. "I want to make sure I get it just right."

"Sammy Jo!" Delaney hissed, realizing she was stalling on purpose.

"Relax, Del," the matchmaking menace coaxed. "Let's see that pretty smile of yours."

"It *is* pretty," Jace whispered against her ear. "As pretty as the sun rising over the horizon."

Delaney smiled at the ridiculous pickup line and a flash of light from the cell phone let her know that Sammy Jo had finally taken the picture.

"Thank you," Jace said as she stepped away. "How about you give me your number so I can send a copy to you?"

Smooth. Definitely smooth. However, Delaney wasn't taking the rodeo hunter's bait. Steeling her resolve, she shot the cowboy an apologetic look and with as much courage as she could muster she warned, "You got the picture. That's enough."

He looked as if he was about to protest, but Delaney quickly escaped out of earshot and made her way around the other side of the fenced arena.

"What are you doing?" Sammy Jo demanded, following at her heels. "If you'd played along you could have had a date tonight."

"I don't want a date," Delaney whispered. She peeked back over her shoulder and realized she was trembling.

"I think you do," Sammy Jo countered. "You're just afraid every man you date will turn out to be a jerk like Steve."

Delaney ignored the reference to her ex. "I'm happy to be alone."

"Someday, you'll change your mind," Sammy Jo predicted, "when the *right* man comes along."

"Jace Aldridge is *not* that man," Delaney said, and let out a small laugh. "In fact, I'm surprised he noticed me at all. It must have been my camera flash that drew his attention."

"Del," Sammy Jo scolded. "You're too hard on yourself."

"The guy's famous," she argued. "Even people who don't follow rodeo follow him. It must be the hair. All the ladies seem to love the way his wispy, dark brown hair falls over his forehead."

"Yes!" Sammy Jo squealed. "And you got your picture with him. You could have sent it in to the magazine and had *your* photo on the cover, too."

"I'll let others enjoy the limelight," Delaney assured her. "I don't need attention."

"You could have at least asked for his autograph," Sammy Jo insisted, "for Meghan."

Delaney laughed. "What would a two-and-a-half-year-old want with Jace Aldridge's signature?"

Sammy Jo shrugged. "I don't know. It could be worth a fortune someday."

Delaney thought of her ex-husband and the money he hadn't paid her. Maybe Sammy Jo was right. Maybe she *should* have asked for the rodeo star's autograph. Then she could have auctioned it off when Meghan was older and needed college tuition—if people still knew who Jace Aldridge was by then.

Too late now. The moment was lost. And after the cold brush-off she'd given him, she doubted Jace would waste any more of his precious time on her again. Within five minutes he'd forget her name, and within ten he'd forget she even existed.

JACE GRINNED AS she walked away. The blond-haired, blue-eyed beauty was interested in him even if she didn't give him her number. He could tell by the way her eyes widened and her lips parted when she gazed at him with that cautious yet yearning expression, which had several beats of his heart tripping all over each other.

He leaned his arms on the rail of the crowded rodeo arena as one of the bronco riders shot out of the gate. The noise level from the stands rose with cheers, applause, and whistles as the buckin' cowboy struggled to remain saddled. But as impressive as the wrangler's ride was, Jace found more pleasure watching Delaney.

She stood to the side of the announcer's box, her camera raised to her eye and her hands twisting the round lens back and forth to make adjustments as she snapped photo after photo. Her friend Sammy Jo stood beside her, and despite the fact that both women's attention was fixed on the excitement going on in front of them, their differences stood out like salt and pepper.

While Sammy Jo had hair almost as dark as his own, Delaney's long tresses were a light blond, like a sweeping halo of sunshine. Sammy Jo certainly had the curves, but Delaney's slim figure appeared more graceful when she moved, which he found more attractive. And while Sammy Jo posed confidently in front of the camera lens, giving the rider in the arena a thumbs-up, Delaney appeared more comfortable behind it.

He didn't relish the media attention or ask to take pictures with every new woman he met but something curiously sweet about the camerawoman had tugged at him the moment he saw her. Maybe it was the attentive way she went about her work, as if she truly cared about the quality or was passionate about the subject matter. Jace had hoped it had been the latter. He pulled up the photo of the two of them together on his cell phone and glanced at the smile she'd flashed at the last second. He may have acted like an attention-seeking fool, but he didn't regret it for one moment.

Not for that shot.

And if she wouldn't give him her phone number, he'd find another way to get to know her better.

Jace got his idea to draw her attention while prepping for his turn to ride. He'd sent a messenger over to the announcer booth beside her and adjusted his feet in the stirrups as he waited to hear, "Ladies and gentlemen, our next competitor straight out of Phoenix, Arizona, wishes to dedicate his next ride this evening to one special cowgirl—a Miss Delaney Collins."

She dropped the camera away from her face and looked right at him the moment the announcer said her name. Except instead of being flattered, she looked . . . mortified. She wasn't wearing a ring but maybe he should have asked if she was single before being so bold. It would make sense that someone as pretty as her would already have a boy-friend. Maybe *that's* why she was reluctant to have her picture taken with him. He wished he could go over and find out, but he had to enter the bulldogging box.

He gave a quick nod to his longtime pal and fellow competitor Bucky Knowles, who had agreed to be his hazer tonight. He trusted few people other than Buck to keep the steer running in a straight line so he could slide out of the saddle and wrestle it to the ground. Most people didn't realize how important a role a hazer played, but he and Buck had both been around long enough to know that one slight turn could make or break a run.

They'd grown up holding on to the tails of steer,

"surfing the dirt" around their daddies' fields together since grammar school. Then when they were older they wrestled steer to the ground right out of the chute—chute dogging, most called it. By the time they each had their driver's license they'd learned to slide from a mounted saddle attached to the back of a tractor driven at thirty miles per hour down onto a fake steer fastened to a second vehicle. The next step, of course, had been to get comfortable performing that same feat from the back of a horse.

Now he and Bucky toured around pro rodeos and often agreed to help one another when it wasn't their own time to ride for score. For there had never been nothin' like the thrill of bulldogging. Nothing else that could pump him with as much adrenaline and heart-pounding excitement.

"Hey, watch the leathers," his gatekeeper warned, pointing to the dangling leather strips hanging down below his stirrups.

Jace adjusted his weight in the saddle and glanced down toward his boot. "Yeah, I had a strap break right before I mounted up and had to replace it. Didn't have time to trim off the excess."

Because he'd spent too much time thinking about Delaney.

But he'd be all right. After all, he was a pro. And once he and his horse raced out of the chute to chase down the steer, Delaney's eyes would be focused solely on him, her camera zooming in to bring his expertise into vivid clarity. Maybe *then* . . . she'd be impressed enough to give him her phone number.

He leaned down and gave his horse, Rio, a good pat.

Then he signaled the gatekeeper with a nod of his head, the chute opened, and the steer burst into the arena. Careful not to cross the breakaway rope barrier until the appropriate time, Jace chased after the five-hundred-pound Corriente, riding up on one side of the animal, while Bucky rode up on the other.

Turfing the steer within four to five seconds usually got him a paycheck, but to win the big money he had to move lightning fast to flip the steer over onto its back within three. His left hand released the saddle horn as he slid off his horse . . . dropped down . . . and got a firm hold on the steer's horns. Everything was perfect. Everything had gone the way they had a thousand times before. Except this time, his foot got hung up in the stirrup.

He kicked with his toe but his boot wouldn't slip out. One of the leathers had wedged itself tight beneath the sole, trapping his foot inside the bell-shaped metal ring like a rabbit in a snare. His horse veered to the left, trying to balance his weight as he hung down the opposite side, and Jace had to let go of the steer to try to free himself. Rio stumbled, and Jace bounced twice along the ground, almost hitting his head. Then with a gut-clenching squeeze, he reached up and grabbed his leg, only half-aware of the roar of the crowd and pounding hooves around him.

"Jace, hang on!" Bucky rode close enough to lay a hand on his shoulder.

His friend tried to hold him up so his own horse wouldn't kick him, but by the time Rio slowed to a stop, he'd already been dragged halfway around the arena.

DELANEY GASPED AND clutched the rail in front of her, her pulse racing. She'd stopped taking pictures after Jace, hanging upside down with his foot caught in the stirrup of his galloping horse, hit the ground a second time.

"He could have been killed," Sammy Jo exclaimed, her eyes wide. "He could have been trampled by the steer or if he'd slipped his foot out any earlier . . . run over by his own horse!"

"They've cut the leathers," Delaney said, her voice breathless. "Jace is standing. Wait. Look." She sucked in her breath and held it, unable to breathe. "His horse is favoring his left leg. He—he can barely walk."

Her stomach squeezed tight as the rodeo star knelt in the dirt and ran his hands over Rio's left hock. The animal flinched and pulled his hoof away. Oh, *no*. That wasn't a good sign. A few of the other cowboys also bent down to take a look, and as Jace glanced her way, his worried expression played havoc with her emotions. Even if he was a hunter and as conceited as she supposed, one thing was certain—he cared about his horse.

"I have to go down there," Delaney said, turning around and scanning the stands behind her for the nearest exit. "I know he's not my horse, but I can't stand seeing any animal in pain and I won't be able to sleep tonight until I make sure Rio is going to be all right."

"But, Del," Sammy Jo called after her. "Security won't let you through."

"I'll find a way," Delaney said, weaving in and out among the crowd. She glanced left, then right, spotted the arched tunnel, and hurried through.

"Del, wait up," Sammy Jo urged from behind.

"There's no time to lose," Delaney said, dodging several more groups of people as she wound her way around the stadium to the private competitor grounds. "You know what kind of poor decisions some of these rodeo veterinarians make!"

She almost bumped into a concession stand boy carrying a large boxed tray of lemonade, but she swerved just in time. Sammy Jo wasn't so lucky. Behind her, there was a crash, followed by a high-pitched squeal. A flurry of irate voices followed, but Delaney didn't turn around; she kept going, and kept a sharp look out for the buckskin horse with his magnificent black mane and tail.

There! Straight ahead, not far from the area behind the roping chutes where they'd first met, Jace stood with a group of others, his face drawn as they examined Rio's injury. At least the horse had managed to walk out of the arena. She couldn't bear the thought of what would have happened if he couldn't.

She considered both the helpfulness and limitations of various homemade healing remedies as she picked up her pace, but just as she flew past the last metal fence post she was brought to an abrupt halt by two men dressed in blue security uniforms who had moved toward one another to block her path.

"Sorry, miss," one of them warned, holding his hand up in front of her. "No media beyond this point."

Delaney glanced down at her camera. "I'm a friend of one of the competitors. I have to see him. You have to let me through."

The security guard shook his head, then raised his walkie-talkie to his mouth to respond to an incoming message, signaling their conversation had come to an end. Delaney wished she had the courage to stand up to them, but what else could she say? What else could she do?

Behind her the ground shook with the thunder of running feet and she turned around just in time to catch a glimpse of the incoming stampede. The herd was led by Sammy Jo. And a small band of angry concession workers chased after her like bulldoggers after a steer, threatening to plow right into them.

The security guards separated as they threw out their arms to prepare for the onslaught, and after reading the silent word, *Go*, on Sammy Jo's lips, Delaney took the opportunity to slink around and sneak right on by.

JACE'S BODY ACHED. He'd have some serious bruises come morning, but it was the ache inside that hurt worse as he looked into Rio's eyes. He ran a hand over his horse's sleek, golden neck, guilt twisting his gut into a tight knot.

It was his fault. He hadn't heeded the gatekeeper's warning about the loose leather straps hanging below his stirrups. He couldn't blame it on his preoccupation with the pretty blond photographer either. No, it was his own ego that was to blame. Taking out his pocket knife to shorten the leathers only would have taken a second, but he'd thought it wouldn't matter . . . that he was too good . . . that something like this would never happen to him.

Rio stood stock-still, his left foreleg slightly bent as he held it a couple inches off the ground. Thank God he'd been able to hobble along and make it out of the arena. One of the rodeo workers had the flatbed truck ready to drive in, in case they'd had to put the horse down, but Jace waved them away.

Now he wondered if he'd just delayed the inevitable.

He'd just stepped back to stand beside Bucky, and an assortment of other concerned rodeo pals to let the veterinarian conduct a thorough examination, when a small blond head popped into their midst. *Delaney?*

She glided toward him and shoved her camera into his hands. "Here—hold this."

Didn't she see that he was busy? That he had other things to—

He hesitated as she spun around, dropped to her knees beside the vet, and asked, "What do you need?"

"Not sure yet," the on-site rodeo vet told her.

"A cold pack?" she asked, withdrawing one from his black bag. "Or a splint?"

"Who are you?" the doctor demanded. "A veterinarian?"

Jace had been wondering the same thing.

Avoiding the question, Delaney continued. "Maybe you want to wrap the leg first with a flexible bandage?"

Frowning, the doctor took the roll of gauze and tape Delaney offered him, and said, "Jace, there's a good amount of swelling and the horse is in obvious pain. There's a possibility the bone fractured from the pull of balancing your weight when you were hanging off the other side."

Jace spit out the remaining dirt he'd collected from the arena floor and wiped his mouth with the back of his hand. Although he'd suspected as much, *that* wasn't the news he wanted to hear. "But you're not sure?"

"I've seen worse," Del assured him, running her hand over his horse's leg. "The fact Rio walked out of the arena on his own says something. He can be given painkillers. And there's no outward signs that it's an injury that can't heal. There's heat and a little swelling, but—"

"*Are* you a veterinarian?" the rodeo vet demanded again, narrowing his gaze upon her.

Delaney hesitated. "No, but I—"

"Jace," the vet said, cutting her off in annoyance, "I can take the horse to the hospital for a comprehensive evaluation with an MRI and CT scan, but before you put out the money you might want to consider the quality of life he'll have afterward. Even if it's just a torn ligament there's a good chance Rio will never compete again. You might want to just put him out of his misery right here and move on."

"Move on?" Delaney shouted, rising to her feet, her expression incredulous. "*Jace,*" she pleaded, her big, blue, beautiful eyes full of heartfelt concern. "You can't make a decision like that without knowing all the details. Certainly Rio deserves a chance, doesn't he?"

Some injuries couldn't be healed and left the horse in continuous pain. Putting a horse down under those conditions often seemed the better fate. However, she was right. Rio deserved a chance. No matter the cost. They'd competed together at pro level the last five years and Rio was solid in the box, scored well, and ran hard. He was also a friend, one who had never let him down, and now it was his turn to return the favor.

"I want him tested," Jace told the vet. "And if the results are promising—"

"He may never race out of a chute again," the vet warned.

Jace continued. "And if the prognosis looks good—"

"Even then," the vet said, shaking his head. "It could take months to recover."

Jace nodded and held Delaney's gaze. "He'll have his chance to live a long, happy life."

Chapter Two

DELANEY CARRIED THE brown rabbit she'd found outside Cabin 5 to the laundry room and set it on the counter where the guests at Collins Country Cabins usually folded their clothes.

Her daughter stood on her tiptoes, gripped the edge of the flat surface with her small fingers, and peered over the edge. "Is he going to be okay?"

"Yes, Meghan," she said, giving what she hoped was a reassuring smile. "After I clean the wound, he'll be back hopping around in no time."

Taking a lukewarm water bottle from her shoulder bag, Del held the rabbit still with one hand and flushed the leg wound clean with her other. She figured her furry friend got in a fight with another animal. Maybe a cat, a hawk, or maybe even another rabbit. The lacerated skin had opened up to a one-inch circle and looked terrible, but it would heal fast. She didn't see any bite marks and the affected area only had minimal swelling.

The rabbit flinched and jerked forward to escape her hold, but she held tight. Then she put the water bottle down and stroked the soft fluffy hair along its back to ease some of his tension. "Meghan, can you get me a towel off the shelf in the corner?"

The screen door screeched open and Delaney's slender, fair-haired mother walked in, her eyes wide as she warned, "Not our guest towels!"

Meghan hesitated, as if unsure what to do. Her lower lip trembled. "The bunny needs a blanky."

"Oh, honey," Loretta Collins soothed, her face instantly contrite. "I wasn't yelling at *you*."

"It's okay, Meghan," Delaney said, avoiding her mother's gaze. Shrugging off her jacket, she wrapped the thin blue cotton material around the animal to dry its leg. "This will work the same as a towel or blanket."

"What is that creature doing in here?" her ma demanded. "Delaney, if your father finds out about this—"

"He won't," Del said, hugging the rabbit close.

Meghan put a finger to her lips. "Don't tell."

Delaney's ma glanced back and forth between them. "I won't tell," she conceded, "*this* time. But, Delaney, you know how your father feels about you turning this place into an animal shelter."

Yes, she knew. Her gruff, hard-nosed father often said, "*It's not safe or sanitary for our guests.*"

"And, Delaney?" her mother continued, meeting her

gaze and nodding toward the counter. "Make sure you spray that with sterilizer to get rid of any rabbit germs."

"Rabbit germs are pee-yew?" Meghan asked.

"Yes," Delaney's ma said with disgust. "Rabbit germs can make you sick. Why don't I take you into the house to wash your hands?"

Delaney wished she had the courage to speak up and voice her opinion about what made a person sick. But she didn't dare talk back to her ma. Or do anything to cause a scene. Her older brother and sister had done that on more than one occasion and it never led to anything but trouble.

Taking the rabbit outside, she released it in the brush behind the row of cabins lining the river, then shook out her jacket and put it back on. The air grew cooler each week, reminding her fall was on its way. Big change from last year when she and Meghan were living in San Diego. Southern California never got as cold as Montana.

Except when one was going through a divorce.

Her cell phone buzzed and she pulled it out of the back pocket of her jeans. "Hello?"

A noisy tirade of angry words assaulted her ears. The only information she clearly picked out was that her caller was one of the editors from *True Montana Magazine*.

"Didn't you get the pictures?" Delaney asked, hardly daring to breathe.

"Most of them, but what about the competitors *after* Jace Aldridge?" the editor demanded. "We don't have any images of them."

Because she hadn't taken any. She'd known when

she left her post she was putting her job and any hope of future work for the magazine in jeopardy, but her concern for the golden gelding had been greater.

"When I saw Mr. Aldridge's horse was injured, I went to assist the veterinarian."

"Miss Collins, we wanted you to photograph the rodeo, not care for the animals. We thought you were a professional."

Delaney stiffened. "I'm sure you'll find the photos I did send are top quality, and the real story from the rodeo is all about Jace Aldridge anyway."

"I'll decide what the real story is," the editor said in a huff. "Not you. That's *my* job."

Glad this was not a face-to-face conversation, Delaney swallowed hard and nodded. "Yes, ma'am."

"Since your photography of the event did not live up to our expectations," the editor continued, "I'm not sure we can pay you the amount we agreed on."

"I'll take a pay cut," Delaney offered, hoping to appease the woman.

However, by the end of the phone call, it was clear the editor did not intend to pay her anything at all.

Delaney thought of her mad dash through security, with Sammy Jo's help, of course, to get to Rio's side. Was it worth it?

Of course it was. If she hadn't intervened, that brash rodeo veterinarian would have had everyone thinking the horse might be better off if he were put down. Her actions might not have gained her a paycheck, but it might have saved a life.

And she could live with that.

Sliding her phone back into her pocket, her thoughts turned to Jace and the devastated look on his face after the horrendous ride. The cowboy's earlier flirtatious banter hadn't had any real effect on her but that look—when she ran up and saw him beside his injured horse—*did.*

His suntanned face had paled, the muscles in his cheeks and jaw pulled tight, and he'd pressed his lips together like she did when she was about to cry. Except cowboys as tough as Jace didn't go around shedding tears in front of each other. No, he held it in, and it was at that moment that her heart went out to the rodeo hero.

She also liked the wise, diplomatic way he'd answered the veterinarian. Instead of jumping the gun and putting a perfectly sound horse down for no good reason, he'd ordered the tests. Which saved her from having to pro-test. *Whew!* She would have done it, if she'd had to. But the horse didn't belong to her; it wasn't her call.

Her wildlife rescue group would have had a fit if they knew she'd taken on the photography job. They'd warned her many times about the sport's cruelty to animals. But Delaney wasn't sure she shared their view. After all, Sammy Jo had raced barrels and always had the utmost concern for her horse's welfare. And it didn't appear as if the accident in the arena had been Jace's fault. She'd ridden all her life and she, too, had got her foot caught in the stirrup once or twice.

Accidents happened.

Digging through her shoulder bag, she took out the

business card Jace had given her and stared at the telephone number beneath his name. Did she dare call and ask how Rio was doing?

Delaney had slipped away when he and the vet loaded the horse into the trailer to go to the animal hospital. She'd told herself it was to make sure Sammy Jo hadn't gotten herself into any real trouble. The angry vendors forgave her friend when they took a look at her big shiny barrel-racing belt buckle. But the real reason Delaney had slipped away from Jace was because she hadn't wanted to talk to him again. It appeared the horse would be properly taken care of and her mission was complete. There had been no more need for interaction and maybe it was best to keep it that way. Even if she was anxious to hear news of the gelding's condition.

She wavered back and forth for several long moments trying to decide what to do, then dropped the card back into her shoulder bag. She wouldn't call. She'd go into town and buy the local Sunday paper instead. No doubt if there was any news about his horse, she could either find it there or listen to the gossips hanging around the general store.

After letting her ma know what she was doing, she grabbed the keys to the family's red rusty pickup. In a small two-block town like hers, news traveled fast and she got an earful, all right. Except the chatter coming from the townspeople's mouths wasn't about Jace or his horse. It was about Fox Creek Outfitters and how the owner, Gavin McKinley, was trying to put her family out of business.

JACE COULDN'T ESCAPE. The local reporters hounded him wherever he went. They called, they flooded his social media, and even pounded on the door of his hotel room. He hadn't ventured out much for fear of being followed, but when he did, he saw the photos.

The front page of the newspapers featured large images of him hanging upside down off the side of his horse, reminding him of his failure again and again. They even showed a close-up of the tangled leather straps around his boot. He thought of the slender, pretty blond he'd met and wondered if any of the photos were from Delaney Collins's camera.

He hoped not. At the time, she'd appeared more concerned about him and his horse than winning a prize shot for her magazine. And he'd like to think that at least one person had more consideration for his predicament than these other bothersome cameramen and reporters. Even if it was her job.

And to think he'd dedicated that ride to her, hoping to get her attention. He got it all right, along with every other media source chronicling the rodeo community. It had been one of those days when he would have welcomed a do-over. Too late now. What was done was done and all he could do was move forward.

Except, not with Delaney. He'd been touched by the look of concern on her face when she rushed in to take a look at his horse, but then she rushed out again afterward without saying goodbye. She probably thought he was a self-righteous jerk and with good reason. He'd acted like one. He'd lost more than a large cash purse at that rodeo.

He'd lost the soundness of his horse, he'd lost a chance at *her*, and maybe even his rodeo career. His friends had all urged him to continue riding, told him what happened was an accident and that they believed in him. Some even offered up their own horses for him to ride in future events.

But Jace didn't want to have to learn the quirks of another animal right now. He didn't want to have to think about cues or how best to communicate with someone new. He and Rio were a team, and besides, he could use this time to think about what he wanted to do with his future. Sooner or later, his body would give out, too, and he would have to find a different career.

Jace put his sunglasses on, and keeping his head down, he walked from his hotel room to the local restaurant for a bite of food. He glanced at his watch. Almost two p.m. The main lunch crowd should have cleared out by now, giving him the privacy he craved, but the Bozeman Stampede had drawn hundreds of visitors into the area. He'd be a fool to think he could remain hidden for long. He'd have to eat and run before anyone recognized him.

It was because he kept his gaze turned toward the wall of buildings that he caught sight of Gavin McKinley's big bold outfitting poster tacked to the bulletin board outside the hardware store, and recognized Delaney's last name hanging out below. He stopped short to look at the advertisement and realized there were two posters on top of one another.

Gavin's poster contained photos of hunters with an elk head, a black bear, and a mountain lion, and proclaimed that if you wanted to hunt there was only one outfitter to choose—Fox Creek Outfitters: The Best in the West. Except whoever had put it up hadn't done a very good job and the bottom fragment of the Collins Country Cabins advertisement still stood out.

Curious, he tore Gavin's poster away and gazed at the one beneath featuring a beautiful two-story log lodge, with a row of outlying guest cabins beside a fantastic fly-fishing river. There was also a stable, a small arena, and an octagon gazebo *"perfect for weddings."* Jace thought that the dude ranch—surrounded by pockets of green trees, open fields rising into soft rolling hills, and panoramic views of the distant mountains—seemed perfect for anyone.

Glancing across the street, he spotted several other posters and realized Gavin McKinley hadn't just covered *one* of the Collins posters, he'd covered *all* of them. And this wasn't even either of the two rivals' hometown. They were both located in Fox Creek, a good half hour from Bozeman, which meant Gavin may have spread his posters across the entire region. No doubt the bothersome outfitter thought he could drum up business while wiping out his competitor's at the same time.

His hunger forgotten, Jace tore each of Gavin's offensive posters down, stuffed them under his arm, and deposited them into a nearby dumpster. Then he jumped in his truck and headed straight for the animal hospital to check on Rio and receive the test results.

The veterinarian at the hospital was more encouraging than the one he'd encountered at the rodeo. "The good news is that Rio's injury should heal just fine," the doctor told him.

Jace released his breath and relaxed as a truckload of worry eased off his shoulders. "Thank God for that," he told the doc. "I don't want to lose him."

"There's no break, but he's strained the tendons all along the side of his leg and will be out of competition for the rest of the season," the doctor warned.

"I already figured as much." Rio nuzzled his nose against Jace's side and he gave the horse's sleek neck an affectionate pat. A year ago the prospect of dropping out of a winning streak, giving up his chance at the championship, and holing up in Montana would have aggravated him to no end, but lately he'd found himself thinking he might need a vacation. "I guess we'll head back to Arizona and catch up on some sleep. Get ourselves some decent home-cooked meals."

Maybe he'd even look into buying his own ranch.

The doctor shot him a hesitant look. "Rio will need stall rest for several weeks before it's safe to travel."

Jace hesitated. "Weeks?"

"You can trailer him to a nearby stable, but I wouldn't recommend you take him all the way to Arizona until he regains some of his strength. A long trailer ride bouncing along the highway could do even more harm to the affected area. Maybe damage his leg permanently."

"Can't he stay here until he's ready to leave?"

The doctor shook his head. "Our stalls are limited and I need the space for other incoming patients. How about your mother's place or your friend Bucky's?"

Jace shook his head. "Bucky's family doesn't have a stable. And my mother sold our ranch years ago and bought a house in town. It's perfect for her, but there's no room for horses."

"That's too bad." Frowning, the doctor said, "I can give you some names, but the number of stables out here are few. Most ranchers keep their horses outside in the fields, not in stalls. However, I'm sure that if you drop your name they will make room for you."

In other words, use his fame. Jace glanced at Rio's swollen leg and then up into his trusted rodeo pal's eyes. "I'll do whatever is best for the horse."

DELANEY ENTERED THE noisy dining room of the main house and searched the scores of people sitting at the rectangular tables for a familiar face. She found only a few. The new guests for the week had arrived, and had apparently brought their appetites along with them. Her mother and grandma stood behind the serving counter, along with the seventeen-year-old Walford twins, dishing out portions of roast beef, fried chicken, mashed potatoes, biscuits, and gravy onto pinecone-patterned porcelain plates.

"You're late for dinner," her mother said, shooting her a worried look. "You know what your father would say."

"That I need to be here to help the family," Delaney replied. She waved the rolled poster she'd confiscated from town. "Ma, I have something I *must* show you."

"Not in the middle of dinner." Her ma handed her an

apron. "Now set whatever you've got there aside and get to work."

Delaney hesitated and glanced across the room at her older sister, Bree. Would *she* let the news wait?

"Delaney!"

Her attention snapped back to her ma and she quickly tied the apron around the waist of her overalls and slipped the accompanying bandana over her hair so no wayward strands would end up as an added surprise in the guests' food.

"I'm not sure I like this new cook we hired," Grandma complained, picking up a piece of chicken from the bowl with a pair of tongs. "I use cornflakes to bread my chicken, not seasoned bread crumbs."

"The cook insists on using her own recipes," Delaney's ma whispered. "At least give her a chance. You can't cook every meal. You'll wear yourself out."

"What do the guests think?" Delaney asked, serving the person in front of her in line for seconds.

"They love it," her ma answered, arching a brow.

Grandma scowled and Delaney fought to hide a smile. Her headstrong grandmother didn't like change any more than she did. And now that they were all back under one roof living together again, there had been many changes.

This time around Delaney, Bree, and their brother, Luke, had each been given a portion of the ranch. One-sixth to be exact. Their grandma, mother, and father held the other three shares. Which meant they each needed to do their part to help Collins Country Cabins succeed, despite the trouble they'd been having with others who wanted to put them out of business.

Another change occurred when just weeks after her return Bree got engaged to their weekend wrangler, Ryan Tanner, who had a seven-year-old son. Her older sister would be a *mom*. Like her. Now they'd have lots to talk about and that three-year gap between them wouldn't feel so large.

And just last month, her older brother, Luke, proposed to their friend and next-door neighbor, Sammy Jo. Never in a million years had Delaney expected to see *him* anxious to marry. But stranger things had happened.

Like her divorce to Steve. She'd once thought he was the one for her. She'd never been so wrong. And now . . . well, she wasn't sure of anything anymore. That's why it was better for her to leave most decisions to the other older and wiser members of her family. They always knew what to do.

Just like Grandma did, when Delaney let her see their rival's poster and explained where she'd found it. Her grandmother's bushy white brows drew together, and after scrunching her face into a sour expression, she commanded in a half snarl, "Everyone get to the kitchen!"

No one questioned Grandma. The matriarch of the family even got Delaney's father's attention. However, that didn't stop him from coming down hard on *her*.

"Delaney, what the devil is this about?"

Ugh. She hated having everyone's eyes on her. Her chest tightened, her palms grew sweaty, and the back of her throat closed up as she tried to speak.

"Spit it out, girl," her father shouted. "We haven't got all day."

Instead of trying to explain, she unfurled the rival out-fitter's poster and held it up in front of her, hiding her face.

"Gavin McKinley went and put his posters over all the ones we spent our hard earned money on," Grandma told them.

Delaney heard Bree gasp first. Then Ma let out a high-pitched squeak. Luke and Sammy Jo's voices murmured back and forth, followed by a deep, guttural growl that could only have come from Delaney's father.

"Who does he think he is?" Jed Collins demanded.

Delaney peeked around the poster and grimaced. "That's not all. I think he's spreading rumors. Several people in town are saying they heard Gavin McKinley call Collins Country Cabins a second rate lodging facility that is constantly having trouble staying open."

"That's not true!" Bree protested. "Ever since we hosted the Hamiltons' wedding a few weeks ago, business is booming. Every cabin is booked several weeks out."

"That's not true either," Ma said, her tone rising into a high-pitched squeak. "This morning we had several cancellations."

"Most likely due to this *smear* campaign," Luke said, his jaw tightening.

"This is an outrage," their father thundered. "What makes Gavin McKinley think he can run our name through the mud?"

"Maybe the fact he's the sheriff's son," Sammy Jo pointed out.

"I could talk to the sheriff about him," Grandma offered.

Delaney thought that might work. Her grandma and the sheriff had grown close and were on the brink of "officially" dating.

"But why would he do this?" Ma asked, her face going pale.

Delaney sighed. "He's mad we're staying open for fall."

"We only decided to do that a week ago," her father said, narrowing his gaze. "Who told him?"

Delaney swallowed hard. "I did. Yesterday. At the Bozeman Stampede. Now Gavin thinks we're going to steal away his business."

"He would have found out one way or another," Grandma sympathized. "But how was he able to produce so many posters so quickly?"

"Stores can print them up in less than an hour," Bree informed her.

"What about us?" Ma asked. "Can we print up more of our own advertisements?"

"We'd do better with a good endorsement from a reputable source," Bree said, and snapped her fingers. "What about the Tanners? Everyone knows they have the largest cattle ranch this side of Fox Creek. Ryan could issue an endorsement."

Delaney thought that might work, too. Another possible solution to their problem.

"As thrilled as I am to have him as my future son-in-law, his personal reputation went through the ringer last month when the newspaper printed that suggestive photo of him in the stable with those three young visiting females pretending to be CEOs," her father reminded them.

"He was set up," Bree defended.

"Ryan's endorsement wouldn't count because he's engaged to Bree and working here on weekends. People would say he's playing favoritism," Ma added, backing up their father.

Luke agreed. "We need a reputable person from the outside, someone not associated with our family. We can invite them to our ranch for a two-week stay and ask for an honest, unbiased review."

Grandma's face lit up. "Someone famous. Like Clint Eastwood?"

Del smiled. "Then you would finally get to meet your hero."

Her eighty-year-old grandma loved the western movies the actor had made, which might be why she found Sheriff McKinley attractive, even if he *was* ten years younger than her—he was a protective gunslinger fighting for justice.

"How about one of those rodeo cowboys you were photographing for that magazine?" Delaney's father asked, his gaze boring into her. "Didn't you meet that guy from Arizona who's in the boot commercial on TV? The one whose mother lives here in Montana and is running for governor?"

"Jace Aldridge," Sammy Jo said, answering for her.

"That was the name on the card I found on the floor," Ma said with a frown. Pulling a white business card from her apron pocket, she asked, "How do you think this got here?"

Delaney's mouth fell open as she glanced into the adjoining dining room and spotted Meghan playing with the contents of her purse.

Sammy Jo followed her gaze and smirked. "Looks like Meghan found the card Jace gave Delaney, the one with his *phone number*. He was flirting with Del at the rodeo."

"Shh!" Delaney warned, giving Sammy Jo a stern frown.

"Is it true?" Bree's eyes widened. "Why, he's the biggest thing to hit the rodeo circuit in the last five years. The press follows at his heels. '*Where Jace goes—*'"

"'*The media follows,*'" Sammy Jo and Bree quoted together, and smiled.

"His reputation is clean," Luke agreed. "He doesn't have throngs of women hanging all over him like some of the other rodeo stars."

"Are you suggesting we invite Jace Aldridge to our ranch?" Delaney asked. Her voice cracked on the last word and had risen almost as high as her mom's.

"He'd be a prime candidate," her father said, his tone suddenly upbeat. "And since he already has his eye on you, there's a very good chance he'd say yes to our proposal . . . especially if you are the one who asks him to come."

Delaney gasped. "Me?"

Bree nodded. "You can be our new public relations liaison."

This was *not* a good idea. Not after she refused to give him her phone number. Besides, as ranch manager, shouldn't her sister be the one to call?

"I think we'd have much better success if you do it, Bree. I'd rather just stay with the horses."

Ma shook her head. "Bree's engaged. So is Sammy Jo. He already likes you and you're the only gal around here free to flirt with him."

"Now you want me to flirt?" Del stared at her ma in disbelief. She didn't want to pretend to like him. She was still recovering from her divorce.

"She does *not* have to flirt," Bree protested. "All she has to do it be herself. But Sammy Jo and I could coach her on what to say and how to dress like a true public relations representative."

Delaney hesitated. "What's wrong with the way I dress?"

"A little style wouldn't hurt," Bree said, shooting a pointed look toward her overalls.

Delaney scowled. If her sister had her way, she'd insist on a complete makeover. She turned toward her brother, hoping he'd protect her. "Luke?"

He shook his head. "You are our best bet, Del. We need that endorsement."

Sammy Jo agreed. "You can do it, sweetie."

Sometimes being the youngest wasn't fair. And she hated it when Sammy Jo called her "sweetie," as if she were thirteen instead of twenty-four.

Ma smiled at her. "You'd be helping the family."

"Who will help me watch Meghan?" Delaney demanded. "I can't talk to Jace about an endorsement with my two-year-old on my hip."

Her father frowned. "Why not?"

Ma shushed him into silence and assured her, "We can all help watch Meghan."

Everyone else nodded, even her father.

"We'll invite Jace to stay two weeks," Bree said, lifting the top page of the calendar on the wall to take a look at the upcoming month of September. "After that, he'll leave and you can go back to giving the guests horseback riding lessons. And all will be well."

Just like that?

Delaney looked to her father, whose gaze was upon her and expectantly awaited her answer. How could she say no? Especially when Bree and Luke had both stepped up to do their part over the last few months to help save the ranch. By default, it was her turn. And as much as she wanted to turn tail and run, she couldn't let them down. She couldn't let them think she was shirking her responsibility. Not when she needed them and the ranch profits to help provide not only for her needs but for her daughter's.

Delaney took the card from her ma. "I'll call him," she said, "but there's no guarantee he'll say yes."

What if he did? And wanted to hunt? Her family might not share her passion for saving animals, but she could not invite that man here and watch him put the wildlife around her in jeopardy. Her anxiety rose higher as she thought of the way he'd stolen her breath when he held her gaze, how her pulse had quickened when he'd drawn near, and the fact he'd already stirred her emotions with genuine concern over his horse. If she wasn't careful—very, *very* careful—her heart could end up at greater risk than her beloved animals.

For while they at least had a chance, she didn't think she could survive having her heart broken a second time.

JACE CAME AWAY from the third ranch on the list the veterinarian had given him disappointed. The facility had an available empty stall, all right. But half the side boards had been broken, the stall door didn't latch properly, and the place in general had been a dump. He wouldn't have Rio recovering in a place like that. Or in a cramped, noisy stable like the first two he'd visited.

He opened the door to his truck and was about to climb in behind the wheel when his phone rang. Lifting the phone to his ear, he said, "Hello?"

No one answered and for a moment he thought maybe the caller had hung up. Then a soft, sweet voice he remembered said, "Mr. Aldridge, this is Delaney from Collins Country Cabins. I'm, uh, also a photographer and we met this past weekend at the Bozeman Stampede PRCA rodeo?"

As if he could forget. He grinned. "I know who you are."

Her family's ranch had been first on the list but the last one he'd wanted to contact. Mainly because he didn't think Delaney wanted anything to do with him. She hadn't even wanted to take his business card. Yet, here she was, calling *him*.

"Mr. Aldridge—"

"It's *Jace*."

"Yes, I know, but I'm calling for business purposes."

So she thought she had to be more formal? He grinned. "I'm listening."

"First—how is Rio?" Her voice cracked on the last syllable of his horse's name.

"I thought you said you wanted to talk business," he teased.

"I'm sorry, I do, but first I just have to know—what were the test results?"

Jace leaned against the side of his truck wondering when she'd get to the part when she admitted that she had been thinking about *him* a lot, too. "Rio's leg wasn't broken."

"And?"

"If Rio can't compete in rodeos, I'll retire him. He'll spend the rest of his days feasting on field grass, rolling in the dirt, and having fun."

Jace heard a sound come through the receiver, almost like a sigh of relief. "That's good. Real good."

Speaking to *her* was good. He smiled, picturing her pale blond hair and sweet face in his mind. A face with blue eyes, delicate brows, a pert little nose, and lips he'd like to cover with his own.

"So what else did you want to talk to me about?" he prompted.

She cleared her throat. "My—my family would like to offer you a complimentary two-week stay at Collins Country Cabins."

He could hardly believe his ears. "You want me to stay at your ranch? For free?"

"My family would be honored."

"I'd planned to head back to Arizona, but the vet said Rio can't travel for a few weeks. He needs a quiet, indoor stall where he can rest. Do you have space for him, too?"

"Of *course*!"

Jace chuckled, impressed once again by her compassion for his horse. No doubt seeing Rio again would make her happy. And the prospect of spending two whole weeks with Delaney didn't strike him as a bad thing either.

Her words and her actions were backed by true emotion, as if a fire burned within her heart, driving her forward. Too many people he met these days were either robotic or indifferent. Busier than they'd ever been but for no real good reason. He feared he might even be one of them. But maybe Delaney could help change that. Everything she did—from adjusting her camera lens, to sidestepping his attention, to dropping down on her knees to assist the vet—was filled with both passion and purpose. Just like this phone call.

Of course he'd accept her invitation, but to uncover the real reason behind it, and he knew there *must* be one, he decided to have a little fun with her first.

"What else do you have to offer?" he asked playfully.

"We'll give you one of our finest luxury cabins with a riverfront view and three home-style cooked meals a day," she said, her voice as vibrant as a radio commercial.

"And?" He smiled as he waited for her reaction.

"You can, uh, borrow one of our horses to go on trail rides. There's fishing. And opportunities for other things," she added with exuberance.

"I hope so." Jace chuckled, his thoughts taking a more devious turn than he imagined she'd intended. "What else?"

She hesitated. "What else do you want?"

"Your phone number?"

"Oh, you can reach Collins Country Cabins at—"

"Not your business phone number," he amended. "I need your personal number."

Again, she hesitated. "My cell phone number? What for?"

"To send you our photo," he said, and taking a leap of faith he hoped he didn't regret, he added, "and to ask you out on a proper date."

"Mr. Aldridge—"

"The name's Jace," he reminded her.

"I don't date the guests, no matter how important they are."

"Bummer," Jace teased, undeterred, and let out a dramatic sigh for her benefit. "I guess I was hoping in my particular case you'd make an exception. How about it?"

She paused, then sidestepped his question with one of her own. "When can we expect to see you?"

Okay, he'd play her little game her way. "The vet said to give Rio a couple more days before I relocate him. How about Thursday?"

"Thursday is perfect."

"All right, then. I'll be there around four o'clock. I just hope I can get Rio into the trailer without too much strain to his leg."

"Do you need help?"

Jace didn't think he and the vet would need assistance, but because she offered, he wasn't going to refuse. "Yeah, I could use your help. I'm sure Rio would appreciate it, too."

"Okay, I'll meet you at the veterinary hospital at three p.m.," she said cheerfully. Then she gave him her phone number. Her *personal* cell phone number. "In case you have to change the time," she told him.

Jace grinned, proud of himself for the mini-victory. Hopefully tomorrow he'd win one more.

Chapter Three

EARLY THE NEXT morning, the phone rang and the first thought that ran through Jace's mind was that Delaney had changed her mind and was going to retract her incredible offer. He hoped not. He'd spent half the night thinking about what it would be like to get to know her better.

A knot formed in the pit of his stomach when he rolled out of bed and glanced at the caller ID, but the call wasn't from Delaney. It was from Bozeman Health, the hospital nearest his mother.

"Jace, you should come quick. Mom's in the emergency room," his older sister said, her voice strained. "She clutched her chest and collapsed in the hallway right in front of me. I thought she was having a heart attack but the doctor says it was just a bad case of anxiety."

"Anxiety from what?" Jace asked. "Running for governor?"

"No, of course not," Natalie scoffed. "You know she can handle that."

Their tough-as-nails, persevering mother had over-come many hurdles in the past, including raising two children on her own after their father passed away. Jace didn't remember him—he'd only been a toddler—but he did remember how resourceful his mom had been to get the money they needed to put food on the table. Grace Aldridge worked two jobs—one at the bank, which taught her how to invest, and another typing transcripts for a lawyer, which opened her eyes to the justice system and inspired her to pursue a political career.

"What's wrong, then? Why is she stressed?" Jace held his breath as he waited for his older sister to answer. Was someone trying to blackmail her? Or threatening a new ploy to convince Democrats to vote for the Republican candidate? Did she have a stalker?

"We'll tell you when you get here," Nat replied.

Women! Why won't they ever say exactly what they mean?

Jace scowled. Arguing and trying to pull the infor-mation out of his sister over the phone would only waste time. Instead, he told her he'd be there as soon as he could, grabbed his belongings, and checked out of the hotel room. But before he started his truck, his sister called a second time with news the hospital had released their mom and he was to meet them at their house.

A few minutes later, just before nine a.m., Jace made his way up the slate steps of the two-story Victorian and found he had to whip out his driver's license for the armed security guard stationed outside her door before the guy would let him in. Since when did his mother need a security detail? His pulse quickened as he continued forward and found his mother and sister seated in the living room. He went straight to his mother's side.

"How are you feeling?" he asked, giving her a hug.

"Better," his mom assured him. "I don't know why I let that letter shake me up like that."

Jace's studied the pale, gaunt expression on her face and his throat ran dry. "What letter?"

Natalie took a folded piece of paper from an envelope on the coffee table beside her and handed it to him. Assorted letters from the alphabet in all different fonts and sizes had been cut from advertisements and pasted together to form one sentence in the middle of the page.

Step down from the candidacy if you want to live.

"The letter was sent to her in a box with a dead rat inside," Nat added. "A dead rat in a rat trap. We figure it's from one of the poaching rings she claims she'll abolish when she's elected governor."

"Did you call the police?" Jace asked. "What did they say?"

His sister shrugged. "They're looking into it."

"I could stay here for a while, until the election is over," Jace offered.

"No, absolutely not," his mother exclaimed. "I won't have you alter your own plans."

"My plans are already altered, due to my recent mishap in the arena," Jace said, taking a blanket off a nearby chair and tucking it around her.

"Mishap? Dragged around the arena and almost killed is what I heard," his mother scolded. "Jace, it's time you took better care of yourself, settled down. There's more to life than rodeo."

His mother never did share his love of adventure. Or bulldogging. Or horses. That was probably the reason she sold their family's ranch and moved to Bozeman a few years after his father died. But by the age of seven, Jace had already been bit by the rodeo bug and continued to spend as much time as he could after school and on weekends at Bucky's ranch.

Unfortunately, his sister didn't. Natalie had never even ridden a horse. Claimed she didn't want to, which was maybe one more reason why they'd never been extremely close. While he and Bucky were riding and wrestling steer, she'd be at the library with her friends attending writing classes and reading books.

"Mom's also been contacted by some animal rights activists," Nat said, her tone holding a note of accusation. "They claim rodeos should be banned and are using your accident as a prime example of how the sport endangers animals."

His mother nodded. "They call themselves Montana Wildlife Rescue and several offshoots of the group have branched out across the state. One of them is located in Fox Creek."

Jace took a seat across from them. "Is it possible they sent you the threat?"

"They do lead protests from time to time, but I doubt they're dangerous. Mostly, they find homes for abandoned horses, nurse injured wildlife back to health, and write articles to promote public awareness."

"I was invited for a two-week stay at a ranch in Fox Creek," he said, wondering if he should speak to this group, try to get them to leave his mother alone.

"A ranch in Fox Creek?" For a moment his mother looked startled. Her eyes widened and she sat straight up in her chair, dropping the blanket he'd tucked around her to the floor. "*Which* ranch?"

"Collins Country Cabins."

"I've heard of them." His mother's expression relaxed, but her tone remained wary. "They're a small ranch with big trouble. Earlier this summer the husband and wife team they'd hired as their ranch managers embezzled their money and fled in the middle of the night when the three adult Collins children came home. They've had trouble staying open for business ever since."

He didn't know about the embezzlement. Poor Delaney. That must have been hard on her family. No wonder she had to take on extra photography jobs.

"They have a stall where Rio can heal," Jace said, picking up the blanket and tucking it around her again. "And I can get from Fox Creek to Bozeman in a half hour if you need me."

"Hopefully we *won't*," Natalie said with a scowl, then she gave him an apologetic look. "But it sure is good to see you, Jace. I missed you."

"We both missed you," his mother said, and arched her brow. "Maybe while you're here you can visit a few realtors and see about buying a ranch up here?"

He grinned. "Instead of going back to Arizona?"

"I can't have you raising my grandchildren three states away," she warned.

"Mom, I'd bet my best buckle Nat has kids before me."

"And right now neither one of us is even dating," Nat chimed in. "Right, Jace?"

"Right," he agreed. "Although I do have my eye on Delaney Collins, and hope she might help change that status in the near future."

His mother laughed. "In that case, I like her already. If you won't stay up here in Montana for me, maybe you'll stay here for her."

Although his mother and sister were all smiles when he left, the threatening letter his mother had received stayed fixed in his mind. Deciding he should do something about it, Jace drove his truck up the familiar dirt lane leading to Bucky Knowles's old ranch just ten minutes away. His best friend's father had been a game warden for Montana Fish, Wildlife and Parks for years, and had recently become an undercover agent. No doubt he'd know the general location of a poacher or two.

When he knocked at the door, both Buck and his father invited him in for coffee. It didn't take long for Jace to explain why he was there. "If you hear of any poachers who might be responsible for the threat to my mother, you'll let me know?"

"Of course," Eli Knowles said, and leaned forward, placing his hand on Jace's shoulder. "But you might be able to help me as well."

"Help you?" Jace looked the man straight in the eye. "How?"

"You said you're going to be staying in Fox Creek?" When Jace nodded, Eli continued. "I've been hearing rumors about a big poaching ring in that area. And you—a wealthy rodeo star who's known to love a good hunt—are exactly the kind of person these outfitters like to lure in with promises of catching big game. You could do some investigating, keep your eyes and ears open as you visit a few of the neighboring ranches."

Jace nodded. "I could find out who threatened my mother."

"Maybe," Eli agreed. "But poaching is a huge problem across the entire state, not just in Fox Creek. There's just not enough game wardens to uncover them all. The threat to your mother could have come from any of them."

"I know," Jace said. "But if I manage to find one illegal outfitting operation, they might have information on some of the others."

"Now don't go getting yourself into any trouble," Eli warned.

Jace grinned. "Do I ever?"

Buck laughed. "Always."

"Remember, if you come across anything, you need to contact *me*," Eli said, giving him a stern look.

Jace gave the man an affirmative nod. "Understood, sir."

"Guess that means traveling with me down to the rodeo in Reno this weekend is out of the question," Bucky said, and slapped Jace on the shoulder. "I wish you luck."

"You, too," he told him, and with a pang of regret Jace realized this would be the first big rodeo he'd miss in over five years. "Win one for the both of us."

THURSDAY MORNING, DELANEY rode her copper-colored horse, Fireball, back to the stable after a glorious walk around the property. She'd checked on the horses in the outdoor paddocks, the cows in the pasture, and the injured animals she'd secretly bandaged and tucked away in the old abandoned toolshed along the far border. Meghan sat in front of her in the saddle and together they waved to the guests as they passed by the cabins lining the river.

"Again!" Meghan exclaimed.

"I'd love to circle around again," Del said, kissing the top of her daughter's blond head. "But I promised Bree I'd get dressed for the special guest we have coming this afternoon."

"Again!" Meghan repeated, and giving in, Delaney smiled.

"All right," she said, wrapping her arms around her child and giving her a hug. "How about this time, you let go of the saddle horn and help me hold on to the reins?"

"C'mon, Fireball," Meghan commanded in her soft, high-pitched, squeaky voice. "Giddyup!"

She'd be a fine, young, talented cowgirl someday, Delaney mused. And meet a handsome cowboy who would sweep her off her feet and take her to live on the finest ranch in the Great Northwest. Just like Bree and Sammy Jo, who were both busy planning their weddings.

Delaney had never cared much about finding that special someone for herself until just a few years ago, and now that she'd survived that disaster, she was content to stay single. She gave the quarter horse beneath her a gentle pat. Fireball would be the only male she'd ever need. She was only sorry she'd ever left him at all. While she'd been living in San Diego, she'd missed him terrible. And now that she was back she vowed never to leave him again. She could always count on Fireball to love her unconditionally—with no strings attached.

"Delaney get in here," Bree shouted from the doorway of the main house after they'd circled around a second time. "You're late!"

"And you promised to let us help you," Sammy Jo said, peeking her head over Bree's shoulder.

Delaney handed Meghan off to her mother, who promised to put her daughter down for a nap, then dismounted and looked at Luke. "Can you un-tack Rio for me?"

Luke gave her a warm smile. "Sammy Jo would have my head if I didn't. Go on. They're waiting for you."

No more excuses. Drawing in a deep breath, Delaney followed Bree and Sammy Jo up the stairs of the main house to Bree's bedroom.

Bree had been a fashion designer in New York before coming back home to manage the ranch this summer. Now in addition to balancing the ranch's financial ledgers, she created her own boot bling jewelry and cowgirl clothing fashions and sold them in their ranch office, in a shop in town, and in an online store on the internet. Delaney considered Bree to be the expert in both business and fashion, so who was *she* to argue with her sister's choices?

But she couldn't help but tremble as she gazed at the assortment of floral, plaid, and paisley dresses laid out on the bed, the collection of cosmetics spread out on top of the dresser next to Bree's jewelry, and the dozens of magazines on the end table offering corporate advice on how to woo a client. Was she ready for this?

"First, ditch the overalls," Bree instructed.

Delaney did as she was told and slipped on the first dress her sister handed her, the white floral print donned with miniature roses. The V-necked bodice hugged her figure, and the attached flirty skirt flounced around her thighs. "I don't have to wear these things the whole time he's here, do I?"

Sammy Jo laughed and swiped a fat, soft brush tipped with pink powder over her cheeks. "Consider them work clothes. As a public relations representative you need to look professional, not like you just milked a cow."

"Then the sooner I get the endorsement, the better," Delaney said as she looked longingly at the faded denim overalls that Bree had kicked into the corner.

Bree raised her brows. "I thought you could look at this as a permanent position. Growing our relationship with the public and the guests who visit our ranch is an ongoing need."

"But I don't even know what to do," Delaney protested.

"First you'll want to give Jace a tour of the ranch," Bree

said, handing her a clipboard of statistical information she could rattle off to him. "Then you'll want to check in with him every day to make sure he is engaging in some of the ranch activities and having a good time."

"There are worse jobs than spending time with a handsome man," Sammy Jo teased.

"He's handsome from a distance," Delaney admitted, "but up close his smile is too wide and his eyes are too sharp."

"How can eyes be sharp?" Sammy Jo demanded.

Delaney shrugged. "I don't know. Maybe it's the angle of those dark brows, or his dark lashes that create the look, but all I do know is that it's too intense, like a hunter with his gaze on the tip of the arrow."

"Or on his prey." Bree laughed. "I love it when Ryan looks at me like that. That's when I know I have his full attention."

Delaney frowned. "I don't want anyone's attention. Especially not his."

"You used to think Jace Aldridge was the most handsome man you ever laid eyes on," Bree teased. "You even had a poster of him on the wall in your room."

"That was years ago, when he was just starting out in rodeo, *before* I knew he was a hunter."

Her sister gave her a pleading look. "We need you, Del. The whole family is counting on you."

"I know." However, in the back of her mind, Delaney couldn't help thinking about that time in middle school when she'd been forced into a part for the school play. Thankfully the teacher hadn't cast her into a starring role, but during the performance she'd tripped and fallen off the stage. Everyone laughed, except the cute boy she secretly had a crush on. He accused her of ruining the whole show and scoffed, "Stay in the background where you belong."

His words had haunted her ever since.

"Now for the hair," Bree said, pulling the bands off the ends of Delaney's braids and spreading her hair apart. "I think we need to go for a looser, more sophisticated look."

"Sophisticated?" Delaney cringed. "I thought you told Ma I should just be myself? Now here you are trying to turn me into some kind of corporate Cinderella."

"We *do* want you to be yourself. We're just polishing up the outside," Sammy Jo said, smiling and picking up a slim black-and-gold tube. "Here, open your mouth."

Delaney tried not to panic as her friend rolled a sticky substance over her lips. "What is it?"

Sammy Jo rolled her eyes. "Lipstick, of course. The color is pink champagne. I think it will go nice with the blush on your cheeks."

Ugh. She'd never worn lipstick in her life. "It doesn't taste very good."

"You're not supposed to eat it, you goose!" Sammy Jo said, shaking her head. "Sorry, I didn't have time to buy any flavored lip gloss to wear over it at the store."

A soft knock rapped on the door and Grandma walked in. "I can't let you girls have all the fun," she said in her gravelly voice. "I have something for her, too."

Moving behind her, Delaney's grandma slipped a silver chain necklace around her throat, and when

Delaney looked in the mirror, she saw it held a dark, hook-shaped object.

"Is this what I think it is?" she asked.

"The claw of a bear," her grandma confirmed, "given to me from my father."

Delaney stiffened. "He didn't kill it, did he?"

"No. He found it down by the river. A mama bear tried to protect her cubs, attacked another bear, and chased it away. She lost a toe in the process, but she won. That mama bear did what she had to do to protect her family."

Relaxing, Delaney said, "Now I'm the mama bear?"

"Oh, no," Bree protested. "That necklace won't go with the look I had in mind for her at all!"

"I like it," Delaney said, smiling. "Thank you, Grandma."

"The claw on this necklace symbolizes courage," the older woman informed them. "And it's going to take more courage than you can imagine for our young Delaney to stand up to that high profile rodeo star and demand he give us an endorsement at the end of his two-week stay."

Delaney gasped. Stand up to him? *Demand* an endorsement? She clutched the bear claw in the palm of her hand and held it tight. "I don't think I can do this."

"Okay, keep the bear claw," Bree conceded, and bit her lip. "We can work around it. Maybe we can give you more of a rustic, romantic look."

"I gave Bree a teal scarf to give her courage when she faced down Ryan Tanner," Grandma told Delaney. "And

I gave Luke the engagement ring he used to propose to Sammy Jo."

"Luke needed lots of courage for that," Sammy Jo confided. "Having the ring in his pocket definitely helped."

"And now you think this bear claw will give me the courage I need?" Delaney asked, glancing at each of their faces.

"They say, '*Courage can only truly come from within,*'" Grandma quoted. "But yes, that necklace gave me the courage I needed when I first met your grandfather and I am sure it will give you the courage you need to face your young man, too."

Delaney's mouth dropped open. "But—I'm not looking to get engaged."

"Of course not," Grandma said with a nod, and smiled. "The best relationships are those we never see coming. Makes us appreciate them all the more when they arrive."

Grandma tapped her wrist and then pointed to the clock on the wall and recited another of her famous quotes, "'*Don't waste time you won't get back.*'"

Delaney suppressed an inward groan. Yes, she'd already done enough of that in her life.

Lifting her chin, she vowed to remain positive, just like her grandma. After all, she was doing this for her family. For Meghan. And for herself. The fate of their ranch rested on her and she would not disappoint them or let fear make her back down. She could do this. She would look her best, act her best, make sure Jace Aldridge had the absolute best time while he was here, and hopefully convince him to give Collins Country Cabins the best endorsement they'd ever had.

At the very least . . . she'd give it her best shot.

JACE WAITED OUTSIDE the animal hospital, and at three p.m., Delaney Collins met him as promised. She arrived in a dusty old red pickup with several dents in the side. But when she opened the creaky door and stepped out, he could see there was nothing wrong with *her*.

She wore a white flowery dress with not a speck of dust on it. Her hair fell loose over her shoulders in shiny, soft waves, and her face was alive with color accenting her natural beauty. She was beautiful. Perfect. A little *too* perfect. She hadn't been wearing that much makeup when he'd last seen her. Someone as pretty as her didn't need to wear makeup at all, but he didn't mind. Especially since she must have taken the time to spruce herself up for *him*. She probably had wanted to make a good impression.

A warm thrill of anticipation shot up his spine and he grinned. "You dressed up pretty fancy to help load a horse."

The rosy color on her cheeks deepened but she didn't comment. Instead, she glanced toward the building and asked, "Is he ready?"

Jace didn't know about the horse, but knew *he* was. Ready to spend time with her. Lots of time. "Rio is inside. The vet is giving him a final look before we leave and said he'd drive out to your place to check on him again tomorrow to see how he's settling in."

Delaney shook her head and frowned. "He doesn't have to do that."

"I asked him to," Jace said, his voice coming out raspy and uncomfortably low. A flood of guilt continued to engulf him every time he thought of the accident and his injured pal. He was afraid that animal rights group might be right. He shouldn't have been so confident about his own performance. He should have cut the leathers when he had the chance. *Before* his ride.

Delaney's expression softened and although she didn't touch him, or even come near, the look of compassion in her eyes reached out and drew him to her more than any amount of dressin' up ever could.

He cleared his throat and opened the wide side door to the hospital. "Shall we?"

Rio hobbled along step by slow step, but other than a few seconds of hesitation here and there, he gave Jace and Delaney next to no trouble when they went to load him into the back of the horse trailer. It was almost as if all his fight was concentrated on supporting his leg as he moved forward. Jace gave him an affectionate pat on the neck and whispered a few lines of encouragement into his dark mane before locking him in.

"He'll be all right," Delaney assured him.

Jace nodded. "I'll drive slow."

This time she *did* touch him. On the arm. "Slow is best," she agreed.

Other trucks on the road passed him, including

Delaney's, but Jace didn't care. His only concern was for Rio and his injured leg. He didn't want to take any sharp turns or hit any potholes too fast. Just one hard stumble could damage Rio's injury beyond repair. And he wouldn't let that happen. From now on, Rio's well-being would come before anyone else's, including himself.

He didn't realize how tight he'd been clenching his knuckles until he came to a stop in the parking lot of Collins Country Cabins and pulled his hands off the steering wheel. His fingers ached, the muscles in his jaw ached, and his gut felt as if he'd taken a punch. Stepping down from the truck, his legs almost buckled. He'd been *that* stiff. Stiff with worry.

Now that they'd made it, Jace relaxed, and took a deep breath. The crisp clean air cleared his lungs and refreshed his brain. He'd had a lot on his mind the last few days. It would be good to get away for a while, away from the circuit, schedules, long drives, flashing cameras, and the limelight. Not only would he have time to spend with Delaney but he'd also have a chance to decide what he wanted to do if Rio couldn't return to rodeo.

"Look! It's *Jace Aldridge*!"

"He's here! Oh my gosh, pinch me! I can't believe this is real!"

"As real as you and me!"

Jace turned his head toward the series of squeals that followed and saw the two redheaded girls just two seconds before they had their hands on him. They each grabbed an arm and gazed up at him with identical sets of starstruck hazel eyes.

"Oh, Mr. Jace, can I have your autograph?" one of the twins asked.

"You can sign your name on my arm," said the other.

Thankfully Delaney appeared. "Nora and Nadine, let the man be."

However, the twins either didn't pay attention to her or didn't care to listen.

"I'm Nora," the first introduced. "And—"

"I'm Nadine!" finished the second. "We're going to be cover models for the new flyers advertising the ranch. Your endorsement will go right beneath our picture on the front page."

"Good to know," Jace replied. *Indeed.* Delaney didn't mention an endorsement when she'd invited him here. He'd thought it was because she wanted to spend time with him. He'd thought she'd only used the *"I'm calling for business purposes"* as a ruse to get him to agree to come. He'd also assumed that maybe she'd just been playing "hard to get."

Disappointment hit him in the chest and it took a moment for him to recover. "Is it true?" he asked, giving Delaney his attention, instead of the girls. "Did you invite me here hoping to get an endorsement for your ranch?"

He had his answer the minute all the rosy color drained from Delaney's face.

"Yes," she admitted. "We *are* hoping. Of course we'd like your honest opinion of Collins Country Cabins. But in the meantime, we hope you enjoy your stay."

Jace winced. Bucky would slap him on the back and laugh his ear off right now if he were here beside him.

He'd say, *"Good one, Jace!"* in that mocking draw of his, and continue with, *"I can tell she's really fallen for you—in your dreams."*

He wouldn't have blamed Buck for saying it either, because he would have said the same to him if their positions were reversed. There was no denying the truth.

Once again, he'd been too confident in himself.

"So how did you two meet?" Nora prodded.

Seemingly unaware that she'd exposed the Collinses' motives, her sister Nadine added, "Are you two dating?"

Delaney glared at the two of them and said, "No, we're just—"

Jace waited to see what she'd answer. Exactly what *were* they? He watched Delaney frown, as if even she didn't know.

"We're just—" Delaney repeated, and her voice faltered.

"Friends," Jace finished for her.

Delaney gave him a startled look but didn't correct him, and he grinned. The fact she needed his endorsement gave him the upper hand, which he fully intended to use to his advantage. She'd have to spend time with him, plain and simple. Lots and lots of time, during which he hoped to become *more* than friends.

"We can be your friends, too," Nora said, smiling. "Would you like us to show you to your cabin?"

Delaney shook her head. "No, we have to unload his horse and get him to his stall."

The twins pouted and Nadine pulled out her cell phone. "Let us at least get our picture with him. Can we, Jace, please?"

Without waiting for an answer, the girl pushed the icon for the camera feature, held her phone up, and snapped a photo of him with her and her sister.

"Someday, we'll all be famous," Nora announced, "and we'll all star in—"

"Commercials on TV," Nadine cut in.

"Or maybe even Hollywood movies," Nora added.

And then, laughing, they gave each other a high-five hand slap and chorused, "Score another one for the Walford twins!"

Jace wondered if he should turn around, get in his truck, and leave, but the twins left first. And the rest of what he assumed was the Collins family had come out of the large main building on his left to greet him.

Delaney introduced her grandma first, Ruth Collins, whose late husband had built the ranch decades before. Then he met Ruth's son, Jed Collins, who looked a lot like her, and Jed's wife, Loretta, who was an older replica of Delaney. Then there was her sister, Bree, and brother, Luke.

All were a little overfriendly and overeager to shake his hand and welcome him. All except the two men in grubby chaps, flannel shirts, and cowboy hats who stepped out behind them and stood off to the side. They were similar enough in appearance with their brown hair and brown eyes and other physical features that he assumed they must be brothers. But not related to the Collinses. Maybe they were close friends of the family, or a couple of the ranch hands.

Bree gestured toward each of them and called, "Ryan, Zach, don't you want to come meet, Jace Aldridge?"

Neither of the two men moved, or smiled, and a muscle twitched along the side of the older brother's jaw revealing some kind of tension. Then after an awkward moment of silence, the one Bree indicated was Ryan informed her, "We know who he is."

Jace narrowed his eyes. *How* did they know him? Had they met somewhere or did they simply mean they were familiar with his name and *weren't* fans? He decided to find out. Walking toward them, he stretched out his hand, but dropped it to his side when it became evident they didn't intend to shake.

Both Bree and Delaney had followed him, and when they, too, noticed his cold reception, both women looked at each other in surprise. Then Bree went to Ryan's side and introduced him. "Jace, this is my fiancé, Ryan Tanner."

"Tanner?" Jace studied the two men further. "I have an aunt who lives somewhere around this area who married a Tanner."

The younger of the pair, the one he assumed was Zach, said, "Yeah, our mother."

Jace did a double take and gasped. "We're *cousins*?"

Delaney shot her sister an incredulous look. "Bree, did you know about this?"

Bree shook her head and stared at her fiancé. "Ryan?"

The muscle along Ryan's jaw twitched again. "His father was my uncle, my mother's brother."

"My father died when we were young," Jace said, seeing a family resemblance between them all now in the shape of their jaw. "I don't remember him."

Ryan scowled. "My mother remembers him and she remembers your mother, too—and what she took from us."

Jace stared at him, not having a clue what he was talking about. "What did she take?"

Ryan didn't answer but Zach raised his chin and said, "Why don't you ask her?"

He would. As soon as her health improved. But for now his mother had enough stress without him adding more to it by peppering her with questions about the past.

Zach moved closer to Delaney. "Are you busy tonight?"

She hesitated, cast Jace a quick look, then said in a sweet, soft voice, "Yes, Zach, I am, but maybe we could get together another time."

Whoa! Were they dating?

Zach tipped his hat toward her as he and Ryan made a move to head off toward the open-sided arena. "I'll take that as a promise."

A promise, my foot! The guy sounded like a fool flirting with her in front of everyone like that. Jace couldn't be sure but judging from the way Delaney looked at the young man, she wasn't as taken with him as he was with her. Then again, maybe Delaney wasn't taken with anyone.

Delaney didn't say anything else, but walked past Jace's truck and unlatched the back of the horse trailer, apparently determined to get Rio out and into a stall before he could change his mind and take the horse back to Bozeman.

And take his much needed *endorsement* away with him.

Chapter Four

WHEW! SHE'D MANAGED to get Rio unloaded and settled into a stall just in time. From the uncertain look on Jace's face after his encounter with the Tanners, she hadn't been sure he'd stay. But he appeared satisfied with the condition of the stable for Rio. And really, with Rio unable to travel, where else could they go? Certainly not to the Tanners' Triple T ranch, so that gave her the advantage.

Rio poked his head out over the half door and rubbed noses with the mare in the stall next to him within the first few minutes. "Look," she said, smiling, "Rio's made a new friend."

Jace nodded. "Just like me?"

She'd invited Jace to the ranch to get an endorsement but the only reason he'd come was for *her*. She'd seen it on his face the moment Zach asked if she was busy. Jace waited for her reply, his eyes questioning, and she knew she had to say something.

"We have twenty-six stalls, an open-sided covered arena, and miles of trails, a couple that lead straight into the state forest. One of them goes up to an old abandoned silver mine where my grandfather used to work," Delaney said, inserting as much enthusiasm into her voice as she could while trying to divert his attention. "What else would you like to know about the ranch?"

Jace grinned and she had the unnerving feeling he knew exactly what she was trying to do. "Are you single?"

"Are you?" she countered, dodging his question again.

"As a matter of fact, I am," he said.

"I suppose traveling the circuit doesn't allow you much time to date?" she asked. "Or at least not anyone you could date steadily?"

"No, it doesn't," he said, and tried leaning his arms on the half door of Rio's stall beside her, but Rio stuck his nose between them and nudged them apart. "What about you?"

Delaney glanced at her watch and gasped. "Oh, my! It's almost time for dinner and there's a few more chores I have to do, but if you go on up to the main house I'm sure you'll love the buffet. We've hired a fantastic new cook and I hear barbequed ribs are on the menu tonight."

"I could help you with your chores," he offered.

"Oh, no!" she said, perhaps a little too quick. But someone who enjoyed hunting couldn't possibly help with the chores she had in mind. Smiling, she reassured him, "As a guest you aren't required to do any work."

"Isn't this a *working* dude ranch?" he teased.

"Don't you want to just relax?" she countered.

Jace grinned. "I just want to be with you."

"Tomorrow," she said, her cheeks heating profusely, "you can help me feed the horses."

"Promise?" he asked.

The look he gave her stole her breath. Why did he have to be so good looking? Nodding, she swallowed hard. "I promise."

Delaney walked out to the toolshed on wobbly legs. If Jace Aldridge could make her weak in the knees his very first day here, how would she survive two whole weeks? Scolding herself for being so vulnerable, she recalled the vulnerability on his face when he learned the Tanners were his cousins.

The revelation seemed to have thrown him for a loop. First his face had shown excitement over the discovery of a new relation, then shock at what they said about his mother, then a profound disappointment when they'd walked away. And after her experience with Steve, she sure knew what it was like to be excited about something, shocked by an unexpected turn of events, then deeply disappointed.

Unable to help herself, her heart had gone out to Jace once again, just like it had at the rodeo when he saw Rio was hurt, just like it did whenever she saw anyone hurt. The fact this heartbroken hero was handsome was just too much for her to handle. She needed to get a grip. Tomorrow, she'd be more prepared. She'd steel her emotions and not let him affect her so much. And the easiest way to do that was to remember that he was a *hunter*.

Delaney checked on the young doe she'd found the

day before limping around with an aluminum arrow sticking out of the edge of its right hindquarter. Had to be from a poacher because the wound was fresh and bow season didn't start until the next day. She'd removed the arrow and cleaned the red, triangular wound the tip had left. All the deer needed now was time to heal.

She filled a bucket with fresh water and placed it in the outdoor pen beside the toolshed. Then left some corn, apples, and berries in a bowl on the ground in case the doe got hungry. The deer could probably jump the four-foot-high wood fence enclosure if it wanted to, but so far over the last two days, she hadn't. Delaney figured her hindquarter was still too sore.

Glancing nervously at the property line, she thought of the other doe, the one she'd lost several years ago when Gavin McKinley trespassed into their territory. She'd love to move her makeshift rehab unit closer to the house, but she also had to keep the animals away from her father, who had the absurd notion they'd pose a threat to their guests.

Delaney checked on a few of the other animals and returned to the house, her mind on the fact Jace wanted to be her "friend." She found Meghan, awake from her nap, and looking like she needed a friend, too. She sat on the floor of the living room drawing pictures with her crayons with her face scrunched and her lower lip sticking out.

Kneeling down, Delaney brushed her hand over the top of her child's head, bent to look at her face, and asked, "Meghan, what's wrong?"

She held up one of the colorful pages full of stick figures with different colored hair and pointed to the first set. "Ryan is Cody's daddy."

"Yes, he is." Cody was Ryan's son from a previous marriage, and when Ryan and Bree married, he'd be Meghan's cousin. Already the two had become so close even though Cody was seven and Meghan not quite three.

Meghan pointed to another set of figures. "Here's you, Bree, and Onkle Uke."

"You mean 'Uncle Luke'?" Delaney asked, correcting her.

Meghan nodded and pointed to another larger figure. "Grandpa is your daddy."

Delaney had a sinking feeling she knew where this conversation was going. With all of the new people coming into their lives this summer, Meghan had become confused about how everyone was related.

"Where's *my* daddy?" her daughter asked.

Delaney gazed down into her daughter's big blue eyes and the hurt Steve had caused them threatened to swallow her up all over again. What could she tell her? That she didn't have one? That he didn't want to be one? That they were alone? She knew the question would come up again sooner or later, but holding out for *later*, she pointed to another of Meghan's drawings, one with two blue-eyed, long-haired, blond figures holding hands.

"You've got a mommy who loves you very, very much."

Meghan drew her little brows together and a V formed between them. "But—"

"How about we sneak into the kitchen and snag one

of Grandma's fresh baked oatmeal cowboy cookies with chocolate chips, raisins, and M&M's?" Delaney asked, hoping to redirect her thoughts.

"Yum!" Meghan smiled, the crayon pictures forgotten.

For now.

JACE OPENED THE door to the refrigerator in his cabin, glanced at the complimentary bottle of sparkling apple cider and box of six homemade chocolate covered sea salt caramels, and decided that was enough for his dinner. No need for him to go to the main dining hall and face any of the Collinses or Tanners again. He wasn't too hungry anyway, not after finding out he had a couple cousins he didn't know about, one with his eye on Delaney.

Taking his treats along with him to the couch in front of the fireplace, he admired the spacious interior of the log cabin with its rustic decor and plush, four-star hotel bed. The Collinses had said they'd given him their best guest rental and he believed them. If he were to buy a house of his own, he'd want it to look just like this one someday. Only bigger. With a garage.

He'd never had his own garage. He'd had barns and sheds, and even a storage unit for a few months while he was on the road, but he'd never had a place where he could kick back and fiddle with the chest of tools from his father that his mother had kept for him. His inheritance. The only keepsake he had to remember him after his mother had sold the ranch.

Of course, he didn't remember his father any more

than he'd remembered the Tanners. He wasn't even sure if he'd ever met the Tanners. If he had, it could only have been when he was very young.

Taking his phone from his pocket, he tapped his sister's number, but for some reason the call wouldn't go through. Frowning, he stepped outside onto the small covered porch, and when that didn't work, he walked out into the open field and held it up toward the sky.

"I'm afraid your cabin is in a dead zone," Bree said, coming toward him. "You have the best cabin but the worst cell phone reception."

He lowered his arm and scowled. "Figures."

"I wanted to welcome you again to Collins Country Cabins," she said hesitantly, "and apologize for my fiancé's behavior, and his brother's."

"What can you tell me about them?" Jace asked. "How long have you known each other?"

Bree shrugged. "I've known the Tanners all my life. They only live twenty minutes up the road and we all went to school together. Dean, Ryan, Josh, and Zach help their father run the Triple T cattle ranch, and on weekends Ryan helps us out with the mini-roundups."

"Wait," Jace said, holding up his hand. "There's four of them? *Four* Tanner brothers?"

"Yup." Bree smiled. "Their mother can tell you they're a handful. Always have been. And of course now there's also Ryan's son, Cody. The youngest Tanner of the bunch."

Jace stared at her, trying to take in the fact he had this whole other side of his family he'd never heard about.

Never thought to ask about. Never knew existed. He shook his head and wondered if Natalie knew or even suspected. And why hadn't their mother told them?

He managed to give Bree a small smile and asked, "And you're sure you want to be a Tanner, too?"

Bree laughed and her whole face lit up with excitement. "More than anything. Ryan and I are set to marry next spring. Maybe you'll come to the wedding?"

"Doubtful. Considering the way my cousins blew me off."

"Oh, they didn't mean anything by that," Bree assured him. "Ryan and Zach both intend to apologize. And it's my fault, really. I hadn't told them you were coming and your sudden appearance just took them by surprise. Once you all get to know each other, everything will be fine."

Jace wasn't too sure about that.

"Ryan said my mother took something," Jace pried. "Did he tell you what?"

Bree bit her lip. Then nodded. "He said your mother stole *his* mother's inheritance."

DELANEY THOUGHT SHE'D be able to manage her new public relations job, take care of her daughter, give the guests at the ranch riding lessons, and still have time to feed and nurse the sick animals in her care back to health on both her own property and the wildlife rescue clinic.

She was wrong. As much as she wanted to, she couldn't do everything, and after a long restless sleep, she woke up this morning and knew she'd have to tell the clinic she had to cut back her volunteer hours.

Montana Wildlife Rescue occupied a small space at the end of the second block of shops in Fox Creek. They worked with the local veterinarian and housed a series of small injured animals until better homes could be found for them. Not only did they have the usual dogs and cats, but they also specialized in helping wildlife such as birds, possums, raccoons, and the occasional abandoned cub. Delaney usually came in three times a week to help, but now she wouldn't even be able to do that.

"It's only for two weeks," she told Carol Levine, head of the facility.

Carol's two full-time employees, Mary Ann and Ben, commiserated, as they, too, always found it hard to juggle job, family, and their other responsibilities. But much like Delany's own father, Carol was a little harder to please.

"We're already short-handed," Carol said, and waved her hand toward all the pens. "How are we going to keep this place clean enough to pass the county health inspection?"

Mary Ann cringed. "And the cat you've been bottle feeding has gotten weaker. She's going to need extra care over the next few days."

Delaney winced. What if the cat didn't make it because *she* wasn't here? Her stomach began to churn. "I'm sorry, but you'll have to find someone else."

Ben groaned. "Looks like I'll be working weekends."

"At least do me one little favor?" Carol pressed. "One that won't take up too much of your time?"

Delaney had learned a long time ago not to say yes to

a favor until she'd heard what it entailed. "What do you need?"

"Come to the rally we have planned on the twenty-fifth?"

"Of course," Delaney said with a nod. The rally was more than three weeks away and she and her family would be rid of Jace by then—and hopefully have his endorsement. There was no reason why she wouldn't be able to make it.

"Great!" Carol exclaimed. "I'd like you to talk about the horrific scene you witnessed at that rodeo last weekend in Bozeman, the one where Jace Aldridge's horse was hurt."

Delaney hesitated. "Me? *Speak?* Wait—how did you find out I was there?"

Ben held up the latest issue of *True Montana Magazine* and opened to the middle where some of her photos were featured. "They added your name to the photo credits."

"I'm sorry I went," Delaney hurried to explain. "You told me not to go, but I—"

Carol pushed her words aside. "I didn't understand until I saw your photos. Brilliant idea to catch these rodeo riders in the very act for which we are protesting. Great job, Delaney. Your photos are going to bring attention to our cause like no other campaign in the past."

Delaney swallowed hard. She'd hoped the readers of the magazine would sympathize more to the heartbreak on Jace's face when he saw his horse was lame. Couldn't they see that he cared? And that he'd been hurt almost as much as his horse?

"It was an accident that could have happened to anyone," Delaney reported.

"Yes, but he's not just anyone, is he?" Carol asked, a sudden gleam coming into her eyes. "Jace Aldridge is famous. And if he hadn't been trying to lean over to grab the steer in the first place, his foot never would have gotten caught and he never would have put extra strain on his horse's leg."

"It is a rough sport," Delaney conceded.

"To top it off, the cowboy not only rides rodeo but he *hunts*," Carol exclaimed, and uttered a few words Delaney wouldn't repeat to emphasize her disgust. "Rumor has it that he's staying in Montana until his horse heals, giving us the perfect opportunity to take action and protest against him."

"I—I can't speak," Delaney said, her throat closing up.

"I couldn't speak when I first heard about the accident myself," Carol agreed. "I was so appalled that for about ten seconds I, too, was speechless."

"No," Delaney said, shaking her head. "I mean—you asked if I could speak about what I saw and . . . I can't. Not in front of a crowd." She glanced at Mary Ann and Ben for help, but they were in agreement with Carol.

"You have the photos you took to back us up," Mary Ann reminded her.

"And your own testimony," Ben added.

Speak out against Jace? The same man from which she was supposed to get an endorsement? Even if she could find the nerve to open her mouth, she couldn't. No matter how much she wanted to protect the animals, she had to protect herself, her child, and her family first.

"You know I have a fear of public speaking," Delaney said, her voice barely audible.

"If you really want to make a difference you have to take a stand and shout out what you have to say to the world. I know that can seem intimidating, but I'll be right there with you. We all will, won't we?" Carol asked, and Mary Ann and Ben nodded. "You don't even have to stand up on the stage if you don't want to. You can just stand in the spotlight on the floor and we'll hand you a microphone."

Take a stand? In the spotlight? With every eye in the crowd staring at her? Judging her? Who would want to listen to *her*? Delaney brushed her sweaty palms down her jeans and took a couple quick, short breaths to quell her queasy stomach—but failed.

Running to the corner of the room, she grabbed hold of the concrete edge of a large potted plant and puked. Then peering at her three friends from under her arm, she shook her head again and repeated, "I—can't—speak."

JACE SKIPPED BREAKFAST but by midmorning his stomach was growling and he needed some food. He thought about calling Delaney to see if Collins Country Cabins offered room service, then remembered he didn't have any cell phone reception. He'd have to walk down the path to the main house and hope they could cook up something for him.

"I don't cook between meals," the chubby, round-cheeked woman in the chef hat chastised him. "Breakfast was over an hour ago and lunch isn't served till noon."

Jace whipped his wallet out of his pocket and offered, "I could pay you extra."

"And I won't be bullied or bribed!" she shouted.

Delaney's grandma entered the kitchen, gave the cook a surly look, and demanded, "What's going on?"

"This cowboy here," the cook said, picking up a spatula and pointing it at him, "thinks he can come in and have me cook for him whenever he wants."

"This cowboy here," Ruth Collins said, throwing the woman's words back at her, "is a very special guest."

"If he's so special, you can cook for him yourself," the chubby woman said, and untying her apron, she threw it down on the counter. "In fact, you can do all the cooking yourself. I quit."

Ruth raised her chin. "Good riddance."

The cook slammed the large wooden door shut on her way out and Ruth gave Jace an apologetic look. "Sorry about that."

Jace's stomach growled from hunger, but he gave Delaney's grandma a partial smile and said, "Not a problem."

"I didn't want her in my kitchen anyway. I usually do all the cooking and that woman never got my recipes right. She thought she could add in her own ingredients and no one would taste the difference. But I did. She isn't half the cook that I am. Now," Ruth said, gesturing for him to take a seat at the kitchen table, "tell me what you'd like and I'll fix it for you."

Before he could respond, a blond toddler came into the room and sat herself beside him. "I want pancakes."

Ruth glanced at the child and said, "Meghan, you already had pancakes."

"I want more," Meghan crooned.

"She didn't eat much earlier," Ruth explained, then said to the girl, "Okay, I'll make you some just as soon as I cook something for Mr. Aldridge."

Meghan turned to look at him and smiled. "Do you like pancakes?"

Her curious, wide-eyed expression made him laugh. "I do," he said, and glanced at Ruth. "Pancakes sound good."

The lines around Ruth's face softened and a twinkle entered her eye as she announced, "Pancakes, it is."

Beside him, Meghan said, "Thanks, Grandma-ma."

"Grandma?" Jace asked. "Is she Bree's little girl? Or Luke's?"

"I'm her great-grandma," Ruth corrected. "And Meghan's the spitting image of her mommy. Now you tell me, who does she look like?"

He stared at the pale blond hair, blue eyes, and sweet, little mouth. "Delaney? Is she married?"

"Divorced."

Jace hesitated, his mind replaying the interaction between his cousin and Delaney the night before. "Not from . . . Zach?"

"Oh, no," Ruth assured him. "Some guy in San Diego."

"And my cousin is . . . ?" Jace asked, arching his brow as he probed for answers.

"Just a friend," Ruth said, and winked at him. "There's nothing really going on there."

Well, that was a relief.

Delaney couldn't have got divorced too long ago; Meghan wasn't that old. Maybe that's why she'd blown off his advances. She was probably just protecting herself and wanted to make sure she wouldn't make the same mistake twice.

"How old are you?" he asked the little girl.

Meghan held up two fingers. "But soon I'll be this many," she told him, and held up a third finger.

"It's been nine months since she got rid of that schmuck," Ruth said, as if reading his thoughts about Delaney and her ex. Then the woman cracked two eggs into a bowl, measured in some flour, and as she stirred the ingredients together with a metal whisk she added, "Believe me, it's for the best. Delaney knows it, too."

Meghan frowned. "What's a schmuck?"

"Someone who isn't very nice," Ruth informed her.

Jace watched Meghan give him a wary look, point to him, and ask her great-grandma, "Is he a schmuck?"

Ruth let out a startled gasp, looked up from her bowl, and met his gaze, then laughed. "I hope not. You're not a schmuck, are you, Jace?"

He grinned. "No. I try not to be."

"Can you do this?" Meghan asked, tugging on his sleeve.

Jace watched Meghan pick up a spoon and place it on the end of her nose. Then she dropped her hands away, and looked at him expectantly, but the spoon fell off.

"Well, let's see," he said, and picking another spoon off the table he tried to imitate her. He had to tilt his head back some, to get the spoon to stay, but he managed to keep the spoon on the end of his nose for a good three seconds before his, too, crashed down to the table.

Meghan laughed as if it was the funniest thing she'd ever seen and he couldn't help but laugh with her. When was the last time he'd done anything like this? Or acted silly? As if he didn't have a care in the world?

If only everyone could be that free. He signed autographs for children at the rodeos, let them pet his horse, but he'd never spent much one-on-one time with any of them. He was always hanging out with adult crowds and on the road driving from one rodeo to the next. His mother's words floated back to him. *There's more to life than rodeo.*

Picking up his spoon, he clinked it against Meghan's in a mock sword fight and thought maybe, just maybe, his mother was right.

WHEN DELANEY RETURNED from the wildlife rescue clinic, Bree pulled her aside out of earshot from the assorted guests engaged in activities about the property. "I just heard from the PI we hired to track down Susan and Wade Randall. He says they were seen crossing the border. They're here, back in Montana."

Delaney gasped. After their former ranch managers had run with the money they'd embezzled from them, the couple had reportedly been heading south. Their PI,

Doug Kelly, had tracked them from state to state, but the husband and wife team continued to elude both him and the authorities. Then last month the Randalls had been caught on a surveillance camera when they'd attempted to rob a bank in Wyoming. The PI suspected the Randalls were returning home because they'd run out of money and wanted to use their connections to get some more.

"Does the rest of the family know about this?" Delaney asked, keeping her voice to a whisper.

Bree nodded. "I just told them."

"What did they say?"

"Dad's worried they'll cause trouble for us all over again—and that it might ruin our chances of getting an endorsement from Jace." Bree gave her a questioning look. "Have you talked with him?"

Delaney had helped Jace unload his horse and had made a weak promise of friendship but that was it. "I'll go talk to him now."

"You need to find a way to keep him busy so he's not distracted by anything else that may be going on. If he talks to too many other people he may hear rumors and start asking questions. Or be deceived by someone the Randalls have hired to sabotage our business."

"Someone like Gavin McKinley?" Delaney asked, wondering if he was on the Randalls' payroll, but Bree shook her head.

"Our rival may be a pain in the butt," Bree said, smiling, "but he's also the sheriff's son. He oversteps his boundaries sometimes thinking he can get away with it, but I doubt he'd ever do anything illegal."

"The Randalls would more likely hire someone new," Delaney agreed, and looked around at all the people. "Like one of our other guests?"

"Exactly," Bree agreed. "So the more time he spends with you, the better."

After checking in with her mother and finding out that Sammy Jo and Luke had taken Meghan on a pony ride, Delaney scoured the property in search of Jace. He wasn't in his cabin, although she'd discovered five women hanging out on his porch awaiting his return. He wasn't with the twins, who tried to apologize to her for mentioning the endorsement the day before. And he wasn't in the barn, the arena, or in the stable with Rio. His truck was still parked in the driveway, so where could he be? Had he saddled one of their horses and gone on a trail ride?

She walked out to the edge of their property to peer down the trail and stopped up short. Jace Aldridge was standing there talking to Gavin McKinley, of all people, who sat smugly up on his gray horse as if he were king of the county. *Ugh!* Was she too late? Before she was spotted, Delaney ducked behind a large round bale of rolled hay determined to find out what the two men were saying.

"I can show you places where you can find elk the size of your truck," Gavin boasted.

Jace appeared interested. "Oh, yeah? I'd like to see that."

No! Gavin was offering to take him on a *hunt*!

"A good hunt may help take your mind off your horse," Gavin continued. "If you come over to my place,

I can show you our wall of trophy heads and outfit you with a bow, a quiver of our finest arrows, and anything else you could possibly need."

Jace smiled. "I *could* use a good distraction."

Delaney winced. *So could she.* Drawing in a nervous breath, she touched the bear paw necklace about her neck for courage. She had to do something quick. She had to step out.

"He can't visit your place today," Delaney said, walking around the hay bale into their view. She looked straight at Jace, who seemed happy to see her, and reminded him, "The vet is coming to check on Rio."

Jace tilted his head back and sighed. "Oh, that's right. Sorry, Gavin. Maybe another time?"

Gavin McKinley cast her a swift, aggravated glance, then returned his attention back to Jace. "How about tomorrow? It's opening day of bow season. What better day to test the equipment?"

"No!" Delaney swallowed hard. "I mean, he's—he's going on a trail ride with *me* tomorrow."

Gavin scoffed, "Going after a trophy head is more fun than a trail ride."

Delaney disagreed with that statement on so many levels she could have spoken from sunup to sundown—if only she had the courage. Which she didn't. But she could try to *flirt.* What had those magazines Sammy Jo brought her said? To lean in, smile, tilt her head to the side, and look up at him, batting her lashes? Okay, so she wouldn't go that far. But she could smile. Hopefully that would be enough.

"If you come on a trail ride with me, I promise we'll

have some fun," Delaney said, giving Jace the biggest smile she could muster.

He rewarded her efforts with a smile of his own. "I'd love to go on a trail ride with you."

"Well, how about the next day?" Gavin asked, his voice faltering. "I could reserve a spot for you on one of our expeditions the next day."

"He just got here. Let him relax first," Delaney said, and leaning in, she tilted her head to the side and gave Jace another smile.

Jace quirked a brow as if to ask what she was up to, then gave Gavin a nod. "I'll let you know."

Gavin looked as if he was about to press him further when all of the sudden a loud rumble to their right turned his head. Jace and Delaney turned their heads, too, and Delaney frowned, wondering what was going on as she watched the large truck and trailer pull up the driveway of the abandoned property next door.

The land used to belong to the Owenses, but when Mrs. Owens went into a mental hospital, it was sold to a wealthy developer who brought in a bulldozer to knock all the buildings down. Both the Owenses and the developer had been suspected of being in tight with the embezzling Randalls. And when the connections between them were revealed, the developer had also left town. Another For Sale sign had been erected, but the land had sat empty now for over a month.

Gavin frowned. "Delaney, who are those people?"

Delaney gasped. "I don't know but they have horses. Lots and lots of horses."

"It's another outfitter," Jace said, his voice low. "The sign on the side of the truck says Woolly Outfitters."

"Another outfitter!" Gavin scowled with disgust. "This area can barely support one, let alone *three*."

"I wouldn't consider Collins Country Cabins a true outfitter," Delaney said, shaking her head. "We don't lead our guests on pack trips or wilderness hunts."

"That's not what your father told me," Gavin said, and spit on the ground beside him. "Jed and I exchanged a few words earlier this morning and your old man made it quite clear that the reason Collins Country Cabins is staying open for fall is so that he and your brother, Luke, can take your guests on hunting trips."

"*What?*" Delaney demanded, unable to believe her father and brother would do such a thing. Then she caught a glimpse of surprise on Jace's face and remembered she couldn't reveal her views on hunting until *after* she got the endorsement. "I mean," she quickly amended, "I didn't realize that's what my family had in mind."

Gavin glanced once again at the new arrivals next door and sat back in his saddle, puffing out his chest. "Mark my words, only one of us will survive," Gavin warned, his voice animated as if the challenge excited him. Then he tipped his hat and gave Delaney a broad smile. "May the best outfitter win."

Chapter Five

JACE DISLIKED GAVIN McKinley more and more each time they met. However, he'd promised Bucky's father, Eli, he'd look into the neighboring outfitters for him to see if they might be involved in one of the area's poaching rings. He kind of liked the idea of being an "unofficial" undercover agent for the Fish and Wildlife department. At least it gave him something to do while Rio healed. After that he'd have to decide whether he wanted to continue with rodeo or find another career.

He'd decided to play up to Gavin to see if he could extract some information, but hadn't expected a new outfitter to arrive next door. The property still had a few fenced corrals but no buildings for hunters to sign up for guided wilderness trips. He supposed they'd see some construction activity over there within the next few days.

Jace hadn't expected the Collinses to become an outdoor outfitter either. While he doubted his hosts could be part of the poaching ring Eli Knowles and his fellow game wardens were after, to be fair, he'd have to keep an eye on them, too.

Right now he had his eye on Delaney as he followed her from the edge of the property line over to the brown weathered stable.

"Gavin is trying to steal you away from me," Delaney said, giving him a sidelong glance. Her tone was flirtatious but the tight expression on her face suggested it was forced.

"Are you jealous?" he asked, hoping if he teased her back she'd loosen up and flirt with him for real.

"I am." She turned toward him and gave a half smile. "We're all afraid you'll leave our ranch and go stay with him."

At least she was being honest. Jace arched his brow. "He *is* the owner of Fox Creek Outfitting, one of the largest outfitters in the county, and his lodge is a hunter's dream, or so he says. What does Collins Country Cabins have to offer if I stay?"

Delaney's mouth fell open as if she thought he was serious. Then she swallowed hard and raised her chin like he'd seen her sister do a few times when making a point, and said, "Me."

"What?" Jace choked back a laugh. He hadn't been expecting that. Especially because she looked as if the word tasted bitter on her tongue. "Delaney, if you're going to flirt at least *pretend* you're having fun doing it."

"I really don't know how to flirt," she admitted. "My ma said it might help our cause, but I don't know what I'm doing."

More direct honesty. *Refreshing.* But she'd been married. He scratched the back of his head as he studied her. "Didn't you ever flirt with your ex-husband?"

Whoops. Too personal. By the dark, stormy look on her face, it was clear he shouldn't have said that. "Sorry," he apologized. "Didn't mean to bring up bad memories."

"Who said it was bad?" she asked, shrinking back. "Who have you been talking to?"

"Cupid?" he teased. Okay, it was a lame answer that grew even more lame with every passing second. *Geez.* He hadn't felt this awkward with a woman in years. Letting out a small chuckle to release some of the tension, he gave her a rueful grin. "Guess I'm not good at flirting either. Every time I'm around you I either say or do something incredibly stupid."

She looked down for a moment, but when she looked up at him again, she smiled. A *real* smile. One that lit her blue eyes and wiped the troubled expression off her face.

"Have I finally said something right?" Jace asked, grinning back at her.

"Look," she said, evading the question and pointing to the white truck parked beside the stable in front of them. "The vet is here."

"In other words, you're not going to answer my question?" he teased.

"No," she said, and let out a small laugh. "I'm not."

Well, he didn't exactly win *her* endorsement, but it was a start. He glanced at the three figures standing off to their right as he and Delaney passed by. Ryan Tanner had his arm around Bree and beside them a young brown-haired boy played with a pack of black-and-white border collie pups. They all looked so content, so happy—that is, until Ryan caught sight of him. His cousin froze and held his gaze for a long moment until Jace finally looked away.

Bree had said his cousins meant to apologize for giving him such a cold reception, but so far . . . they hadn't. And Jace wasn't sure they ever would.

"Have you ever had someone hold a grudge against you for something that wasn't your fault?" Jace muttered.

To his surprise, Delaney nodded. "Yeah," she said, and let out a sigh. "My father."

He didn't know what she meant by that, but didn't ask, fearing he'd ruin the progress they'd already made. But maybe in time, if she continued to talk to him, she'd tell him.

Delaney entered the stable first and greeted the vet as if he were an old friend. "I wrapped his leg with some of the special herbs you gave me for some of our other horses," she said, bending down beside him as he removed the gauze around Rio's lower leg.

"I see that," the vet replied. "Great job, Del, as always."

Jace drew close and gave Rio an affectionate gentle scratch behind an ear. "How's it look?"

"Better each time I see him," the vet reported. "I won't need to come out again unless there's a problem." Then after giving Delaney a wink, he added, "He's being well cared for."

After the veterinarian left, Jace helped Delaney fill the grain buckets so when the other horses who spent most of their daylight hours out in the pasture were brought in for the night, their dinner would be ready for them.

"Why didn't you become a vet?" Jace asked, scooping a measured amount of grain into the last bucket and closing the stall door.

Delaney pressed her lips together and didn't reply.

"Another bad subject?" he asked, searching her face for a sign.

"The two are tied together," she said, and dragged a hose over to start filling secondary buckets with water.

Jace figured that was all he was going to get out of her, but then she continued. "You see, I failed chemistry."

He shook his head to indicate he didn't understand, and truly he didn't. He thought they had *great* chemistry together—when she let her guard down.

"I'm not good at math either—equations, formulas, or any kind of measurements." Her gaze drifted toward the grain they'd just measured out. "That's why I use a scoop. It's premeasured."

"Math just happens to be my strong suit. I'm usually pretty good at putting two and two together." He took the hose from her hands to take over the watering. "I could teach you."

"It's too late now," Delaney said, and shrugged. "I don't have time to go back to school. I'd been going to the University of Southern California until my chemistry professor gave me a big fat *F*. My roommate thought a trip to Las Vegas would cheer me up. I'm not impulsive and I don't like to gamble, but that night I was too upset to care. The next thing I know—" She broke off and frowned.

"What?" Jace prompted. "You woke up with a hangover?"

"No, something worse," Delaney grumbled under her breath. "We'd met these guys and one of them took an instant liking to me, and somehow convinced me to enter one of those little chapels that stay open all night and—" She broke off again and scowled.

"You woke up married," he finished. "Why didn't you get it annulled?"

"Because at the time, he seemed nice enough," she said, then drew in a deep breath. "And a few weeks later I found I was pregnant."

Jace raised his brows. "Oh."

"We didn't even know each other," Delaney said, her voice filled with regret. "He flirted, but I didn't. We weren't even friends."

"I've made a few mistakes in my life," Jace admitted. "I think we all have."

"We stuck together for two years and tried to make it work, but one thing's for sure," she said, her tone hardening, "I'll never marry again unless it's to someone I really know, who also knows me, someone I'd consider my best friend." She placed her hands on her hips and gave him a direct look as he hung up the watering hose. "So you see, that's why I don't know how to flirt. I've never really done it. I'm not even sure I can. And that's also why I don't trust a guy I've just met who flirts with *me*."

"Well, then, we'll have to get to know each other," Jace teased. "Would that be okay with you?"

Delaney rolled her eyes, but instead of being annoyed, she laughed.

Jace drew closer. "Can I take that as a 'yes'?"

"I—I have to take care of a few more chores and then I'll see you at dinner."

"Evading my questions again?" he asked, watching her cheeks turn a rosy pink. "How about you let me help you?"

"No," she said, shaking her head, then smiled. "I mean, no thank you. After all, you are our guest, and are supposed to be relaxing, not working, and enjoying yourself during your stay."

"I *am*," Jace assured her, and brushed a finger softly over her cheek. "Believe me, I am."

DELANEY LEFT THE stable, and when she was sure no one was watching, she hurried down the path, past all the cabins, past the open field, and into the grove of trees where she had hidden her own private animal clinic. She went into the old toolshed first and checked on the raccoon with the broken leg. Another portioned-off section housed a pheasant with an injured wing. Walking outside, she unlatched the gate to the square, wood fenced enclosure where she'd kept the young doe and after a quick examination decided it was time to set her free.

The arrow wound did not get infected, which had been her main concern, and was already scabbing over. The doe could rejoin her kin back in the woods and heal the rest of the way on her own. Leaving the gate open, she walked behind the doe and shooed it out of the fenced pen.

Part of her wished she could keep the doe locked up safe forever, where no hunters could ever do her harm, but she also knew the deer was a wild animal who would never be happy unless it was free.

Whew! She'd had a close call with Jace back there at the stable. He'd wanted to come but she couldn't bring a *hunter* along. She didn't think he'd kill a confined animal, but who knew? She didn't really know what kind of man he was. Except that he was flirtatious. And persistent. Who knew what else she might say, if she'd extended their time together? Yes, it was best for all their sakes not to let him too close.

A loud ring echoed across the land, and Delaney jumped with a start. The familiar sound was from Grandma ringing the triangular metal dinner bell and no doubt, if she didn't hurry, she'd be late for dinner once again.

Back at the house, she ran into the kitchen, washed her hands, then picked up an apron and joined her mother and the Walford twins behind the serving counter.

Her mother clucked her tongue and said, "Delaney, if your father finds out you were late—"

"He won't, unless you tell him," she said, and glanced toward the twins for backup. "Isn't that right, girls?"

"Yes! Yes!" Nora agreed. "Del, you aren't still mad at us for spilling the beans about wanting the endorsement, are you?"

"We didn't know we weren't supposed to say anything," Nadine explained. "We thought Mr. Aldridge already knew that's why you invited him here."

"Speaking of our famous cowboy," Nora said, leaning into Delaney's ear. "He's looking at you."

She followed the teenager's gaze. Dozens of guests filled the seats of the rectangular wood tables, but at the far end of the room, Jace leaned against the far wall. "Why isn't he eating?"

"He told us he was waiting for you," Nadine said, and wiggled her brows.

Delaney proceeded to serve the line of carnivorous guests who had yet to get their evening meal, which tonight was hamburgers, made from ninety-seven percent lean choice beef from a Black Angus she'd named Gabe.

"Can you believe Grandma fired our cook?" Ma demanded, her voice rising higher and higher in pitch. "Now she's back in the kitchen and I'm afraid she's going to cook herself into the grave."

"She loves cooking," Delaney said loyally.

Nora and Nadine both giggled, and Nora said, "We think she loves the sheriff. He came over to see her today and—"

"She blushed every time he looked at her!" Nadine finished.

Delaney laughed. "How did the sheriff look at her?"

"Just like Jace is looking at you!" the twins chorused in unison.

Del glanced over toward the wall and her heart skipped a beat. He *was* looking at her. The dark-haired cowboy with the straw hat didn't take his eyes off her. *Oh, no.* He was making her feel incredibly self-conscious and flattered all at the same time. And if she was honest, she'd have to admit . . . she kind of liked it. But what did he want with her? From the way some of the other women at the tables were looking at him, it seemed as if he could have the pick of the litter.

"Don't be silly," Delaney's ma scolded the twins. "Mr. Aldridge is *not* looking at . . . well, goodness! It looks like he is. Careful you don't get emotionally involved, Del. You know he's only here for two weeks."

Delaney gasped. "*I'm* not the one who's staring."

"He's staking his claim," Nora squealed, and her sister agreed. Then the twins prattled on about the new cameras they got for their birthday.

"Can you give us photography lessons, Del?" Nora asked.

"Please, please, please?" Nadine added.

Delaney agreed, only to get them to stop begging her. "Tomorrow," she told them, then stiffened. "Ma! What's Meghan eating? Did you give her a *hamburger*?"

Her mother's face took on a worried look as she glanced at the table where Meghan sat with Bree, Ryan, and Cody. "She likes it."

"Ma," Delaney said, thinking of poor Gabe. "You know how I feel about eating meat. I thought we agreed you needed to respect my wishes as the parent."

Her ma winced. "Our beef has high nutrition, which Meghan needs if she's going to grow into a healthy adult. Besides, she *asked* to try it."

"*Ma!*"

"I'm so sorry, Del," her mother said, her face filled with remorse. "I tried to serve her something else but she helped herself and took a bite before I could stop her, and then she liked it so much that I didn't have the heart to take it away."

Delaney tried to swallow her outrage. Would her mother let her daughter eat rat poison, too, if she wanted? No! Of course not. But if she argued any further, she'd most likely cause a scene, heads would turn, and more people than just Jace would be watching her.

She'd talk to both her mother and Meghan again later in private. Just like she would talk to her father and brother about taking their guests on hunting expeditions.

As the guests thinned out and left the dining hall to return to their cabins or to join in song around the bonfire Luke had lit outside, a shimmer of anticipation shot up her spine. *Jace was waiting for her.* And when he left his post across the room and slowly walked toward her, a grin spread across his attractive, suntanned face.

"Can I get you a plate?" he offered as she took off her apron.

"Um, sure," she said, wondering how she could use this meal to her advantage and encourage him to give their ranch a line of praise.

"Mom," Meghan said, tugging on her hand so she'd look down at her. "I ate a hamburger."

"I saw," Delaney said, and lowered her voice, "but you know we don't—"

"Cody eats hamburgers," Meghan interrupted, as if anticipating what she was going to say.

"Yes, but that doesn't mean that *you* have to."

"Are you going to eat a hamburger, too?" Meghan pointed at the plate Jace placed on the table in front of her.

"I didn't put anything on it," he said, nodding to the condiment table, "because I didn't know what you would like."

Delaney stared at the juicy, charbroiled meat wedged into one of her grandma's sliced golden rolls, and froze. When Jace asked if he could get her a plate, she thought he'd meant an *empty* plate, so she could serve herself. But he'd gone ahead and filled plates of burgers and chips for each of them.

She sat down in a chair before her knees buckled. What was she going to do? She could just tell him she was a vegetarian, but she wanted him to *like* her. That was the goal, right? So that he'd be eager to write them the endorsement? But she feared once he found out how different their values were, he'd shoot on over to Gavin's place faster than an arrow could fly. Just because Rio couldn't leave didn't mean Jace couldn't.

He pulled out a chair to sit beside her when Delaney suddenly put out a hand to stop him and gave him a big smile. "Could you please get me a napkin?"

"Of course," he said, and headed back toward the serving table.

Moving fast, Delaney then took the offensive slab of Gabe's remains off her plate with a fork and quickly slid it under the table where her sister's puppy, Boots, waited for handouts. She didn't like the idea of handing off Gabe to another, but at this particular moment it was either her or the dog. And the dog didn't seem to mind half as much as she did.

When Jace returned, he handed her a napkin and frowned. "Where's your hamburger?"

Delaney patted her stomach and gave him a big smile. "I ate it."

"You ate it?" he repeated in obvious disbelief. "What did you do? Wolf it down?"

"I was hungry." She gave him a big smile to distract him, but it didn't work.

"Can I get you some more?" he offered, still staring at her.

"Oh, no," she said quickly. "I still have the potato chips to eat."

He hesitated, then sat down in the chair beside her. "A gal with a healthy appetite. From your slim figure, I never would have guessed."

Beside them Meghan laughed, pulled Bree's dog out from under the table, and announced, "Boots likes hamburgers, too."

Delaney froze and her gaze darted toward Jace, but he didn't appear to suspect anything. He was too busy engaging Meghan in a sword fight with their forks.

JACE ASKED DELANEY if he could use the landline and she led him to the ranch office and closed the door so he could make his phone calls in private. If he wasn't mistaken, she almost looked relieved to be rid of him. Sitting down in the chair behind the large wooden desk, he groaned.

He'd thought coming here would be nice for both him and his horse but so far nothing had gone as planned. Before dinner he'd followed Delaney to the patch of woods where she kept her animal hideaway. He'd been careful to keep out of sight, so she wouldn't see him, but why hadn't she wanted him to come with her? What did she think he would do? Shoot the animals she was caring for right in front of her?

He had no interest in hunting game with a clear disadvantage. In fact, he wasn't in the mood for hunting at all since Rio's injury. He used to hunt on his friend Bucky's ranch to put food on the table for his family and help thin out the deer population so they wouldn't all die of starvation, but he'd never *enjoyed* putting an animal down, no matter what the media said. And after seeing the pain in Rio's eyes, he couldn't bring himself to hunt right now even if offered the best package deal made available to mankind.

Of course, the local outfitters didn't have to know that. In fact, he'd almost enjoyed playing along when talking to Gavin McKinley and pretended interest just to see how far the man would go. If Gavin wasn't offering poaching trips, then he might know someone who was and be able to tip him off on who sent the threatening letter to his mom.

He still needed to talk to his mother about his long-lost cousins, who added another layer of tension to his stay each time they looked at him. While waiting for Delaney to finish serving dinner to the guests, Ryan's son,

Cody, had come up to him and asked for his autograph. He didn't even think the kid knew they were related, but that didn't stop Ryan from giving him another cold stare.

Picking up the phone, he called his mother's number, determined to find out if there had been other threats. While he had her on the phone, he thought he'd ask about the real story with the Tanners, too. But his sister, Natalie, answered his call instead.

"Mom's not home right now," Nat told him. "She's speaking at a dinner tonight in Helena hosted by her supporters. She's ahead in the polls and it looks like she may have clinched the governor's seat."

"The election isn't for another two months," he reminded her. "There's still plenty of time for the competition to sway votes."

"Jace, whose side are you on?" Nat scolded.

"Mom's, of course. But I do worry about her being a target for some of the crackpots out there. Any more letters?"

"No," his sister assured him. "And Mom's acting as if the incident never happened."

"That's good." Then he remembered the second reason he'd called and asked, "Hey, Nat. Guess who I ran into out here in Fox Creek?"

"Knowing you, it could be anyone," she teased. "*Mr. Rodeo* knows everyone."

"I didn't know we had cousins."

She hesitated. "Who?"

"Tanners," he replied. "From Dad's side of the family. What do you know about them?"

"Mom never talks about Dad's relatives much. I knew he had a sister, Lora Lynn, who married Bo Tanner, but she and Mom never got along."

"Aunt Lora had four boys: Dean, Josh, Ryan, and Zach. I've met the last two, who look to be around the same age as us, and Ryan's seven-year-old son, Cody."

His sister gasped. "How did you meet? How did you find out you were related?"

"Ryan works here, at Collins Country Cabins, on weekends. He's engaged to Delaney Collins's older sister, Bree. And he wasn't too friendly. He said Mom took something from them."

"*Our* mom?"

"Yeah. Any idea what it could be?"

"None. But now that you've got my curiosity going, I promise you that as soon as Mom comes home I'm going to find out."

"I was hoping you'd say that," Jace said, and grinned. "You're always better at digging up details than I am."

"I'll take that as a compliment," Nat said, as if amused. "By the way, speaking of details . . . how's it going with Delaney?"

Jace hesitated. "I don't think she trusts me any more than the Tanners."

THE FOLLOWING DAY, Delaney kept her promise to the Walford twins and gave them a lesson in photography. Both girls had received identical cameras from their uncle for their seventeenth birthday and held them up to their eyes, trying out different types of lenses, and adjusting the apertures and dials.

"Too bad we didn't have these when Dreamy Devin was here this summer," Nora crooned.

"Too bad he went off to college," Nadine agreed.

"When do you two go back to school?" Delaney asked. She'd gotten used to the teenagers' quirky ways, but it would be a relief to have some peace and quiet around the ranch.

"*Wednesday!*" they chorused.

"We'll be high school *seniors*," Nora added, as if she could hardly believe it. "And we'll rule the school! But Bree said we can still help out on weekends."

She did? Delaney sighed. So much for a respite. Oh, well, she might as well accept it and hope for the best. Smiling, she asked, "Maybe you'll meet some cute boys in your new classes?"

"Not like Devin," Nora said dramatically. "He was so handsome—"

"No one we meet will ever be as handsome as him," Nadine finished for her.

Delaney smiled. "My grandma always says, '*You never know what might be waiting around the next corner until you get there.*'"

"My, gosh, you're right!" Nora exclaimed, and nudged Nadine's arm. "Who are those boys coming toward us?"

Nadine turned her head and Delaney followed their gaze. A few of their newest guests had teenage sons. Both girls rotated their camera lenses to zoom in on them, and started clicking pictures as fast as their fingers would let them.

Nora giggled. "I'm so glad our uncle wanted us to learn how rewarding it is to go on a nature shoot—"

"And capture life in all its gorgeousness," Nadine added, clicking more photos of the boys.

Nature shoot? Delaney's mouth popped open as she realized that was the answer. *That's* how she'd distract Jace from hunting. She'd give him a camera and take him on a *nature shoot* to teach him to appreciate the wildlife around him—without killing it.

Delaney brushed her hair, dabbed on some of the makeup Sammy Jo left her, and yes, even put on the dreaded lipstick. Then she changed into her best sparkly western-style blouse, a gift Bree had given her to update her wardrobe, and went down to the stable to tack up the horses.

The other guests who had signed on for the trail ride gathered in the staging area. Luke led their assigned horses up to the raised platforms to make it easier for them to get on. Then a few minutes later, Jace arrived. With a gun. A Winchester 30-30 lever action rifle like her father's.

Delaney swallowed hard and forced a smile. "Glad you made it. We almost thought we'd have to leave without you."

"We?" Jace looked at each of the guests. "I thought when you offered to take me on a trail ride, you meant a *private* trail ride."

Is that what she'd implied? "I—I take the guests on trail rides every day." She glanced at the threat in his hands. "Not . . . hunting expeditions."

Jace gave the weapon a quick glance. "Your father insisted I bring this just in case I saw something."

Ugh. Anything to get the endorsement.

"Jed wouldn't take no for an answer," Jace said, hoisting the rifle strap over his shoulder. "He's a hard man to refuse."

Yes, he was. But it was bow season. Guns couldn't legally be used for another two weeks. What was her father thinking?

"I'll take the others," Luke offered, "and you can take Jace."

Delaney gasped. "But—"

"Whatever it takes," Luke reminded her.

Yes, she'd promised to do whatever she had to in order to please their special guest and get his endorsement. "Thank you, Luke."

"You're welcome," her brother shot back, and grinned.

Jace tipped his hat toward her, then mounted the chestnut gelding Luke brought over to him. "Ready when you are."

Delaney hadn't considered that when she led the trail ride she'd be riding in front and Jace would be able to watch her the entire time, making her self-conscious once again. However, his constant gaze didn't deter her from her goal of slapping a camera into his hand. As long as he held the camera, he wouldn't be able to pull the trigger of the gun.

"You never know what you might see," she said, echoing her father's words as she handed him a simpler model Canon than the camera that hung about her own neck. "I thought you might appreciate looking at nature a different way."

She half expected him to refuse, but apparently she had enough of her father in her that he accepted without a single protest. In fact, he reminded her of the twins as he looked at the camera like a new toy and snapped several photos of her.

"Can you show me how to print them out, too?" he asked, lifting his gaze from the viewfinder.

"Of course," she said, and relief flooded through her that at least this one day the animals would have one less hunter to contend with.

"When?" he pressed, his expression eager. "Tomorrow?"

"Soon."

Jace grinned. "Why is it so hard to lock you into a date?"

"I never make plans without checking my schedule," she said, finding it hard to suppress a smile.

"Where do you keep your 'schedule'?"

"Someplace safe where you can't steal it." This time she did smile and Jace smiled back.

"What are these other settings for?" he asked, tapping the dial on the top of the camera.

She rode closer and leaned toward him and pointed. "This one adjusts the shutter speed to catch fast-action sequences, such as a fox chasing a rabbit. The next is a macro setting enabling you to zoom in close on an object, like the wings of a bee. The third is a manual mode that you can use for special effects, like if you wanted to turn the texture of the cascading water in the river to silk."

"How does that work?"

Delaney shook her head. "I can't show you how to change the aperture on horseback. We'd have to get off and—"

"There's an old fencepost where we can tie up the horses," Jace said, nodding toward the trail ahead.

She supposed they could take a quick break. Delaney had led him down the open trail that followed the river on purpose. She figured it was one more way to keep him out of the woods and away from the animals.

"The river is one of our ranch's best features," she said, sliding out of the saddle. "Our guests love the clear blue water, the trophy-sized trout, canoeing, kayaking—"

Jace helped secure the horses. "What do *you* like to do?"

Delaney smiled. "Skip stones."

The corners of Jace's mouth curved up into a smile. "Are you any good at it?"

"Come and see." There were many things she feared she *wasn't* good at, but she did take pride in this particular skill. Handing Jace her camera, she walked toward the water and scanned the riverbank for a flat, smooth, round stone. Then after finding one to her liking, she held it between her thumb and forefinger, and gave Jace a quick glance. "Ready?"

He nodded, his eyes lit with amusement. "Ready . . . aim . . . fire!"

While she wished he'd used another term, she reminded herself that she was doing a good job of distracting him from doing any *real* firing, and gave the rock a swift toss across the river. Flying low, it bounced along the surface, hitting the water six times before sinking.

Jace clapped, his face full of admiration as he walked up close beside her. "I guess I should have tried the camera's fast-action mode but I wanted to see this with my own eyes."

"What about you?" she asked. "How many times can you skip?"

"I've never spent much time by a river." Jace frowned. "There are a lot of things I've never done."

"Don't you love hearing the sound of the rushing water beside your cabin while lying in your bed at night?" Delaney asked, hoping to point out the advantages of staying at Collins Country Cabins.

"I *do*."

He appeared to be impressed, so she kept going. "And don't you love the way the sunshine makes the river sparkle?"

"I love the way it makes your eyes sparkle," he teased.

"I'm trying to get you to appreciate what's right in front of you," Delaney said with a sweep of her hand.

He laughed, his gaze never leaving hers. "I am."

Frustrated by the heat rising into her cheeks, she said, "How about I show you that manual mode?"

He handed her camera back to her and raised the one she'd given him to his eyes. "What am I looking for?"

"A horizontal scale of numbers should appear along the bottom of the viewfinder."

"I don't see anything," he said, pulling the camera away from his face.

Stretching one arm between his, she leaned against him in order to see what she was doing, and turned a different dial on the camera. "Look again."

But instead of peering into the camera, he turned his head and looked at her. Delaney froze as his gaze held hers. Just inches apart, she had to admit her first assessment of the cowboy was wrong. He was handsome, whether he was far away or close, even more so close. She just hadn't seen it before.

He seemed to be looking at her as if for the first time again, too. "I could get used to this," he said, and grinned.

Delaney pulled back, sure her face must be as red as her family's new hay barn. "We should get back to the horses."

But as they continued to ride, Jace continued to flirt with her. When they stopped along an upper ridge to admire a few remaining wildflowers and Jace rode up beside her, she pointed. "See that yellow flower beside that big rock?"

He nodded. "Scarlet paintbrush."

"If you zoom in close you can see every spiked petal," she said, and gazed up at him. "Isn't it beautiful?"

"It is," he said, without even a glance at the plant. "So are you."

Her cheeks heated again and Sammy Jo's encouraging voice screamed in the back of her mind, *Flirt!* But she couldn't do it. All she could do was laugh and tell him, "I have no idea what to say to that."

Jace grinned. "Again—love your honesty. Although I suppose you could say a simple, 'Thank you.'"

Delaney smiled. "Okay then, thank you."

Was it possible she'd misjudged him? Believed he was worse than he really was? After all, she'd seen with her own eyes how much he cared for his horse. And how much he'd wanted his cousins to like him. And how much he'd wanted to use the camera to take her picture.

"You really are, you know, beautiful." The way he looked at her almost made her believe it. Except Bree had always been the beauty queen around the house, not her. She was the pigtailed tomboy who didn't mind when her horses slobbered apple and carrot juice all over her. The one who volunteered to muck out the stalls. A gal who climbed up to sit on the roof of the barn to watch the moon.

A few of the horses whinnied and a second later a group of horses and riders rode toward them coming from the opposite direction and intending to pass them.

"Jace!" Gavin McKinley called. "You should have come with us. One of our guys got himself an eight-point buck with the first draw of his bow."

"That's impressive," Jace said, giving the man a nod as if interested.

"Let me introduce you to Alicia," Gavin said, coming up beside them with another rider. "She'd like to be your personal trail guide."

"I sure would," the voluptuous blond bombshell purred. "How about tomorrow, cowboy?"

Delaney stiffened and glanced at Jace. Was he attracted to this blatantly seductive woman? It was clear from Gavin's expression that he hoped so.

She thought of the dresses, jewelry, makeup, and magazines Bree and Sammy Jo had brought over. They'd been *right*. She was going to need every advantage she could latch on to in order to keep Jace from giving his endorsement to someone else. *Oh, if only she knew how to flirt!*

By some miracle, Jace shook his head. "Maybe some other time. I promised Jed and Luke Collins I'd go out hunting with them tomorrow."

What? She couldn't let them, but silenced her tongue. For now, all that was important was that Jace had rejected the rival's offer. She had several hours available to come up with a plan to stop Jace from hunting with her own family. "That's right, Gavin," she said, backing up Jace's decision. "My father is a hard man to refuse."

Gavin grimaced. "But, Jace, we're talking about big game here, with a beautiful woman by your side. What more could you want?"

Jace gave the man a level look and nodded toward Delaney. "I've already got a beautiful woman by my side. Promise me something no one else can and maybe I'll come along on a hunt with you."

"Playing hard to get, are you?" Gavin let out a hearty laugh. "Okay, Jace, I'll wait to talk to you in private, when there aren't so many *others* around."

The outfitter nodded in her direction, making it clear he meant when *she* wasn't around. How dare that man! And what about Jace? His words inferring she was as beautiful as Gavin's sexy blond gave her an unexpected jolt of warm pleasure, but what about what he said after that?

"Promise me something no one else can"? Was Jace insinuating he might be interested in going after some illegal kills with this guy?

Her stomach squeezed tight, just like it did when her friend, Carol, from the animal shelter asked her to speak at the rally. Nauseating bile rose into the back of her throat and she feared she might be sick again. She squeezed her eyes shut, took a few deep breaths, and after a moment got it under control.

And to think she'd actually considered that maybe Jace wasn't so bad. *Men.* She couldn't trust any of them. She wouldn't have anything to do with them if she could get away with it, but she remembered the promise she'd made to her family. No matter what she thought of Jace, she had to be nice to him and somehow make him believe her ranch was better than anyone else's.

Gavin signaled for his group to move on, and as he rode his horse past her, he smirked, and taunted softly so only she could hear, "You don't have what it takes to keep him."

Alicia blew Jace a farewell kiss off her hand and with a sinking feeling Delaney feared the rival outfitter might be right.

Chapter Six

"ONKLE JACE SAID Rio is a rodeo horse!" Meghan squealed, twirling around the bathroom in her palomino-print dress. She'd wanted to wear a dress because she'd seen Delaney wear a dress at dinner the night before, and had also seen how much Jace had liked it.

"Jace is *not* your uncle," Delaney corrected.

Meghan stopped twirling, came over to look in the mirror Delaney was using to put on her makeup, and frowned. "He gives high fives and piggyback rides like Onkle Uke."

Yes, she'd seen him do that the evening before when everyone was walking out to toast marshmallows around the bonfire. He'd pretended he was a horse and Meghan had giggled more that night than she had in a long time.

"*Uncle Luke,*" Delaney corrected, trying to help her with her speech. "And just because Jace plays with you *doesn't* mean he's your uncle. Jace is not related to us. He's not family."

Meghan gave her a dubious look. "He's my friend?"

"Not even that."

"Who is he?" Meghan asked, looking confused.

Delaney set her tube of lipstick down on the sink. "Just a cowboy."

Meghan smiled. "Cowboy Jace?"

"Yes." *Cowboy Jace.* That's all he would ever be to both of them.

Delaney glanced in the mirror and smacked her lips together. She had been unable stop her father and brother from taking Jace out on a hunt, even though she'd tried telling them they should all be in church this fine Sunday morning instead of out in the woods killing things.

She only hoped plan B had more success.

JACE FOLLOWED JED and Luke Collins on horseback along the trail between their ranch and the property next door to their right. Sure enough, the new outfitter had brought in a mobile trailer unit to act as a temporary office, and already had hunters lining up for business. The owner, Isaac Woolly, who sported a white woolly beard to match his name, introduced himself as they rode by.

"Odd time of year to be settin' up, don't you think?" Jed asked, coming to a stop beside Isaac. "In a few more weeks the snows will arrive and you'll need a plow to get anyone in or out."

Isaac shook his head. "We've got a plow ready to go

and next week we're bringing in snowmobiles. Woolly Outfitters is going to be a year-round outfitting facility."

"Maybe we should look into getting some snowmobiles," Luke said under his breath as they continued riding. "Collins Country Cabins could be a year-round facility, too."

"Do you know how much those things cost?" Jed argued. Then he glanced back at Jace and his scowl changed into a friendly grin. *Too friendly* as he asked, "What do you think, Jace? Would you recommend we stay open, too? Do you think that would attract more customers?"

"Not with subzero temperatures and two other outfitters nearby," Jace said truthfully. "You'd spend more money in fuel for heat and gas for the vehicles than you'd make on cabin rentals. A few adventurous souls might come out, but most people fly south for warmer vacations during the winter months."

"Exactly what I thought," Jed agreed.

"Unless we got ourselves some good advertising with a good endorsement," Luke suggested, and he rode on ahead of his father, giving the older man a quick grin along the way.

Jace chuckled, knowing it was *his* endorsement they were after, just like so many others over the years who wanted him to endorse this product or that. He found the whole fame thing a nuisance. Only his mother, sister, and his friend Buck seemed to like him for who he really was these days.

Next they passed the property belonging to Gavin

McKinley, and he, too, had hunters lined up in front of his large western-style lodge, wearing their orange caps and vests, and looking at each other's newfangled bows.

Back at the ranch that morning, Jed had offered him a compound bow, but Jace pulled his own sixty-pound recurve bow and quiver full of thirty-inch broad-tip arrows out of the back of his truck. Both Jed and Luke had given him a look of disbelief as if he were crazy. Most every hunter used a compound bow for its arrow speed and accuracy, but those weren't qualities Jace was looking for today.

"Well," Luke had said, still looking skeptical, "there *are* a few guys out there who claim using a recurve allows them to draw back their arrow faster."

Not that Jace intended to do that either.

Farther down the trail, right before it branched off into state forest, Jed pointed to a cattle ranch with several sheds, a stable, and a small, single-story house. "That's the Triple T ranch owned by the Tanners."

Jace studied the property. "I didn't realize they were so close."

"About twenty minutes if you use the road and drive around," Luke informed him. "But Ryan usually takes the trail and can ride his horse over in about ten."

"This trail connects all four properties to state forest land?" Jace asked as they turned into the woods.

"Don't forget Sammy Jo's property on the other side of us," Luke added. "We all grew up riding these trails together and know every inch. But there is one place in particular we'd like to show you, a place where Dad and I always find the best deer."

"I'm sorry Delaney didn't bring you out here yesterday," Jed said as the wooded trail circled an open meadow. "She's a little confused right now. Her divorce messed her up some and she doesn't know what a man wants. She doesn't realize sometimes a guy needs to get into the backcountry and hunt."

"What's that over there?" Jace said, pointing.

It looked like a bright blue shirt peeking out from beneath a bush. He wouldn't have known what it was except for the sleeve. Only a keen eye could have spotted it, but he'd always had the vision of a hawk. A pink pair of pants lay in the brush a few yards ahead. Child-sized. He scanned the trail circling the meadow and spotted several other articles of clothing of various colors and sizes wadded up and tucked beside logs, piled on rocks, and hanging from tree limbs. It looked as if someone had cleaned out their closet. Who would do that? Litter the land with clothes?

Now that he'd pointed them out, Jed and Luke saw them as well, and from the look they gave each other it was clear they also knew who the items belonged to.

"We won't find any deer around here," Jed barked, his voice gruff. "Not with the human scent on all these clothes stinking up the place. We'll take you to a different spot."

Jace nodded and followed them along the outside rim of the forest. Once they reached their location of choice, Luke tied the horses to a high hitch line between two trees and Jed took Jace up toward an outcropping of rock with a view of the wispy golden fields below.

"The deer come out here to feed on some of the left-over wheat," Jed told him, and sure enough, about an hour later, a big ole six-point buck came into view. Jed moved aside, giving him room, and said, "He's all yours."

Jace had agreed to come, hoping he could talk to them about the poachers in the area, but hadn't discovered anything. He wasn't in the mood to hunt. Hadn't intended to hunt. That's the real reason he'd brought along the recurve instead of the compound bow. But Jed put the pressure on by issuing instructions like a drill sergeant and looked at him expectedly as if he couldn't wait to see him take the shot, making him once again a hard man to refuse.

Raising his bow, Jace drew out an arrow, placed it along the notched rest, drew back the string, and was ready to let the arrow fly when all of the sudden the buck reminded him of another deer. The young doe he'd seen Delaney release from her secret animal shelter hidden in the grove of trees along the edge of the Collins property.

He also remembered Meghan saying the dog liked hamburgers, too—right after Delaney tried to convince him she'd eaten hers in about two seconds flat. It occurred to him he'd *never* seen her eat meat. The night before, she'd only dished salad onto her plate. Geez, Delaney was probably a vegetarian!

Then there was the horrified look on her face when he'd shown up for the trail ride—with her father's gun and the way she'd shoved the camera in his hands and gushed about the precious wildlife. And the image of all the clothes, filled with human scent, leaped forward with vivid clarity. The pink child-sized pants. Obviously, they'd been laid there on purpose by Delaney.

She didn't want him to hunt for sport.

Jace slid his aim to the left and released the arrow just short of the buck's hind end, effectively scaring the animal off into the trees so Jed wouldn't try a shot with his own bow.

"Looks like I missed," Jace said, inserting a note of disbelief into his tone. Then he turned and leveled his gaze on Jed, who no doubt guessed the truth, and a silent understanding passed between them. Dropping his bow down to his side, Jace added, "I think it's best we don't tell Delaney about this."

Jed almost looked relieved. "No," he agreed. "We won't tell Delaney."

Upon their return, Jace scanned the people milling about the ranch but there was no sign of Delaney. She was probably hiding, unable to bear the sight of him bringing in a fresh kill. He wanted to tell her she needn't worry, but he caught sight of Meghan playing with Boots, the black-and-white puppy, and walked over to her first.

"Hi, Cowboy Jace," Meghan greeted, pushing the puppy off her lap so she could stand up to give him a high five with a slap of her hand. "I have to call you Cowboy Jace because Mommy said you aren't my onkle or my friend."

"She did, did she?" Jace asked, and scooped the toddler up into his arms. "Who do you think is a friend?"

Meghan reached up and pulled the tip of his hat down over his face. "Someone who plays with me."

Pushing his hat back up on his head, Jace grinned. "Don't I do that?"

Meghan giggled. "Yeah. You're my friend."

"We'll be secret friends," he said, setting her back down. "But you can still call me Cowboy Jace."

"Okay," Meghan agreed, and smiled up at him with those incredible blue eyes she'd inherited from her mother. "Maybe if you play with Mommy, you can be her secret friend, too."

Jace laughed. "Yeah, maybe. Do you know where I can find her?"

"She's right here," a voice said from behind.

Jace spun around and watched her gaze search the area around him. "No luck today?" she asked, obviously referring to his hunt.

"Not until now," Jace said, taking her hand. "I guess I'm only lucky when I get to spend time with you."

DELANEY DIDN'T KNOW what to make of Jace's bold flirtatious statements. No one had ever been so persistent in pursuing her before. She didn't know if he really meant it, or if he was teasing, or if it was a game he played to see how uncomfortable he could make her. Because whenever he said she was beautiful, or that he wanted to get to know her better, or that he was lucky to spend time with her, she didn't know what to say, how to act, or how to even breathe.

She blushed on a regular basis now. All Jace had to do was look at her and heat would shoot up into her cheeks, then cascade over the rest of her, making her feel all warm and bubbly inside.

But as long as his fascination with her kept him from hunting, that was all that mattered. She'd been incredibly relieved when he'd come back empty-handed after his trip out to the woods with her father and brother. Emptying her laundry basket to scare off the wildlife with both her and Meghan's scent had been a desperate, spur of the moment decision. Apparently it worked. For a while anyway. Coming up with new strategies to keep Jace away from the animals was a constant struggle.

He'd only been back a short time when Alicia, the sexy blond from Fox Creek Outfitters, rode her horse down the property line trail. Cupping her hand around her mouth, the woman called out, "Care to come on a trail ride with *me* this afternoon?"

Delaney didn't think she'd ever been bold enough to cut anyone off in midsentence before, but when Jace started to reply, she said, "He can't."

Just two words, yet those two words had been firm and powerful, and got the job done.

Jace glanced over at her with surprise, and if he *had* wanted to go with the blond, he could have. But he didn't. He shook his head and gave Alicia an apologetic look. "Sorry, not today. I promised to give Delaney a lesson in archery. Isn't that right, Del?"

He'd called her by the shortened nickname only her family used. But she wasn't going to correct him in front of Alicia. She had bigger concerns than what name he called her at the moment. "I—I, uh, yes. I can't wait," she said, nodding her head vigorously. "And I'd be . . . very *upset* if you . . . canceled on me."

Alicia hesitated for a split second, then licked her lips and gave Jace a slow, ever-widening smile. "Seems like I'll have to take a number and get in line. Let me know when it's my turn, cowboy."

If Delaney had her way, that woman would *never* get her turn. Not because of Alicia's extreme sex appeal, or because she couldn't stand the thought of Jace turning his attention on someone *else*, but because . . . well, because the woman worked for Fox Creek Outfitters. She was one of Gavin McKinley's minions, sent to steal their endorsement. Yes. No doubt about it. *That* was the reason she didn't want Jace to go off with Alicia, the only reason. After all, what other reason could there possibly be?

She continued to glare at the woman until she rode out of sight, then realized Jace had said something. He waved a hand in front of her face to get her attention and she did a double take. "I'm sorry, what did you say?"

He laughed. "I have to go into town for about three hours, then I'll be back for your archery lesson."

"Three hours," Delaney repeated. "Right. I'll see you then." Three hours happened to be the perfect amount of time for her to ride out to the woods and recollect her clothes.

Later that afternoon, Bree came out to the stable to let her know Jace had returned, but when she went to meet him, Delaney wasn't expecting to have to make her way through a crowd.

"Ready for your lesson?" Jace asked, giving her a mischievous grin.

She glanced at the row of archers lined up across their open field, shooting arrows at ten equally spaced round targets pinned to stacked hay bales. "What's all this?"

Jace shrugged. "While I was in town I thought I'd pick up some archery supplies."

Delaney stared at the assortment of bows, arrows, quivers, leather armguards, and targets their guests were using and tried to calculate the cost. She gave up after only adding the first few numbers. "You must have spent a fortune."

"Not that much," Jace assured her. "The bows aren't meant for anything other than target practice and the arrows have blunt plastic tips at the end. Except for Meghan's. The ends of her arrows have big suction cups so they'll stick to the special children's target I bought for her and Cody."

"You even bought the kids a set?" Delaney glanced toward her daughter, who was having trouble holding on to all her arrows, but still having the time of her life. As were the guests who had rented cabins 6 through 8.

She'd been worried about that group. They'd arrived a few days before, and consisted of three different families, but they'd been listlessly hanging around the ranch as if they had nothing interesting to do. Now they were all laughing and smiling like a completely different set of people.

"Great idea for a fun afternoon," the father of one family said. "I haven't shot a bow in years."

"I haven't shot one ever," said his wife.

"Can we take them home?" asked one of the teenagers with them.

Jace shook his head. "Sorry, but they belong to Collins Country Cabins. We need to keep them here for our other guests."

Delaney noticed he said *"our,"* as if he were a part of her family, but didn't draw attention to it. She was just thankful he'd helped give their guests a good time. Because if they had a good time, chances were they'd tell all their friends and next year Collins Country Cabins might have even more bookings than this one. Which was exactly what her family needed.

"If you give the receipt to Bree," Delaney told him, "I'm sure she can write you a check to reimburse you."

Jace frowned. "This is a gift."

"Did you see that?" Cody called over to them, his eyes lit with excitement. "I just got a bull's-eye!"

"Great job," Jace called over to him, then he glanced at Delaney's daughter. "Meghan, do you need help?"

She threw down the bow and walked up to the target and stuck her suction-tipped plastic arrow onto the special laminated circle that had come with her play set. Then she turned around, looked at them, and said proudly, "I got a bull's-eye, too."

Delaney laughed and then locked gazes with Jace. Her ex never played with Meghan as much as he did. Not ever. "Think you'll ever want kids one day?"

Jace nodded toward Meghan. "If they're like *her*, then sure. Although my mother would faint from shock if she heard me say that."

"Doesn't she think you'll ever settle down?"

Jace grinned. "My mother *hopes*."

A few more people from the ranch came out to watch and other families wanted to take their turns, which started a friendly competition between them.

"Jace, can you show me how to line my arrow up straight again?" Cody called over to them.

"If anyone's going to teach you how to shoot, it's going to be *me*," a man's stern voice said from behind.

Delaney watched Jace turn and face Ryan. Both men stared each other down a second. Then Jace offered, "Then why don't you join us?"

A muscle flexed along the side of Ryan's jaw, then he gave Jace a nod. "Thanks. I will."

As Delaney watched Jace try to hide a smile, her heart skipped a beat and her throat closed up, tight with emotion. She, too, yearned for acceptance from the ones she loved and knew how much that small step forward must have meant to him.

He looked at her as if *she* meant something to him. Then he took a lightweight bow out of a bag, and a few arrows, and stepped in close behind her. "Let me show you how it's done," he said, wrapping his arms around hers and helping her place her hands on the bow. "Keep the bow in your left hand, and with your right, you hook the feathered end of the arrow into the string like this."

She stared at the bow and arrow in her hands and paid attention to what he was saying, but in the back of her mind all she could think about was how nice it was to be wrapped in someone's arms, not just anyone's, but someone who seemed to care about her.

"Then you see that little ledge in the middle of the bow?" he asked. "Place the shaft of the arrow on the ledge, keeping it straight, then pull back and—"

He put his left hand around her waist and his right over the fingers she used to pull back the arrow. Never would she have ever imagined she'd participate in archery. Never would she have ever thought she'd *enjoy* it.

"Let it fly," Jace whispered, his mouth against her ear.

The arrow flew forward and missed the target by a half foot, but when she turned her head to look at him, she knew an arrow of a different kind, *Cupid's arrow*, had hit its mark. Her heart still reeled from the impact.

"Can we do it again?" she asked, her gaze drifting toward his mouth and then back up to his eyes.

"Oh, yeah," he said, his voice deep and raspy, as if he had a hard time getting the words out. "We can do it as many times as you want."

ON MONDAY, JACE waited at one end of the stage while his sister waited at the other. There was no way their mother was going to escape their questioning this time. They had her trapped, and only had to wait until she finished her Labor Day campaign speech in front of the crowd gathered in front of Bozeman's city hall before they could speak to her.

"Poaching has spread across our state like wildfire," Grace Aldridge spouted into the microphone, "ravaging our wildlife and destroying natural habitations as well as our ecological landscape with no regard for rules, respect, or resolutions, all for the sake of money."

Her supporters, made up of generational ranchers and vocal environmentalists, nodded their heads in agreement and clapped after each and every line. Jace glanced at his watch. He had wanted to spend more time with Delaney, but it looked like this business with his mother would take up the entire day.

"I thank you for your time, your energy, and most of all I want you to know how much I value your support," she shouted boldly. "If elected governor, I promise you these poachers *will* be caught and brought to justice for their actions. Changes *will* be made. Our land will flourish with life and our natural resources will be protected, pristine, and plentiful once again."

Jace admired his mother's tenacity, just *not* when she was being tenacious toward him. He'd left numerous phone calls over the last couple of days and Natalie had doggedly followed her around the house whenever she didn't have to work on her new novel, but still their mother had continued to elude them.

"Mom, if we can have a *word*," Jace said, sprinting up on stage the moment she was done and offering her his arm to escort her off, "Nat and I have something we have to say to you."

"All right," his mother said diplomatically, "first let me speak to my financial backers, then we'll have lunch and we'll discuss whatever is on your mind."

Another hour passed. Lunch was interrupted by several townsfolk wanting to shake her hand and offer their encouragement. Then when they arrived back at her house, the cleaning lady needed to talk to her about some kind of problem in the bathroom.

Jace rolled his eyes and shared a commiserating look with Nat, and said, "There's obviously something she doesn't want to tell us."

Nat agreed. "Do you think she *did* steal the Tanners' inheritance?"

Their mother must have overheard them, for she suddenly appeared from around the corner of the dining room and met them in the kitchen. "What's all this about stealing?"

Jace handed her a cup of tea and gestured for her to sit down on the stool opposite them at the kitchen counter. "You've stalled long enough," he told her. "Now, you know we love you, but you have to tell us what the Tanners meant when they said you stole their mother's inheritance."

His mother's gaze dropped to her cup as she took a spoon and stirred the tea bag around and around. "Lora and I never got along. She didn't want me to marry your father. She said I was too ambitious and self-seeking. But I only did what I had to in order to protect my own."

"What did you do?" Natalie pressed, taking the spoon away from her.

Their mother looked up, gazed at them each a moment, and sighed. "When your father died, our only income came from the ranch and at that time I hadn't acquired any skills that I could use to support us. For four years I struggled to hire ranch hands willing to work for less than satisfactory wages, until I couldn't hold on to our place any longer and finally one day I sold it."

Jace nodded. He'd been mad at his mother for selling the ranch, but he knew even at age seven that they had to eat, and vowed to help his mother put food on the table by catching squirrels, rabbits, and other small game over at his friend Bucky's ranch until he was old enough to use a bow or gun to bring in some bigger game.

"We moved into this house," their mother said, sweeping a hand around the room, "and suddenly had cash in our pockets, but I knew it wouldn't last long. I knew it would take me a while to learn new skills, get a good paying job, and launch a career that could end our financial worries. So I had to be careful with what we spent."

"All of that makes sense," Natalie said, and frowned. "So what's the problem?"

Their mother took a deep breath and explained, "Half of the money from the sale of the ranch was supposed to go to your father's sister."

Jace gave her a direct look and said, "You never paid her."

His mother shrugged. "Their parents' will wasn't specific. Lora married Bo Tanner and went off to his ranch to live with him. They seemed to be doing okay. They had a large cattle ranch that brought in enough profit to keep them afloat. I suppose it was always assumed that if Lora and your father's parents' ranch sold, they'd divide the profits, but when your father died, Lora and Bo didn't seem to need the money half as much as we did."

"She had a right to her share," Jace argued.

"And look at us now," Natalie exclaimed. "We have more than enough money. Why didn't you ever pay her back?"

"She wouldn't speak to me for many years," their mother said with a shudder. "Then after a while, it just seemed too awkward."

"So you kept it?" Jace stared at her in disbelief. "Information like this could jeopardize your political career."

"And you have enough going on with the threat from the poachers," Nat warned.

"I know," she said, and broke down in tears. "I know."

"Mom," Jace said, and swallowed hard. "We all make mistakes. But if you don't give the Tanners back what you owe them, *I will*."

Chapter Seven

DELANEY THRUST THE hoe into the ground to help her grandma uproot the rest of the dying, shriveled vegetable vines in her precious garden. The growing season in Montana was always short, hampered by frost until late spring and cut off early by frost in the fall, but Grandma was a stubborn old lady and insisted on trying to grow her vegetables anyway. *"Where there's a will, there's a way,"* she often quoted whenever anyone got on her about it.

Sammy Jo volunteered to help since the Happy Trails Horse Camp where she'd taught children to ride all summer had now closed for the season. With the kids back in school, the type of guests staying at Collins Country Cabins had changed, too. Instead of catering to families, the reservations were for adults interested in either hiking or hunting. And thanks to Gavin's ongoing smear campaign, those reservations were few. This morning they'd had even more cancelations.

Although Delaney knew her family needed the money from having booked cabins, part of her was glad for the extra time available this week, which having fewer guests provided. She had to admit, she was proud of herself. Each day she'd managed to keep Jace busy with some kind of activity to keep him from hunting. She'd taken him on another photo shoot and he'd helped her improve her accuracy in archery.

There had only been one intense, breathless moment where she feared she might fail. Jace had been setting up to practice his archery alongside her using his recurve bow with his sharper, real hunting tipped arrows, when a buck with a beautiful rack of antlers stepped out from a pocket of trees. Jace had his bow up and ready, his arrow loaded, and had been aiming at the target in the foreground when the deer appeared. She'd been afraid he'd see the animal, shift his aim, and shoot. So with her heart leaping into her throat, she grabbed Jace's arm with both hands and pretended to sneeze, just as he fired. The arrow skittered off in one direction and the deer skittered off in another.

"Sorry about that," she'd lied.

She doubted he'd even seen the deer, doubted he suspected how she really felt about hunting, and doubted he knew anything about her many animal rescue attempts while they were together. Especially since he just gave her a good-natured smile like always, and teased, "It's okay. I know how hard it is for you to keep your hands off me."

She'd laughed in return, partly because she secretly loved his flirtatious teasing, and partly because she knew she'd won another round in keeping the animals safe.

He'd been here ten days, with only four more to go. Four more until she asked him for an endorsement and then he left . . . to continue on his way.

"Shoo!" Grandma said, nudging her dappled gray miniature pony, Party Marty, aside. "I know you love me, but I can't work with you rubbing right up against me."

Sammy Jo laughed. "Bree told me Delaney was looking pretty cozy with Jace out there on the archery field."

"Just doing my job," Delaney said, hiding a smile. "I think it's safe to say we'll have the endorsement for the ranch within the next day or two."

"I think dressing up for dinner and wearing the makeup and jewelry has helped," Sammy Jo said with a nod. "I knew it would work. You look both professional and beautiful, exactly what was needed."

"Nonsense," Grandma argued. "It's the bear claw necklace that's doing it. Delaney's changed into a different person over the last week and a half. She's stronger on the inside, a little less fearful, a little more ferocious."

Sammy Jo shook her head. "I don't think Del could ever be considered ferocious."

"I don't think so either," Delaney agreed. She pulled up the stalk of a potato plant with a gloved hand, and shook off the dirt clinging to the cluster of little round golden potatoes hanging from the roots. "If I'm different it's because I'm just acting out the part I'm supposed to play."

"Or you're in love," Sammy Jo teased.

Love? After only ten days? Ridiculous. *Entranced*, maybe, but not in love. She had to admit she was attracted to the man. Everything from his dark hair, green eyes, strong husky physique to the way he treated both her and Meghan, and even their guests, was *very* attractive. He'd make a great boyfriend, except for the fact he liked to hunt. But so far he hadn't, and maybe, just *maybe*, she could convince him never to hunt again. Realistically she didn't know if that was possible, but whenever he looked at her she dreamed impossible dreams.

He'd sent her the photo of the two of them together from his cell phone and had called her the night before to ask her on a date. A *real* date. She hadn't dated since that fateful night she went to Las Vegas and met Steve, if you could even call that a date. She preferred not to think of him. Which meant she hadn't been out on a date since high school unless you counted the few times over the summer when Zach Tanner had asked her to come hang out. She preferred not to think of him either. Zach showed interest in her, but wasn't ready to be the father of a little girl like Meghan. He wanted to have fun, not be tied down. In fact, he was a lot like Steve.

As her thoughts returned to Jace's finer qualities, a high-pitched scream pierced the air, followed by another. Delaney turned her head toward the sound and gasped. *"Meghan?"*

"It's not her," Grandma said, dropping her hoe. "She's with your ma."

"Sounds like the twins," Sammy Jo said as the three of them rushed out of the garden.

A gunshot echoed off the hills, making them run faster, to see what was the matter. All Delaney could think of was saving the animals. Today was Saturday, which was why the twins were here and not at school. She'd told them to feed the cows and horses, which meant they were in the back pasture. But it wasn't gun season for another five days, the day Jace was scheduled to leave, so why would someone be shooting so close to home?

When she rounded the corner of the stable and glanced into the field beyond, her stomach nearly fell down beneath the soles of her boots. She froze, her head in a tizzy as she glanced at Jace standing beside a dead animal carcass, a gun in his hands.

"I didn't shoot it," he said, meeting her gaze. "But whoever did, left it here after only taking its antlers and the smell drew in a pack of coyotes."

"He scared them off," said Luke, and Delaney noticed that he and their father also carried guns.

"That's why I gave him a gun to take with him on your trail ride last week," her father said, a grim expression spreading over his face. "For protection."

"It was?" Delaney cast Jace a quick glance, her heart relieved it wasn't to hunt after all.

Her father nodded. "At the time, I didn't want to alarm you, but we've been finding dead carcasses all along the border of our property."

Delaney stared, horrified, at the unmoving body that lay before her, and wondered if it was the same deer she'd helped save when she and Jace were practicing archery and she'd sneezed. She couldn't tell because the rack of antlers had been cut off, leaving the head a bloody mess.

"Poachers," Grandma whispered, furrowing her bushy white brows.

"Yeah," Luke said with a nod. "And by leaving the bodies on our property it seems someone is trying to set us up to take the fall."

"Gavin McKinley," their father growled. "Or that new outfitter next door. Come to think of it, the carcasses started showing up about the same time our new neighbor arrived."

"We came out to feed the horses, just like Delaney said," Nora squealed, her eyes wide. "And then I asked, '*What's that?*'"

"And I said, '*I don't know,*'" Nadine continued. "When I turned around, I tripped and grabbed her hand. Then we both almost—"

"*Fell right on top of it!*" they shrieked in unison.

Both twins trembled from head to toe and Delaney directed, "You two go back to the house and stay with my ma and Meghan. Don't let Meghan come out."

As the twins ran off, Sammy Jo asked, "What do we do now? Contact the Department of Fish and Wildlife?"

Delaney knew what she had to do. Her wildlife rescue group would want to know about this and she had to get to town to fill them in on all the details.

"Yes, we're aware of the problem," Carol Levine said when Delaney met with her that afternoon. "Just yesterday, Ben and Mary Ann were called out to a piece of property, not too far from yours, and a family showed them the body of a dead bobcat. Its head had been cut off.

We figure some poacher wanted to mount it to a plaque and sell it for money."

"But that wasn't the only problem," Mary Ann explained. "The cat left behind a couple of cubs in a den not ten feet away."

Delaney gasped. "Oh, no! Isn't it late in the season for cubs?"

Carol shook her head. "Although spring is typical, bobcats can mate all year long. We figure this mother was on her second litter of the year."

"What did you do with them?" Delaney glanced around at all the cages and Ben motioned her over toward a special pen in the back.

She unlatched the wire cage door and reached in to scoop one up, then held it in her arms and her heart practically melted on the spot. The brown kitten with black-tipped ears and adorable round blue eyes was the size of a house cat but with only a short little tail. And while it had a series of black stripes around its cheeks, the majority of its body, especially its cream belly, was covered in black spots. "Oh, they're so adorable, only a few weeks old."

"We're bottle-feeding them for now," Carol said, looking over her shoulder. "But they require constant attention and at two months they're going to need to eat meat."

Delaney thought of the fresh deer carcass her father had butchered into chunks and placed in the freezer, not wanting the poacher's kill that morning to go to waste. "I know where we can get some venison," she told them. "I can bring some by on my next trip into town."

"Actually," Mary Ann said with a smile, "we don't have the personnel we did while you were working here and we know you've turned that old toolshed on your family's property into a great little shelter."

"Why don't you take them home with you?" Ben asked, handing her the other cub in addition to the first. "No one knows how to care for these cute little guys better than you."

Carol agreed. "You have a way with animals, Delaney. A gift."

"My father would kill me!" she exclaimed.

Carol smirked. "Then don't let him find out."

Her father wasn't the only one she was worried about. What about Jace? Could she spend time with him and still tend to the cubs?

JACE WAS IN the stable tending to Rio when Delaney's grandma came out to pay him a surprise visit.

"Put some of this on his leg and I guarantee you'll start seeing a difference in the way he walks by the time you have to leave," Ruth Collins said, handing him a white tube.

Not seeing a label, he asked, "What is it?"

"Some of my homemade mineral-infused hand cream. It's a natural healing remedy great for any kind of wound, but especially sore muscles and chapped hands," she said, and nodded toward his fingers. "You should put some on yourself and take care of those chapped knuckles of yours."

He looked into the eye of his horse, who stood in the stall beside him. "What do you think, Rio? Should we give it a try?"

Rio twitched his ears and let out a snort.

"I gotta say, it does work," Ryan said, coming up the aisle and leaning over the half door of the horse's stall. "She gave me some, too. I told her I didn't need to go greasing up my hands like some woman, but the cuts in my fingers did heal and I've been using it ever since."

"Well, okay, then," Jace said with a nod. "If it has Ryan's endorsement, I'll give the cream a try."

"You men can tease me about it all you want," Ruth warned. "But I know who you'll be coming to see when your mineral lotion runs out and your hands start bleeding again."

Ryan cleared his throat. "My mother would like to see you, Jace. You're invited to dinner tonight. I'm supposed to issue the invitation on behalf of the entire family."

"Well, then, tell her I accept." Jace ran his hand through Rio's black silky mane and swished it back and forth. "There's something I need to give back to her."

His cousin turned to leave, then glanced back over his shoulder and added, "Bree's going to be there. And Delaney and Meghan are invited, too."

"My, won't that be something," Ruth predicted with a chuckle. "Can't wait to hear about Zach's reaction to all this. There might even be some cousin-to-cousin combat. Jace, you might be back for another tube of my mineral cream to heal your hands a whole lot sooner than I thought."

Jace didn't want any trouble with the Tanners. He had to admit he was curious to see what his aunt and his other cousins looked like, but his main goal was to deliver half of the inheritance owed his aunt Lora and then get out of there.

"You look nervous," Delaney commented as they knocked at the door of the Triple T ranch. "Are you nervous?"

He swallowed the lump in his throat and shook his head. "Of course not."

"Nothing to be nervous about," Bree told them, pushing the door open and walking right in. "We're all family."

Except, in his experience, family didn't usually stand around in a horseshoe formation gawking at you the moment you stepped through the door. Bree took his arm, pushed him forward, and initiated the introductions.

"Doesn't he look just like you?" Bree asked, her voice overflowing with enthusiasm.

Lora cupped a hand over her mouth as she looked at him, then her eyes grew moist and she said, "He looks like my brother. Only his hair is darker, much darker."

"So is my sister's," Jace said with a nod.

"I'd like to meet her, too," Lora said with a smile, and invited them all to sit down at the table. "We're having steak and potatoes, a staple around here since we live on a cattle ranch. I hope that's all right with you?"

"I'll eat whatever you're serving," Jace assured her. He pulled out a chair to sit beside Delaney, but Zach stole his seat by sitting down first. Recalling Ruth's warning about him in the stable, he decided it was best to sit somewhere else and circled to a chair on the other side of the table across from her.

Lora glanced at Delaney and Meghan. "We also have salad for you."

"Oh, that's right," Zach said, and grinned. "Bet you didn't know Delaney was a vegetarian, did you, Jace?"

Delaney's mouth dropped open and she gave Zach a look of horrified disbelief, then looked across the table toward *him*.

"Actually, I did know," Jace said, hiding a smile as Delaney's mouth dropped open further. "Vegetables are part of a good, healthy diet."

"That's not going to stop *you* from eating meat, though, is it, Jace?" Zach taunted.

Jace glanced at Delaney, wishing he could do just that. If it made her happy, he'd eat only vegetables for the rest of his life. But it was also the first time he was a guest in his aunt's house and she'd already gone through the trouble of cooking an extra portion just for him. He really didn't want their new relationship to start off on the wrong foot. He hesitated, undecided what to do.

"Of course it's not going to stop Jace from enjoying his dinner," Delaney said, sticking up for him. When everyone turned to stare at her, the color left her face and her lower lip trembled, but she continued. "Not eating meat is *my* choice, but I know how the world works. We have cattle on our ranch, too. And I'm not going to tell anyone else how to eat."

"Well said," Lora's husband, Bo, agreed. "So . . . Jace, I hear you're a steer wrestler?"

Jace nodded, while his aunt Lora dished him a plate of food. "Been bulldoggin' most of my life."

"Ryan used to compete in the local rodeos back when he was in high school," Bo informed him. "In fact, all my boys competed in rodeo at one time or another."

Dean, the oldest of his cousins, gave him a quick look and said, "Yeah, winning could put instant cash in your pocket for the weekend."

Dean placed a slight emphasis on the word "cash" and after Jace finished chewing his first mouthful of steak, he put down his fork, wiped his mouth, and said, "Thank you for the invite to dinner, but that's not why I've come."

His aunt gave him a quizzical look. "What do you mean?"

Taking an envelope out of his shirt pocket, he laid it on the table beside her. "In here is a check for all the money I believe my mother owes you—your half of the inheritance that you should have received from the sale of your parents' ranch. I've even included interest."

All four of his cousins stared at the envelope and the room went so quiet even little Meghan stopped chattering.

"Is this *your* money, or your mother's?" Lora prodded.

"Does it matter?"

"I believe it does, Jace," Lora said, and pushed the envelope back toward him. "I know why your mother withheld it from me. She was scared. But I had four boys to feed and we didn't have much money at that time either.

We could have worked together. Instead, she withdrew and didn't associate with us, robbing me of the chance to get to know you and Natalie."

"I didn't know about the inheritance until five days ago," Jace told her. "My mother told Nat and me that she's sorry."

Lora nodded. "I think we all are."

AFTER DINNER, THE Tanners insisted on giving Jace a tour of the house, the grounds, the cattle, and exchanged life stories and holiday memories, which should have been shared, but had regrettably been missed. At the end of the tour, Lora and Bo led the way back into the house and everyone gathered in the living room.

Bree pulled Delaney aside and whispered, "I think it's going well, don't you?"

Delaney nodded and glanced toward Jace. The Tanner brothers had stepped up to the plate to make their cousin feel welcome. Except Zach, who continued to goad him by acting like he was her boyfriend.

She walked halfway across the room, determined to sit beside Jace by the fireplace, when Zach grabbed her hand and pulled her down beside him on the couch. Reaching beneath their seat, he pulled out two guitar cases, opened them, and handed the first guitar to her.

"How about some music," Zach said, not really giving her an option. "Has Jace heard you play?" Turning toward his cousin, he added, "Delaney and I play together all the time."

"Only a few times," she corrected, shooting him a frown.

Zach laughed. "Sorry, I guess I just wish it were more."

Delaney gasped, appalled he had the nerve to flirt with her right in front of everyone. In front of *Jace*! To cover her embarrassment, she strummed a few chords, then chose a song to play, a popular country-western ballad titled "Only Yours," which had recently been making its way up the music charts. Zach played accompaniment, following her lead, while everyone else sat listening, clapping their hands or tapping their foot.

She hadn't made it halfway through the song when a rich, deep baritone joined in and she was so surprised that for a moment she missed a note. Glancing up, she saw Jace looking straight at her with a look of pure adoration on his face and *oh, my,* the cowboy could *sing*!

He had a clear, beautiful voice, and as Delaney recovered from her surprise and continued to strum strings, she knew in her heart she could sit there and listen all night long. There were nine other people in the room, but it seemed he sang the words just for her. And when he got to the line, *"I'd give anything to be only yours,"* he winked at her, like he had at the rodeo when they'd first met.

Zach responded by leaning his head in toward hers so that they were almost touching, an intimate gesture too close for comfort. She leaned away and wished she had the courage to tell him to stop, but she didn't want to cause a scene and have everyone look at her again. Even though they *were* looking at her, and trying not to laugh, as the two men competed for her attention.

Then Dean, Ryan, and Josh decided to join in the fun and sang, too. It was amusing and created a bond between Jace and the three oldest cousins, but Delaney's fingers grew tired, and after an hour, she put the instrument away.

Jace grinned. "Maybe I'll have to teach you to sing, so you can sing along with us."

"Maybe in addition to photography I'll have to teach you how to play guitar," she challenged.

Another way to keep Jace from hunting!

"Aren't you going back to Arizona soon?" Zach asked, arching his brow.

"Give the guy a break," Ryan said, coming to Jace's defense. "And stop flirting with Delaney."

Ryan's brother Josh added, "Yeah, can't you see she's not interested?"

"You are embarrassing her, Zach," Dean, the oldest of the brothers, agreed. "And we can't have cousins fighting over the same girl."

Bree laughed and looped her arm through hers. "Time to go?"

Delaney smiled and pretended to glance at her watch. "Yeah, I have to go home and get Meghan to bed."

"I don't want to go to bed," Meghan said, climbing up into Jace's lap and giving him a high five. "I want to hear another song."

Delaney looked at the two of them together for a

moment. It was obvious who her daughter thought was the better man. She never climbed up into Zach's lap.

"How about I sing you a song on the ride home?" Jace offered.

"A bedtime song?" Meghan giggled. "Okay, Cowboy Jace."

Cowboy Jace. Yes, Delaney thought, warmed by the title her daughter had given him. *If he wasn't a hunter, he'd be more than the better man.*

He'd be perfect.

JACE ENTERED THE Collinses' guest registration office, closed the door behind him, and picked up the phone. He'd received an urgent text message from his sister while driving back from the Tanners' informing him that their mother had received another threatening letter.

"It says, '*Drop from the race or we'll hurt Jace,*'" Natalie read aloud when he called. "Mom doesn't know what to do. She took it to the authorities and thinks maybe you should be assigned a bodyguard."

"There's no way I want some security servant following me around day and night," he argued. "No one's going to hurt me."

"Don't be too confident," Nat scolded. "Every time you're overconfident it gets you into trouble."

Except tonight. He'd been a little bolder than he intended, but the smile on Delaney's face and dreamy look in her eyes when he sang to her had been worth it.

"What if they threaten me next?" his sister asked, a

note of fear in her voice. "What happens if Mom's elected governor and she passes initiatives to go after these poachers? What will happen then?"

Jace had been having too much fun with Delaney to do any real investigating into the poaching rings. He'd hoped maybe the first letter his mother received had just been sent to intimidate her, nothing more. But now that the second letter threatened *him*, he had to wonder if the poachers were trying to set up the Collinses because *he* was there. Was his presence a threat to Delaney's family?

He thought of the carcasses Jed and Luke had found along the edge of the property and the deer they'd found outside the horse pasture that morning. He didn't know if it was the same group of poachers issuing the threats, but it was time to find out.

After he finished talking to his sister, he called Bucky's dad to let him know what was going on, then placed a call to Gavin McKinley.

"Got some extra time tonight to show me that trophy wall you've been talking about?" Jace asked, keeping his tone friendly.

"Sure," Gavin exclaimed. "Come on over."

The hike up the trail to Fox Creek Outfitters didn't take long and when he arrived Gavin threw open the door. "Jace, I'd like you to meet my father."

Jace walked into the spacious timber framed lodge, eyed the badge on the older man's shirt, and shook his hand. "Good evening, Sheriff."

Sheriff McKinley gave him a rueful grin. "Gavin says

he's been trying to coax you to come out on a hunt with him but you've been distracted by fairer conquests."

"The Collins women are beautiful, wouldn't you agree?" Jace asked him.

The sheriff chuckled. "They are indeed. Ruth and I have been friends for many years. And I got to know the other Collinses very well this past summer with all the trouble they've been having."

"I bet Fox Creek Outfitters hasn't had any trouble," Jace mused. "After all, who would dare mess with a company owned by the son of the town sheriff?"

"You're right," the sheriff said, slapping his hand on his son's shoulder. "I've got him covered."

"I bet you do." Jace looked up at all the animal heads mounted on the paneling that rose two stories high and whistled. "Geez. When you said you had a trophy wall, you weren't kidding."

Gavin pointed to the head of a mountain lion with its mouth wide open as if ready to sink its sharp teeth into its prey. "Got that one last season," he boasted. "He's worth a fortune."

"Do you ever sell them?" Jace asked, as if interested.

Gavin shrugged. "Sometimes. But usually our guests like to go out on a hunt and get their own. We've got horses, ATVs, and all the equipment you need. The only thing I could use more of is beds. I've got fifteen rooms here at the lodge and hope to expand Fox Creek Outfitters by building some cabins."

"Like Collins Country Cabins?" Jace pressed.

"Yeah, they've got twenty-six, right by the river, too.

Lots of animals go down to drink at that river." Gavin let out a grunt. "I'd buy their ranch from them if they'd ever sell, but it doesn't look like that's going to happen any time soon."

"Especially now that Bree, Luke, and Delaney have come back home," Jace added.

"Yeah, you're right about that." Gavin arched his brow and gave him a hopeful look. "Which is why I'd like to make you an offer."

Jace narrowed his eyes. "What kind of offer?"

"How about half of Fox Creek Outfitters?"

"Become a partner?" Jace asked, glancing first at Gavin, then the sheriff, who nodded his approval. "Are you serious?"

"With your name we could build this place into the *premier* outfitting company of the entire state," Gavin said, puffing out his chest.

"And when you aren't off on the rodeo circuit you could come here and hunt whenever you want," the sheriff added.

Jace hesitated. "I have to admit, when I came over here tonight I wasn't expecting this."

"You told me to make you an offer you couldn't refuse," Gavin reminded him, then pinned him with a direct look. "So what do you say?"

Chapter Eight

DELANEY PUT ON a robe over her nightgown and followed Bree downstairs. When Grandma called a family meeting, they listened, no matter what time of the night. Thankfully Delaney had been able to tuck Meghan into bed first. The evening at the Tanners' had worn her little girl out. Delaney had almost been asleep herself when Bree knocked on her door and told her to hurry.

"What's wrong?" Delaney whispered, padding down the hall in her slippers.

Bree shrugged. "No idea."

Their father must have overheard them because the moment they came into the living room to join the rest of the family, he bellowed, "I'll tell you what's wrong. We still don't have our endorsement, that's what's wrong."

Delaney froze, then slowly made her way to the far end of the couch beside her grandma, who usually protected her.

"How *are* you doing with that, Del?" Luke asked, his face drawn and filled with concern.

"Jace knows we asked him here hoping he'll give us an endorsement," Delaney said, and smiled, remembering her wonderful evening at the Tanners'. "And I—I think he's having a really good time. He loves the cabins, the property, the river, the stable for Rio. He's been happy learning photography and practicing archery."

"You haven't let him go hunting, which everyone who has ever read an article about him knows is *what he likes to do*," her father spat.

Delaney winced. "You and Luke took him hunting."

"And thanks to *you*, he didn't get anything," her father said, waving his hands in the air. "You didn't fool anyone by dumping out those clothes in the woods."

She gasped, realizing she'd been caught. "He doesn't need to hunt. He's been having a good time with me and you should see him with little Meghan. He gives her piggyback rides, and high fives, and plays with her, and—"

"I see the way you look at him," Ma accused, her tone hard.

"She fell for that lousy ex of hers fast, too," her father added, as if she wasn't in the room.

Delaney swallowed hard. "I never loved Steve."

"And this guy, you do?" Ma asked, raising her brows.

"Of course not, I've only known Jace a week and a half!"

"You only knew Steve one day and you *married* him," her father shouted.

Delaney stared at him, her eyes burning, and remembered why she hadn't wanted to come back. "You're never going to forgive me for my past mistakes, are you?"

Her father didn't answer, and Bree said quickly, "What's done is done. We can only move forward, right, Grandma?"

"Right," Grandma agreed. "With newfound wisdom and courage."

"Feel-good quotes aren't going to help us get that endorsement," Ma argued. "And you're wrong about Jace not needing to hunt, Delaney. Do you know where he went after he dropped you off tonight?"

Delaney hesitated, alarmed by the tone of her mother's voice, and with dread sinking like a stone in her stomach, she slowly shook her head.

"He went over to Gavin McKinley's," her father barked. "Luke followed him."

Jace went to see Gavin?

Delaney turned to sneak a look at Luke, not wanting to believe it, but her brother nodded, his expression solemn, and said, "It's true."

JACE DIDN'T KNOW what he did wrong. During his stay he'd humored Delaney by taking the camera and letting her teach him some photography. He'd flirted with her while he taught her archery. And he'd repeatedly refused Gavin McKinley's offer to hunt so he could spend more time with her. Geez, he'd even humbled himself to *sing* to her.

Most women he knew would have been flattered. But today Delaney avoided him, and more than once, he caught her looking at him as if he were some kind of vile snake. He'd spent the day with Luke, who took him down to the river to fish. Is that why she was mad at him? Was she against fishing as much as she was against hunting?

He wasn't very good at fly-fishing, but it did give him a chance to ask Luke why he used a cane and discover he'd torn his ACL in a motorcycle accident shortly after he'd gotten out of the military. However, that didn't stop him from riding his horse or even catching fish. While Jace didn't catch any, Luke caught three.

Jace thought about his meeting with Gavin. The Collinses were worried he might endorse Fox Creek Outfitters instead of them. However, there was no chance that would ever happen.

He'd already made up his mind to give the Collinses his endorsement, and honestly thought they did have better cabins, guest facilities, food, and pleasurable company than any other ranch he'd visited. Even so, he wasn't about to give them their precious endorsement until his two-week stay was up. He kind of liked having Delaney try to win it from him, and by waiting, he would have more time to try to win *her*. But at this rate, he might need more than two weeks.

Alicia had come by again this morning to ask if he was interested in a ride up to the silver mine. He'd said no, but Delaney had seen her talking to him.

Could she be jealous of Alicia? He'd smiled at Gavin's head trail guide and acted friendly, but he would have done the same to anyone. Did the fact the woman had breasts the size of basketballs and platinum dyed Barbie doll hair even fairer than Delaney's have anything to do with it? Women were often jealous of each other's looks. No, that couldn't be the problem. He'd already told Delaney he thought that she was beautiful. Honestly, he would prefer her slim, graceful figure and natural blond hair over Alicia's any day.

The one thing Alicia did have in her favor that might have intimidated Del was that she knew how to flirt. Did Delaney mistake his friendliness and think he'd flirted back with the other woman? Or was he totally off target and he had done something else to make Delaney mad at him?

Unable to sleep that night, he tossed the blankets on his bed aside, sat up, redressed, and pulled on a pair of boots to go find out. But when he walked up the path toward the main house, he found most of the windows were dark. What if Delaney was already asleep? How would he get her attention without also waking Meghan?

Despite his restlessness he was about to turn back when he caught a slight movement out of the corner of eye. He glanced up at the top of the stable thinking he'd seen a bat, but then identified the figure sitting up there in the moonlight to be human. Who would be up on the roof at this time of night? And why?

The mysterious dark figure removed their cowboy hat and the moonlight illuminated a head of long, pale hair. *Delaney?*

Intrigued, he changed course and headed straight into the building beneath her. Rio nickered a soft greeting and Jace ran a hand over the velvet end of his nose. Then he continued down the aisle and up the ladder to the hayloft. From there, an open window at the far end led him out onto a small balcony, from which he could finally make it up onto the roof.

"I don't want to startle you," he said, keeping his voice low as he crept forward. "But I was wondering if you'd like some company?"

She spun with a jolt and for a moment Jace feared she'd fall over the edge to her death. His heart raced and he couldn't breathe. In fact, he almost slipped off the slanted shingles himself.

"Careful," she said, pointing. "There are a few loose boards, and if you don't stay to the right, you might fall straight through and become stall mates with Rio."

Keeping left, he made his way toward her. "Thanks for the warning."

"What are you doing up here?" she asked, as if he were crazy for following her.

The moonlight lit her face enough so he could look straight into her eyes. "I could ask you the same thing."

"I couldn't sleep."

"Me neither." He cleared his throat. "What did I do?"

"Nothing."

He let out a soft chuckle. "Is *that* the problem? Did you *want* me to do something?"

"What do you mean?"

"Were you hoping for a kiss?" he prompted.

"What?" She did a double take, gasped, then sputtered, "Whatever would give you that idea?"

Oops. Guess his confidence had tripped him up once again. "I thought you might have been a little jealous when you saw Alicia this morning."

"Me? *Jealous?*" Delaney laughed and shook her head in disbelief. "To be jealous, that would mean that I would actually have to—" She broke off and stared at him, then quickly glanced away.

"It would mean you would actually have to *like* me," Jace finished, and an uncomfortable weight pressed in against his chest. "I guess there's no chance of that?"

Her gaze dropped to his mouth and back up to meet his gaze. "I—I don't know."

He nodded, and looked up at the moon, so full, so bright, so far away from them. They sat there in silence and he didn't expect Delaney to say anything more. Then she let out a half sob and said, "Sorry I avoided you today." Then she let out a sigh. "My family is going to *kill* me."

"Don't worry," he said, letting her off the hook. "I'll still give you the endorsement."

A single tear fell down her cheek and she swiped it away with the back of her hand and asked, as if in shock, "You will?"

"I'll write an official statement before I leave," he assured her.

She continued to stare at him for several long seconds. Then she smiled.

"You have no idea what kind of trouble our family has had over the last few months," she said, her tone rising with more enthusiasm with every word. "I was living in San Diego, Bree in New York, and Luke in the Florida

Keys. We'd each left home one by one after graduating high school because our father, well, you've met him. He's got a gruff way about him and is always making us feel like we can never do anything right.

"Then he hired this couple, Susan and Wade Randall, to help him out and he made them his ranch managers. He didn't know it, but they'd been embezzling money, didn't get the building permits or hire on the summer crew they were supposed to, and put special supplements in the horses' grain so that my father's horse would throw him. We think they wanted my parents to sell the ranch to them but they didn't expect us kids to come home."

Jace had never heard her say so much at once in all the time he'd spent with her and didn't want to stop her now. "Go on," he encouraged.

"My father ended up in the hospital after his horse reared and when it was clear the ranch wouldn't survive without our help, Grandma agreed to divide the owner-ship of the ranch between us. She hasn't filed the official paperwork yet, but each month I've been getting my own share of the profits. Which is good because Meghan's father isn't paying any child support."

"What?" Jace asked, thinking of his own mother and how she'd struggled. "You're supporting her on your own?"

"That's right," Delaney said with a nod. "That's why I need my family's ranch to succeed. I wanted to be a vet-erinarian and work at the San Diego Zoo, but the closest I ever got was shoveling poop out of the cages."

"You said you volunteer at an animal shelter?" he asked.

"Yes, but what I really want is to open one of my own," Delaney said, her voice soft.

He nudged his shoulder against hers. "Like the one you're hiding in the woods?"

Delaney's eyes widened. "You know about that?" She didn't ask him how he knew, but continued. "I want one I don't have to hide, but it's the best I can do. My father thinks I should focus on the guests instead of the animals, but I have always found the animals more appreciative, and less judgmental."

"They offer unconditional love?"

"Yes," she admitted. "They do. Except I won't even be able to keep my little hideaway shelter if this ranch fails to bring in more profits. Susan and Wade Randall ran off in the middle of the night when Bree started looking into the ranch's financial books, but they still have all these other people who have been helping them to put us out of business. Maybe even the poachers who are trying to frame us. Bree hired a private investigator to track the Randalls, and he says it looks like Susan and Wade might be moving back into the area."

"Why would they do that?" Jace shook his head. "Wouldn't they be afraid they'd be caught?"

"My grandma thinks they're a couple of half-crazed vultures moving in for the kill." She took his hand in hers and gazed at him with such intensity it rooted him to the roof so he couldn't move. "So you see why we need this endorsement? Without it, my family will lose the ranch and I don't know what will happen to us."

"You'll need more than my endorsement," Jace told her.

She nodded. "You're right. We'll need a miracle to survive against two other local outfitters offering outdoor activities. But if you let us use your name, and give us the endorsement we need, it would certainly help."

"I'd love for you to use my name," Jace said, and wondered how "Delaney Aldridge" would sound to her. He didn't ask, but instead, raised her hand to his lips and gave it a light kiss. "No strings attached. No conditions. No judgments."

"I guess now you know why I couldn't sleep," Delaney said, and smiled again. "What's your excuse?"

"While growing up my mother always told my sister and me that we could never go to bed angry. All our fights and disagreements had to be resolved before sundown. I couldn't sleep because I thought you were mad at me and I didn't know why."

"Luke followed you last night to Gavin McKinley's lodge," Delaney informed him.

"Del, I wasn't looking to hunt," he said, realizing that's what she must have thought. He decided it was time to let her in on his own secret. "I promised a friend I'd look into the local outfitters to try to find out who's been poaching."

Her somber expression changed to one of surprise. "Is Gavin a poacher?"

"I'm not sure," Jace admitted. "But he has grand dreams of future expansion and offered me half of Fox Creek Outfitters."

Delaney gasped. "What did you say?"

"I told him that I started out hunting to provide meat for my family. Then I continued to hunt over the years to help thin out the population so the remaining deer wouldn't starve to death from lack of food. I let him know that the media had blown my desire to hunt out of proportion and that I donated the meat of the fallen to the homeless shelters, so the people there could eat, too. But *never* have I hunted for sport or for the pleasure of obtaining a mounted trophy."

"You turned him down?" Delaney whispered.

"Yes," Jace said, and grinned. "I turned him down. Gavin wasn't too happy about my decision."

"No, I bet he wasn't," Delaney said with a shake of her head. "But I am."

He gave her a rueful grin. "You're not still mad?"

"Not anymore. In fact," she said, and smiled as she tilted her head toward him, "I might even like you."

"Whoa! Watch yourself," he teased, wrapping his arm over her shoulders. "You almost sounded as if you were *flirting*."

She didn't reply, but her smile widened, and as she continued to gaze at him in the glowing moonlight he had an incredibly good feeling their future might be just as bright.

DELANEY WOKE UP smiling the next morning and made her way down the stairs with an extra bounce in her step. Her good mood must have been contagious because

Meghan looked at her and giggled. Swooping her little girl up into her arms, Delaney danced into kitchen, spun around, and exclaimed, "I've got a good feeling about today, Grandma."

"That's quite a turnaround from last night," her grandma teased. "Any special reason?"

"Yes, any special reason?" Jace asked, a glimmer of a smile lifting the corners of his mouth as he came out of the pantry stirring the contents of the bowl tucked in the crook of his arm with a wire whisk.

"Are you cooking?" she asked, unable to keep the surprise from her voice.

He grinned. "You're a master at sidestepping other people's questions, aren't you?"

She smiled. "Are you making pancakes?"

"Sidestepping me again?" he teased. "You know, you're not going to be able to sidestep me forever, Delaney."

She wasn't sure she wanted to.

Jace had almost kissed her after they descended from the roof of the stable and prepared to go their separate ways. He'd taken both her hands in his and leaned his head in close as he said good-night, giving her heart a jolt. But a couple guests who Jace had befriended during archery practice had come up the moonlit path and called to him.

"Tomorrow," he'd promised a second before the men caught up to them.

She'd smiled, not sure if she was relieved or disappointed, then slipped away.

Afterward she'd lain in bed dreaming of what it might

have been like to kiss the rodeo star. Or would kissing Jace be a mistake? After all, she had Meghan to think about. She didn't go around casually kissing men but wasn't sure she was ready for another relationship either. And the hunting issue still lay between them. Jace had claimed his reasons for hunting were noble, but he hadn't said he'd *stop* hunting either. She wasn't sure she could live with that.

Beside her, Meghan sucked in her breath and exclaimed, "Jace, are you making me pancakes?"

"I sure am, Megs," he said with a grin, and tossed Delaney's grandma a nod. "I have a good teacher, and I thought I'd make breakfast."

"For everyone?" Delaney asked, thinking of all the pancakes they'd need for their dozens of guests. Why, he'd be in the kitchen all morning, instead of spending time with her.

"No," he said, shaking his head. "Just for the three of us."

The three of us. Delaney smiled, and another one of her impossible dreams popped into her head. The dream of a family—a loving, caring, unified family of her very own.

Delaney could hear the sound of the front door opening, and a moment later Bree called out her name. "Come quick!" her sister shouted. "We've got a deer trapped in one of the cabins!"

A deer? Trapped in a cabin?

"Meghan, stay with Grandma," Delaney instructed, and shot a worried glance at Jace, thinking it would be better if *he* stayed with her grandma, too.

No such luck. As if reading her thoughts, Jace handed

Grandma the bowl of pancake batter and said, "I'm coming with you."

They passed Loretta as they followed Bree to Cabin 26, the one farthest away from the main house. "It sounds like the deer is tearing the entire cabin apart," she shrieked, her face full of panic. "I think we need your father to get his gun."

"I have one in my cabin," Jace told her.

"No!" Delaney shouted, and glared at him. "At least give me a chance to try to save it."

Sometimes animals couldn't be saved, but Jace didn't tell her that. Instead, he followed her the rest of the way to Cabin 26 to assess the situation.

Loretta Collins was right. From the loud thumps, crashes, and squeals coming from within the cabin, it sounded as if lamps, chairs, and tables were being destroyed.

Delaney pushed through the crowd of gaping, wide-eyed guests who circled the cabin and stopped up short by the front porch. "How did it get in there?"

Bree pointed to a group of three women. "When they came back after breakfast they opened the door and saw the deer inside."

"I thought I was going to be gored by its antlers," one of the women exclaimed.

Jace spotted the open cabin door and frowned. "Why won't it run out?"

One of the other women said, "It's stuck!"

"What do you mean, 'stuck'?" he demanded, following Delaney toward the door.

All three women motioned to the tops of their heads and it didn't take long for Jace to see what they meant. The deer had put its head through the thin, wood paneled wall separating the kitchen and bedroom and as the buck twisted this way and that, trying to free itself, the large set of antlers kept it trapped. As he and Delaney approached, the buck let out a bloodcurdling yelp and kicked its back legs out at them.

"He's bleeding," Jace said, shooting Delaney a glance. "His neck is sliced from the wood."

"We can save him," Delaney said stubbornly.

He admired her tenacity, but he had no idea how they could get close enough to free the deer without getting hurt themselves. He swallowed hard and said, "Del, I know you don't want to hear this, but it might be better to put the deer out of its misery."

"You didn't put Rio down without trying," Delaney argued.

"This is a wild animal!"

Delaney narrowed her eyes. "Who *also* deserves a chance to live."

"It's a buck," Jace said, staring at the eight-point rack sticking through the wall as if the deer's head were already mounted. "He could get shot by a hunter the moment we free him."

"He deserves a *chance*," Delaney insisted.

Jace glanced at the deer's neck again. There seemed to be a lot of blood, and it was splattering everywhere, down the paneling, onto the floor, the kitchen counter. Then he looked into the deer's panic-stricken eyes. The deer was suffering, surely Del could see that.

"You go around to the other side while I stay here in the kitchen and talk to him," Delaney instructed.

"*Talk* to him?"

"Jace, *please*," she begged, her whole face filled with compassion for the poor animal she wanted so desperately to save. He hesitated, and her expression hardened. "Help me," she said, her voice low, "or you can leave this ranch and take your bloody endorsement with you."

He'd never seen Del so serious. His heart pounded in his chest and he flicked his gaze toward the deer again. The animal trembled, but wasn't thrashing about as much. Either it was too terrified, or it didn't have much time left.

"All right," he said, his adrenaline pumping into high gear as he met her gaze. "Let's do this."

DELANEY STAYED BY the deer's head in the kitchen while Jace ran around the other side of the wall into the bedroom to deal with the back half of the animal.

"Don't move," she pleaded with the buck in a whisper. "Please don't move."

She reached a hand up and touched the side of its head. The deer flinched, and kept his eye on her, and uttered another cry, but she kept talking to the animal. And as she did, she moved her fingers toward the splintered opening and picked away the sharp pieces of wood as fast as she could. Other pieces of wood fell away in the opposite direction, and when she saw Jace's fingers, she realized he was trying to do the same thing.

"*Yow!*" Jace's shouted. "He tried to kick me."

"Watch out," she called, grabbing hold of a large broken piece of the wood paneling that was giving way around the deer's antlers. Then she pulled with all her might and the piece of wood came free, opening a large hole.

"Almost," Jace called to her.

The deer thrust his head back and forth again and, on the second try, more of the wood split off and the buck withdrew its head through the opening toward Jace. Delaney ran into the other room and spotted Jace on top of the bedroom dresser, which he'd used to keep himself above the deer's body while he worked on widening the opening.

"Delaney, get back!"

She pressed herself into the hall closet and the deer jumped over the bed, darted past her into the living room, and out the door. A shout of surprise sounded from the crowd outside, and Delaney ran out onto the front porch just in time to see the deer, unharmed except for the few slices to its neck, run into the nearest patch of woods.

The overwhelming surge of relief knowing the deer was free brought tears to her eyes and made her feel almost giddy, as if she'd drank an entire bottle of champagne or as if one of her impossible dreams had come true. She supposed one had.

Jace stepped out onto the porch beside her and she

smiled. "The cuts around its neck weren't nearly as bad as I first thought," she said, her voice choked with emotion. "They should heal over in no time and he's *free*! We did it, Jace. You and me. You—you *helped* me."

She looked up at him, and realized that with his dark hair falling down over his forehead and his beautiful green eyes he really was the most handsome man she'd ever seen.

"Thank you," she whispered.

Jace didn't say a word but held her gaze, then he slowly reached out and touched her lower lip with the tip of his finger. She didn't move, didn't try to pull away, but parted her lips ever so slightly and realized the look in his eyes wasn't the same as when he'd flirted with her in the past. It was far more serious, more penetrating, as if he were seeing straight through her to the person she was on the inside for the very first time. *And he admired her.*

She took a small step forward and he leaned his head toward hers and captured her mouth in a kiss so warm, so tender, so exhilarating, that the euphoria of emotion she'd already been feeling skyrocketed to a whole new level. A round of clapping erupted around them, and lifting his head, Jace grinned. "Remember how I said last night that I'd kiss you 'tomorrow'?"

She nodded.

"I always keep my promises," he said, and looked like he might kiss her again.

Except today, someone called *her* name.

Delaney glanced over the crowd and spotted three figures who wore green Montana Wildlife Rescue T-shirts staring at her. *Carol, Mary Ann, and Ben*. Jumping away from Jace, she sucked in her breath. "Carol, what are you all doing here?"

"Your ma called," Carol said, her expression tense. "She said you needed help. We happened to be in the area and came as fast as we could."

"We rescued the deer," Delaney assured them.

"Looks like we should have got here sooner to rescue *you*." Carol glanced from her to Jace, then back to her again. "Delaney Collins, how *could* you!"

Delaney hesitated, unsure what she meant. "How could I what?"

Giving her a look as if it should have been obvious, Carol pulled her aside and asked, "How could you kiss *that man*?"

Chapter Nine

"JACE HELPED ME get the deer out of the cabin," Delaney said, touching the bear claw necklace about her neck as she stood up to the three she'd always considered her friends.

"Are you that fickle that you'd kiss a hunter for doing one good deed?" Carol argued.

Apparently Jace overheard. He frowned, then gave her friend a pointed look. "I'd prefer *not* to be labeled a hunter."

Carol shot him a look of disgust. "You think if I called you a 'rodeo star' that would be any better? I've seen how you rodeo people treat your animals. You run them into the ground until they're of no use to you, and then get yourselves a new one."

Delaney shook her head. "You can't slap a title on someone and make snap judgments about them. A title doesn't define who a person is."

"Isn't it your philosophy that everyone deserves a chance?" Jace added.

Reaching out to take his hand, Delaney lifted her chin like her stubborn sister, Bree, and told Carol, "You don't even *know* him."

"I don't know *you*," Carol retorted with unconcealed disappointment.

The woman Delaney had considered a mentor for so many long years turned on her heels and left. Was Carol now jumping to conclusions and making snap judgments about *her*? Mary Ann and Ben hesitated, cast Delaney an apprehensive glance, then followed Carol's lead.

"I'm so sorry, Del," Jace said softly. "I know that must have hurt."

"It *did*." She drew in a deep breath to steady her breathing. "Speaking out always does."

Swallowing the lump hovering in the back of her throat, Delaney noticed Bree waving her hand to get their attention.

"Come take a look at this," Bree shouted.

Luke and their dad, only just arriving at the scene, hurried to join them. "Of course the deer had to be inside one of the new cabins," Luke complained, poking at some of the debris with the tip of his cane. "I just finished building this one seven weeks ago."

"It's going to cost us," Delaney's father said with a scowl. "As if we needed an added expense."

Jace picked a syringe off the cabin floor and said. "I think you've got bigger worries."

Delaney stared at the fibrous tailpiece at one end and the sharp hypodermic needle sticking off the other and gasped. "A tranquilizer dart?"

Bree nodded. "That's what I wanted to show you. It must have fallen from the deer during his kicking frenzy."

Delaney thought her sister must be right.

"Someone must have knocked the deer unconscious with the tranq dart," Luke said, giving them each a look of warning, "then carried him in here to wreak havoc when he woke up."

Delaney nodded, thinking her brother must also be right. Her older siblings always were.

"That's some prank," Bree exclaimed, shaking her head.

"It's not a prank," their father said, his tone ominous. "Someone did this for a specific purpose."

"Someone who is trying to put us out of business?" Delaney asked. "The rival outfitters?"

Luke nodded. "I think Del's right."

Really? She leaned in to hear her brother tell her why.

"I think whoever it was wanted to see Jace hunt," Luke continued. "They could have put the deer in here to tempt him."

"It would have tempted any hunter," Delaney's father agreed. "I heard that buck had himself a fine rack. But why do you think it was meant for Jace?"

"If I shot the deer, Delaney would never forgive me and tell me to leave," Jace said, looking straight at her.

"Chances are I wouldn't give Collins Country Cabins an endorsement after that."

JACE SUSPECTED THAT if anyone had wanted to prevent the Collinses from getting the endorsement by sabotaging his relationship with Delaney, it had to be Gavin McKinley. After all, the only other outfitter in the area was Isaac Woolly's company next door, but Isaac didn't know either one of them half as well as Gavin. He didn't know they were attracted to each other.

"I think I should pay our friend Gavin a visit," Jace told Delaney after they left the cabin. "And see if he has any tranquilizer darts lying around."

"I'll come with you," Delaney said, her beautiful blue eyes filled with concern. "Right after breakfast. I have to check on Meghan."

There was nothing he would have liked better than to have Delaney stick by his side the remainder of the day. Except after they'd finally eaten the pancake breakfast he'd promised her and her little girl, Jace discovered he had a surprise visitor.

"Jace," Natalie said after being introduced, "I need to speak to you. *In private.*"

He could see from her agitated expression that what she had to say was important. Had his mother received another threat?

Excusing himself with a promise to meet up later, he left Delaney at the house with Meghan and escorted his sister to the privacy of his cabin.

"You didn't tell me she had a kid," Natalie scolded. "What if you date her and it doesn't work out? How will that child feel when you leave?"

"I don't plan to disappoint either one of them," Jace said, closing the door and taking a seat beside her on the couch.

"Yeah, well, it happens," Nat said, her face contorting as if fighting off tears. "People you think you know and trust disappoint you."

"Okay, Nat," he said, noticing she *did* have tears in her eyes. "What's up? Who disappointed you?"

"I told Mom that Aunt Lora wouldn't take the money from you," Natalie said, shaking her head. "But she still hasn't set a date to meet with them and return their share of the inheritance herself."

"I'll talk to her," Jace promised.

"You know how stubborn she can be," Nat warned.

"Some of her persistence has also rubbed off on *us*," he reminded her. "We won't let up on her until she does the right thing."

"What if she doesn't? How will I look Aunt Lora in the eye without feeling guilty?"

"Aunt Lora and the rest of the Tanners have assured me that no matter what happens it won't affect how they treat you or me. They want us to be part of their family."

"Are you absolutely sure?" Nat asked, her expression worried.

Jace nodded. "They're anxious to meet you."

"Maybe we'll also end up being part of the *Collins* family," Nat teased, "if you develop a relationship with Delaney."

WHILE JACE WAS busy with his sister, Delaney took the opportunity to sneak off to the old toolshed to check on the raccoon, the pheasant, and bottle-feed the bobcat kittens. Then she went to the stable to feed the horses and found Rio kicking his stall.

"Easy, boy," she soothed, running a hand gently over his pink satin nose. "You don't want to hurt one of your other legs, too."

The buckskin snorted and tossed his head, making the front tuft of his black hair fall over his eyes, reminding her of Jace. She reached up and smoothed the hair back so he could see and then decided to take him out of his stall for a short walk. Two weeks had passed since he'd been injured, and thanks to her herbal wraps and her Grandma's handmade mineral lotion, it appeared the horse's leg was in the process of healing. Rio still couldn't put his full weight on the leg with the strain, but he looked like he was able to hobble around a little better.

Delaney slipped a halter over Rio's nose and the horse got even more excited. He kicked the wall of the stall with his rear leg as if impatiently telling her to hurry. Sliding his half door open, she took the lead rope and slowly led him step by slow step into the aisle and through the double doors. Luckily his stall had been on the end so he didn't have far to go.

Once outside, the horse appeared to calm, enjoying the cool breeze that ruffled his mane and tail. She ran her hand down his neck and back, admiring his soft coat. With the colder temperatures coming in, all of the horses' hair had grown long and thick. Most of them already wore their blankets and soon the temperatures would drop so low the animals would have to be stabled. They all had to enjoy what time they had left.

"I don't blame you, Rio. I'd get cranky and restless, too, if I had to stay inside on a nice day like this," Delaney told him.

The horse snorted again and then raised his head with his ears perked forward. Delaney followed Rio's gaze and then she heard it, too, the sound of pounding hooves coming their way.

Seconds later she spotted Sammy Jo, with her long, dark curls flying out behind her, racing her palomino across the field that connected their two families' properties together. Rio appeared interested in the newcomer, as if he knew Sammy Jo's horse, Tango, was a rodeo veteran, too. Or maybe he was just eager to prove he was the better man. Calling out with a loud whinny, Rio held his head high.

Slowing to a stop a few feet away, Sammy Jo slid out of the saddle and pushed her hat, which had fallen down over her back while riding, up onto the top of her head again. "My, my, look who we have here," Sammy Jo exclaimed, glancing at Rio. "Part one of your perilous pair. Where's part two?"

"Jace is in his cabin," Delaney said, smiling, "and he and Rio are *not* perilous."

"Perilous to your heart," Sammy Jo teased, then nodded toward the horse by her side. "How's he doing?"

"His leg is healing, but he's not very happy. The stall's making him stir-crazy and he wants out."

"Of course he does," Sammy Jo cooed. "He loves bull-dogging and wants to chase himself a bull." Arching her brow, she added, "How's the flirting with part two coming along? Have you been doing everything I taught you?"

"No," Delaney said, shaking her head. "But he kissed me anyway."

"He did?" Sammy Jo asked, and let out a high whoop showing her delight. "When?"

"This morning, right after he helped me save a deer that was stuck in one of our cabins."

"Talking about getting stuck," Sammy Jo said, her tone turning serious, "I got stuck in traffic trying to get past the end of your driveway a little while ago on my way into town."

"Traffic?" Delaney frowned. "On *our* road?"

"Yeah, whoever would have thought, right?" Sammy Jo let out a short laugh, but then her expression sobered once again. "Actually, it's not funny. There are dozens of protestors lined up in front of your ranch waving picket signs and chanting, 'Save our wildlife' and 'End animal cruelty.' Some of them are holding a twenty-five-foot banner that reads Collins Country Cabins Harbors Heinous Hunters, Poachers, and Reckless Rodeo Rogues. I personally took offense to that last one."

Delaney's mouth fell open. "They aren't all wearing green T-shirts, are they?"

"Afraid so," Sammy Jo said, and winced. "It appears Carol, Mary Ann, and Ben are leading the pack, and there's another group of Montana Wildlife Rescue supporters rallying together in town. They say threats to the animals in our area are at an all-time high, whether wild or domesticated, and it's time for everyone to take action to bring balance back to the environment."

"Oh, no," Delaney said, and the back of her throat closed, nearly choking her. "Because I've helped them in the past, my father's going to blame *me*."

She was right. Standing in the hallway outside the living room, she overheard her family discussing the situation unfolding outside, and her father said, "They wouldn't even know about our ranch if Delaney didn't volunteer at the local clinic."

"I'm afraid it's my fault," her mother said, her voice shrill. "I'm the one who called her Wildlife Rescue friends to come help get the deer out of the cabin. I didn't know they'd get mad at us and think we had anything to do with the deer getting stuck."

"They weren't mad about the deer," Bree told her. "They were mad when they saw Delaney kissing Jace."

"What's wrong with that?" Grandma demanded.

"They didn't know he was staying here with us," Bree explained. "And they think Delaney betrayed them by kissing the enemy. Jace rides rodeo and hunts, two things they hate. Now they're bad-mouthing our ranch because he's here."

"We can't tell him to leave without getting his endorsement," Delaney heard her father grumble.

"We can't get his endorsement and *then* tell him to

leave either," Luke cautioned. "But if we *can* get Jace to give us that endorsement, I think we'll have enough good publicity to counteract the protestors' complaints."

"Maybe we should let Bree try to talk Jace into giving us the endorsement," Ma suggested.

"What about Del?" Grandma demanded.

"She was supposed to get help us create *good* public relations, not *bad*!" Delaney's father bellowed. "Maybe we should let Bree talk to Jace and send Delaney off on a vacation until he leaves and the protestors settle down."

"No!" Delaney shouted, stepping out to join them. She walked directly toward her father, and if she weren't so angry she might have been afraid, but all she could think about was that he didn't think she could get the job done. And she would *not* let him make her feel like a failure again.

Growing up, he never thought any of his kids could do anything right. The ranch work always had to be done *his* way. Then after he'd driven both Bree and Luke away with his perfectionism and gruff dictator-like manner, he'd said *she* would have to stay at the ranch because she couldn't make it out in the world on her own.

She left for college in San Diego to prove him wrong. Then when her grades slipped, she feared he was right and that she'd have to come home. Until she met Steve, who offered marriage as a convenient solution. But when Steve filed for divorce, her father said that was her fault, too, because she *"didn't have what it takes"* to keep him. Just like Gavin McKinley had threatened that she *"didn't have what it takes"* to keep Jace. Coming home and having to rely on her family again, and admit that *yes, she'd failed*, had been one of the most humiliating moments of her life.

And she would not let her father or the rest of her family think she could not pull her share of the responsibility around here.

"Jace *is* going to endorse our ranch," Delaney told them.

"When?" her father demanded. "His two weeks are almost up and so far the only thing you've managed to get out of him was a kiss."

"I promised you that I would get that endorsement," she said, standing up on her tippy toes and looking her father straight in the eye. "And I will. Right *now*."

She gave him one last infuriated look, then turned on her heel and marched down the path to Jace's cabin, and pounded on the door.

JACE WALKED TOWARD the door of his cabin, wondering if Natalie had forgotten something and returned. She'd only left fifteen minutes before, long enough for him to remove the splinter he'd received while trying to free the deer and put on some of Ruth Collins's homemade mineral lotion to help his finger heal.

His mystery guest pounded on the door again. This time with more strength.

"Coming," he called. Then unlatching the lock, he swung the door out and there she was, the one he'd been waiting for, standing on his front porch. Taking her hand, he drew her inside, and relocked the door behind them.

"I'm sorry for the interruption earlier," he said, stepping toward her. "We seem to have had a lot of them over the past few days."

"You are absolutely right," Delaney agreed, her voice firm. "That's why I can't wait a minute longer."

He grinned. "Neither can I."

"So should we just get right to it?" she asked, her expression as innocent as ever.

He did a double take. "Geez, I didn't expect you to be so straightforward."

"Jace," she pleaded. "I need that endorsement."

"Endorsement?" he asked, fighting to hide a smile and choking on his response at the same time.

"Of course," she said with a frown. "What did you think we were talking about?"

He placed his hands on either side of her waist and pulled her closer. "For a minute there, I thought you couldn't wait to kiss me again."

Color rose into her cheeks and she smiled as her gaze drifted toward his mouth. "Why did you kiss me, Jace? What is it you see in me or am I just another pretty face?"

He brushed back her hair with his hands and then cupped her cheeks. "I see that you are the most compassionate, honest, persevering, cleverly resourceful woman that I have ever met."

"Resourceful?" she asked, as if puzzled.

"Your attempts to keep me from hunting," he said, and a surge of warmth spread over him as he recalled the memories. "Let me see, like trying to keep my hands on a camera instead of a gun, grabbing my arm and pretending to sneeze so I'll miss a six-point buck with my bow, or emptying your dirty laundry basket out in the woods to chase off any animal within a half mile radius?"

"That's called being desperate," she said, and laughed.

"Delaney," he said, drawing his head closer. "If you didn't want me to hunt, you should have just said so."

"Would you have listened?" she asked.

"I did," Jace assured her. "I heard the message through your actions loud and clear."

All of the sudden she jumped in place. "My father was pretty loud and clear today when he said I needed to get that endorsement. You *will* write us one, won't you, Jace?"

"I promised you that I would."

"Right now?"

Jace closed the distance between them and brushed a kiss over her lips, then drew back and sighed. "If that's what you really want."

Delaney hesitated, then shook her head. "The endorsement can wait."

"Are you sure?" he teased, his mouth hovering just inches above hers.

She smiled, and wrapping her arms around his neck, she whispered, "Kiss me."

"Maybe I should add '*demanding*' to your list of attributes."

"Kiss me," she repeated. "Please?"

"If you insist," he said, gazing down at her, but keeping his mouth just a hairsbreadth out of reach. Her breath was sweet upon his lips, fresh and enticing and—

"Jace Aldridge," she sputtered, her voice sharp. "Stop teasing me and kiss me already!"

He chuckled, enjoying the intense look of yearning in her eyes. "Geez, Del. You're a little spitfire beneath that innocent, quiet, shy demeanor, aren't you?"

"Only when it matters," she countered.

"And this does?" he asked, skimming his mouth across her lower lip.

"Definitely."

Jace captured her mouth with his, and wrapping his arms around her shoulders, he pulled her in against him. Delaney tightened her grip around him, too, and as time lapsed and the world around them fell away, he realized he didn't want to leave this week, he didn't want to go back to the rodeo circuit, and he certainly didn't want to go back to Arizona.

He wanted to stay right where he was, like this, with Delaney by his side.

Forever, if she'd have him.

Chapter Ten

DELANEY FOUND MEGHAN in the front of the house with Ma, Grandma, and Party Marty, her grandma's ever-present miniature companion. Meghan had her arms around the pony and was giving him a hug when she joined them.

"We've been keeping our eye on the protestors," Grandma said, pointing at the crowd circling along the road near their driveway.

"I'm sorry your father was so hard on you," Ma said, her face taking on a worried expression. "He's afraid of losing this ranch as much as the rest of us and holding on to it sometimes seems like an uphill battle."

"A battle we will continue to fight," Grandma proclaimed, giving Delaney's ma a stern look.

"Thank you for watching Meghan so much for me lately," Delaney said, bending down to scoop her little girl into her arms. "I feel guilty every time I leave her side."

"What you're doing is important," Ma said, and raised her brows. "Any news?"

Delaney smiled. "*Yes.*"

Ma let out a sigh of relief. "That will make your father happy."

Meghan tangled one of her hands into Delaney's hair, playing with the ends, and asked, "What news? Where were you?"

"I was with Cowboy Jace," she told her.

Meghan's eyes grew wide. "Without *me*? He was my friend first."

"Can't he be a friend to both of us?" Delaney asked.

"Did he give you anything?" Meghan asked suspiciously.

She thought of their kiss, but she wasn't about to divulge that particular detail to her two-year-old; instead, she could mention the other gift he'd given her. "Cowboy Jace gave me a paper."

"He gave *me* a horse," Meghan said, proudly taking a tiny two-inch plastic figurine from her jacket pocket. "This is Rio."

"It *does* look like Rio, doesn't it?" Delaney asked, and marveled once again how kind Jace was to her little girl. He'd make a wonderful father someday. So different from Meghan's real father, who didn't want anything to do with her, a man who never even wanted her to be born.

Putting Meghan back down to walk on her own two feet, she said, "Let's go see Aunt Bree. I need to give her something very important."

Delaney wasn't sure if she should enter the ranch

office or not. She overheard several women arguing before she even got to the door. Deciding Bree might need either moral support or a distraction, she slipped in quietly with Meghan behind the three women standing before the office desk. Sammy Jo sat beside her sister and noticed her as soon as she came in.

"This is the brave woman who helped get the deer out of your cabin," Sammy Jo said, motioning for the other women to turn around. "You should be thanking her instead of making threats to sue."

Delaney gasped. "You plan to sue us?"

One of the women scrunched her nose and informed her, "All of our personal belongings are trampled. My new designer suitcase has a *hoofprint* on it."

"My clothes were destroyed," announced another. "Even my underwear."

"The beast broke my laptop," said the third woman. "I had it on the coffee table in the living room and found it smashed in pieces all over the floor. Then there's all the blood! There's no way we can sleep there tonight."

Delaney looked at Bree. "Did you offer them another cabin? We have lots of empty cabins."

"You'll have a lot more after I file a lawsuit," the first woman threatened.

They couldn't survive a lawsuit. They had enough bad publicity from the protestors. From the look on Bree's face, she knew it, too.

"We'll refund the money for your cabin rental," Bree offered. "And reimburse you *twice* the replacement cost of your damaged items."

"Twice?" the three women chorused, and looked at one another.

Then each of them broke out in a smile and the woman who had threatened the lawsuit exclaimed, "Let's go shopping!"

After the three left, check in hand, Delaney winced. "Bree, how can we afford that?"

Her sister shook her head. "How could we afford not to? We don't have the money to hire a lawyer and get involved in court fees. We're already spending enough on the PI we hired to track down Susan and Wade Randall so we can try to get some of our embezzled money back."

"I'm going to need a private detective of my own," Sammy Jo complained. "Every morning this week, Luke has gone MIA. I've wanted to talk to him about wedding plans but he keeps disappearing. You don't think he's getting cold feet, do you?"

Bree laughed. "Absolutely not. He's head over heels in love with you. Which reminds me . . . Del, can you take our engagement photos?"

Sammy Jo nodded. "Yes. We figured it would be easier if we could do Luke and me at the same time as Ryan and Bree."

"Of course," Delaney agreed. She was to be a bridesmaid and Meghan was to be a flower girl in both their weddings. Ryan had proposed to Bree first and planned a spring ceremony, but Luke and Sammy Jo couldn't wait and decided they'd marry this Christmas.

Bree gave her a wistful look. "What about Jace?"

"Cowboy Jace is my friend," Meghan told them.

Delaney smiled at her daughter and handed Bree the piece of paper Jace had given her with his endorsement for their ranch. "I think right now he's everyone's friend."

Bree and Sammy Jo talked back and forth excitedly as they read the kind words Jace had written about their ranch, but Delaney's thoughts were on the words he had *really* wanted to write. The ones only she knew about.

After Jace had kissed her at least a dozen times, he'd pulled back with a grin and said, "We better get that endorsement written before your father comes looking for us."

She wasn't thinking of her father at that moment. All she wanted to do was keep kissing Jace. But he had a point. They'd been kissing for over an hour and if she didn't return soon they'd send out a search party.

Retrieving a pad of paper and a pen out of a drawer in the kitchen, Jace leaned over the counter and asked, "What do you think I should write? That Collins Country Cabins has the most beautiful women, the finest flirters, and the best kissers?"

Delaney had smiled, then she placed a kiss on his forehead, another on the tip of his nose, and a third on his chin. "I told you that I don't know how to flirt."

"Oh, but you do, Del," he said, giving her another quick kiss on the lips. "You most certainly do."

JACE HAD SEEN a couple flashes from a camera go off from someone in the crowd who stood watching the scene with the deer unfold. But he'd thought it was a natural gesture from a guest who was excited by what was happening and wanted a shot to show their friends. Today, he realized one of the "guests" must have been a reporter looking for a juicy story to sell newspapers. But it wasn't the story of how he helped save the deer that covered the front page. Instead, they'd featured a picture of him kissing the guest ranch owner's youngest daughter.

Delaney hadn't known they'd had a reporter within their midst either. When the twins first showed her the newspapers, she'd dropped her plate of scrambled eggs and toast all over the floor, her face had gone stark white, and he'd pulled out a chair for her to sit down so she wouldn't faint.

"Oh, Miss Delaney!" Nora squealed, bending down to help her sister, Nora, clean up the mess.

"We didn't mean to startle you, Miss Del," Nadine added. "I'd give anything to have my photo on the front page."

"And," Nora said, and giggled, "it's so romantic!"

"I never wanted to be in the spotlight," Delaney said, meeting his gaze. "The focus should be on the deer."

"Welcome to my world," Jace said, and set all the newspapers into one pile so she wouldn't have to look at them again. "The media is biased. They say what they want, label you how they want, tell the whole world you're an avid hunter if they want."

"In the text beneath the photo it explains how the ranch managers embezzled our money earlier this summer and how I had to come home to work the ranch," Delaney said, and grimaced. "Then they call me a modern-day Cinderella who has been swept off her feet and caught kissing famous rodeo star Jace Aldridge."

"I always wished I could be like Cinderella," Nora said dreamily as she stood up holding the dustpan she'd used to clean the food off the floor. "So that I could—"

"Meet a handsome prince!" Nadine exclaimed. "And live—"

"Happily ever after!" both twins chorused in unison.

Some of the color returned to Del's face and she appeared to relax. "You two have been watching too many of Meghan's fairy-tale movies on TV."

"Don't you believe in fairy tales?" Jace teased. "Sometimes dreams really do come true."

She smiled and gave him one of those adorable, longing looks. "I *want* to believe."

So did he, which is why he planned to do everything in his power to make her happy and feel secure. First, he'd have to find out who put the deer in the cabin and see if the same poachers who were messing with her family were the ones threatening his mom.

"Aren't you two supposed to be in school?" he asked the twins.

Nora suddenly coughed, an obvious *fake* cough, and Nadine pretended to sneeze, although her acting was ten times worse than Delaney's.

"We're sick," Nora told him. "But it's not contagious or anything."

"You don't *look* sick," Delaney said, giving them each a frown.

"Oh, Miss Delaney," Nora squealed. "We just couldn't go to school today."

"Not when we saw who arrived at the ranch last night," Nadine added. "A father and his two sons who are—"

"Absolutely *gorgeous!*" Nora finished, and pointed into the side of her cupped hand to indicate their location.

Jace glanced over at the middle-aged man and the two younger guys who accompanied him. The boys looked to be only a year or two older than Nora and Nadine. But they weren't his sons. The older man with them glanced up and caught Jace looking at him. Then smiled.

"Excuse me," Jace said, rising from his chair and giving Delaney an apologetic look. "There's someone I want speak with."

Then moving into a seat at the table with Bucky's father and the other young men, he said, "Welcome to Collins Country Cabins."

Eli Knowles let out a chuckle. "I was wondering when you'd notice us. Jace, let me introduce you to Clint and Clay Maier, undercover agents in training."

"Like me?"

Eli gave the boys a nod. "They're friends of a friend."

After they shook hands, Eli said, "With all the reports that have been coming in, we figured we needed to get closer to the action. These poachers may have a hidden agenda other than killing for sport or making a profit."

Jace frowned. "What do you mean?"

"Have you considered what might have happened if you had shot the deer, three days before gun season?"

"You'd arrest me for poaching?" he teased.

"No," Eli warned, "*think*, Jace."

"The media twists stories around to say whatever they want," he said, clenching his fist. "They might not portray it as a mercy killing. The rival outfitters could have framed the Collinses for poaching and put them out of business."

"Or," Eli offered, "they could have framed *you*, the son of a candidate running for governor. This could have ruined your mother's campaign."

He thought about the second note they'd sent his mother. *Drop from the race, or we'll hurt Jace*. The poachers could have set him up to ruin his reputation to keep his mother from taking office. "You think this is all political?"

Eli shrugged. "We have to look at it from every angle."

Bucky's dad was right. There was more than one possibility. He'd have to keep his eyes and ears open and not make any swift assumptions.

When he returned to his own table, each of the twins, one on either side of him, grabbed his arm. "Jace, you didn't tell them we *like* them, did you?" Nora exclaimed, her face almost as white as Delaney's had been when she'd seen the newspapers.

"No," he assured them. "Your secret is safe with me."

The twins released his arms and let out identical sighs of relief.

"By the way," he said, amused by all their dramatics. "Their names are Clint and Clay."

"Clint and Clay," Nora repeated. "The names kind of

roll off your tongue when you say them, don't they? Just like Nora and Nadine."

"Oh, Jace," Nadine said, giving him a big smile. "You were helping us get information, weren't you? How can we ever thank you?"

Jace glanced at Delaney's bemused expression, and then looked back at the twins and asked, "Give us some privacy?"

DELANEY COMBINED THE special powdered formula her wildlife rescue group used for orphaned wild animals with the correct dosage of water. Then she fed the bobcat cubs one at time, holding them in the crook of her arm like a baby. They certainly were adorable. The cub she held wrapped its little paws around the bottle as it drank and looked up at her with those round blue eyes. The cub's eyes were as blue as Meghan's and her own. And how could anyone resist that cute little pink nose, and the black tiger-like stripes on its face?

Now that the cubs had been exposed to humans, the chances of them being reintroduced into the forest were slim. But they'd had no choice. At this age, the cubs would never have survived on their own. Perhaps when they were older, the cubs could be used to help educate the public during nature talks and special events. For now, she'd enjoy them and do her best to keep them safe.

She let both the raccoon with the broken leg and the pheasant with the broken wing go free. Both had healed remarkably well and no longer needed her protection.

This would make space for any new animals that she found or give the cubs a larger area to play.

Back at the ranch, she used the green motorized utility gator to carry the hay out to the fields to the horses for their morning feed, and then went into the stable to check on Rio. When she came out again, a couple of loud whoops and whistles turned her head toward the open field where Jace had set up the archery targets the week before.

Except this time he had set up a herd of fake steer. Luke must have helped make them because short logs formed the bodies, and the legs, neck, head, and horns were made from scrap lumber, probably left over from one of Luke's building projects. Her brother had repaired two cabins, a deck, and built the octagon gazebo at the request of the Hamilton wedding party this past summer, but she'd never seen him build anything like this.

Jace stood in the midst of them, instructing a crowd of their guests how to lasso a rope around the steer's neck. When one of the guests asked him about steer wrestling, he took one of the wooden figures, grabbed it by the horns and rolled onto the ground, turning the thing upside down with its legs in the air. Meghan broke into a fit of laughter and then ran over to him and tackled him, telling him that *he* was a steer.

Delaney couldn't stop herself from laughing either. Walking toward the group, she noticed all the guests were wearing new brown felt Stetsons. Meghan wore one, too.

"Where did all the hats come from?" she asked, joining Bree and her father, who stood off to the side watching.

"Jace bought them and handed them out to everyone,"

Bree told her. "He said everyone at a dude ranch needs a proper cowboy hat."

"The guests love him," her father said, and let out a chuckle. "Maybe we should hire him full-time to be our head director of activities."

Delaney shook her head. "We can't afford him. Jace would only stay on for big bucks."

"I can take him hunting again," her father offered.

"I meant *money*," Delaney amended, and then saw the glint in her father's eye and realized he'd been teasing. Her father had been in a good mood ever since Jace gave them the endorsement.

Bree laughed and nodded toward the rodeo hero. "I think he'd stay on for *you*, Del."

Would he? His time was up in two days, but Jace had not mentioned leaving or staying. She assumed he'd pack his things, load Rio back into the trailer, and head out. But later that day, when she and Jace were alone, she found her sister was *right*.

"I've decided to buy a house here in the area," Jace announced. "My mother's running for governor and claims it would look better for her campaign if I settle in up here instead of Arizona. But I think the reason she really wants me to stay is because she and my sister like seeing me on a regular basis. They hate it when I just check in one weekend each month."

"Is there any other reason you might want to stay in Montana?" Delaney asked, arching her brow.

"Well, I did promise my friend's dad I'd look into the poaching and see if I can discover who might be behind it," he added, then he grinned, and pushed her against the six-foot-high round hay bale that stood in the field, blocking them from everyone else's view, and kissed her for several long minutes.

"Anything else?" she whispered, trying not to get her hopes up.

"Actually, there are two other reasons I'm staying," he said, his voice dropping into that smooth baritone level she loved. "The two most important reasons are you and Meghan. I am just getting to know you, Del, and I don't want to go. I want to know everything about you, everything you've been through, everything you hate, everything you love. I want to know it all."

She laughed and rolled her eyes. "That would take an awful long time."

"I've got time," he said, and held her gaze, his face serious. "But I guess I forgot to ask you a question. Probably because you sidetracked me again, as you have a habit of doing."

Smiling, she wrapped her hands around him and said, "Ask me."

"Do *you* want me to stay?"

Her heart leaped in her chest and she'd never been more sure of an answer. "Yes, Jace, I do."

He pretended to let out a deep sigh. "That's good," he teased. "Because I already paid Bree for another month in advance. I figured that might help her recover some of the money she had to pay those three women who were angry about the deer in their cabin."

"You knew about that?" Delaney asked, surprised.

"I was next door to the ranch office throwing in a load of laundry in the washroom and couldn't help but overhear."

"Are you always this nice?" she asked, thinking of all the ways he'd helped her family since he'd arrived.

He brushed the side of her face with his finger and grinned. "I guess *you'll* just have to stick around to find out."

JACE WOKE UP before dawn the next morning, dressed, and peeked out his cabin door. There they went again, Jed, Luke, and four other men carrying bows and wearing orange hunting hats and vests, but each day they came back by noon with nothing. Sometimes, like the day before, Jed was back for breakfast, and the other guys would come back later. But Jace had been here almost two full weeks and still the men brought back no game? They were either exceptionally bad hunters, or they were up to something else. And today he was determined to find out what it was.

Quietly closing his cabin door, he followed behind them at a safe distance, ducking behind a bush, tree, or hay bale whenever one of them turned around. He couldn't follow them across the open field until they'd disappeared into the next grove of trees. But he didn't worry about them getting too far ahead. Tracking animals had always been one of his strengths, and tracking humans was even easier.

Their path led to a corner of the ranch property Jace

had never been to before. It was a good distance from the main trail that led toward the other land owners and was hidden by a small grove of trees by the edge of the river. Lucky for him there were also a few big boulders nearby to hide behind. If he could just sprint over to them without being seen . . .

On his way across he realized where they were going. There, in front of him, was a cabin in the woods. It looked like most of the other guest cabins, except this one was slightly larger and constructed from fresh wood. One of the men picked up a hammer and nailed a two-by-four across what looked to be the framework for the front porch. Another took a saw and cut several other pieces of lumber into varying lengths. Obviously the men were not hunters; they were carpenters. But why would they need to hide a cabin all the way out here?

One possibility he did not think of before now crossed his mind and made him shudder. What if the Collinses *did* want him to shoot that deer in the cabin? Delaney would have been furious, ending their relationship, and he could have been framed for poaching. All of the other carcasses had been found on *their* property. Was there a chance that Jed and Luke and maybe even these friends of theirs were the poachers all along? The ones threatening his mother? Had they invited him here in order to frame him so it would ruin her career like Bucky's dad had said?

He crept over to the cabin wall closest to him and intended to peer around the corner to see what the others were doing, but as soon as he stuck his head out, Luke grabbed him and pulled him out into the open. Quite a feat, since the guy used a cane to assist him when he walked, but Jace had been caught unaware.

Luke let out a deep breath. "Jace! I didn't know it was you. I heard someone sneaking around and thought it might be Sammy Jo."

Jace glanced across the faces of all six men, and realized he hadn't been very smart about this. He should have brought Eli Knowles and his two young men with him. What if these men *were* the poachers and he'd discovered their lair? Even though he wrestled bulls for a living, and would take them on if he had to, there was no denying he was outnumbered.

"Why would you think it might be Sammy Jo?" he asked, trying to keep calm.

"She's been getting suspicious this last week," Luke told him.

Jace hesitated. "Suspicious of what?"

"We're building Sammy Jo and Luke their own cabin," Jed informed him. "So when they get married in a couple months, they have their own place on the property."

"With privacy," Luke added with a grin. "But it's a surprise. Sammy Jo and none of the other women know."

"And we'd like to keep it that way," Jed warned.

Jace wanted with all his heart and soul to believe them, not only for Delaney's sake but for his own. It wouldn't do him any good to be at odds with Delaney's family if he wanted to continue to spend time with her. "Can I take a look inside the cabin?"

He didn't wait for an answer but headed over to the

front door and walked right in. The foul smell that greeted his nose confirmed his suspicions before he saw the body of the dead antelope on the floor, its horns removed, of course.

"Care to explain this?" Jace demanded as Luke and his father jumped back, with similar wide-eyed looks of both shock and anger.

Luke shook his head. "We're innocent!"

"Try telling that to my friend here," Jace said, nodding toward Eli Knowles and his "sons" Clint and Clay, who stepped through the door behind them.

Looked like he had backup after all.

Chapter Eleven

"DELANEY COLLINS!" HER father barked, marching up the aisle of the stable. "You've been hiding something from us. Did you think we wouldn't find out?"

She dropped the bucket of horse brushes in her hand and they fell to the dirt floor with a *thunk*. Had he seen her kissing Jace? Would he scream that she was crazy for getting involved with someone again so soon after her divorce? She didn't think nine months was too soon, but she and her father often had differing opinions.

"Don't pretend you don't know what I'm talking about, young lady," her father continued, his voice stern as his narrowed gaze bore down on her. "The animals in the toolshed?"

She gasped, and then held her breath, unable to breathe from fear over the fate of her young cubs. "You—you didn't *hurt* them or set them *free*, did you?"

"Nah, they're exactly where you left them," he assured her with a grimace. "But they have to go, Del."

"I've kept them out of the way," she protested. "And I promise you, they won't pose any threat to the guests."

"Do you know where I just was?" he demanded.

She realized something other than her cubs must have roused his temper, and shook her head, afraid to answer.

"Luke and I were out at the far left border by the big rocks building a surprise honeymoon cabin for your brother and Sammy Jo, and we were nearly arrested for poaching!"

"What?" She shook her head, not understanding how that could be possible.

"Jace followed us," he said with a grunt.

Her Jace?

"And he brought his friends, who are undercover agents for the Department of Fish and Wildlife. They're posing as guests right here at our ranch!"

She thought back to the three men he'd gone over to speak to at the other table during breakfast. "But how can they think that *we* are poachers?"

"Because of all the carcasses found along the edge of our property and the antelope we just found inside Luke's new cabin."

What a tragic loss of life. She cringed, the sorrow registering deep in her gut. "An antelope? Inside?"

"It was dead. With its horns cut off. They sell for big money these days. And believe me, it was more of a surprise to us than to Jace and his friends."

"We aren't in trouble, are we?" she said, her fear turning to dread. "You told them you didn't kill it?"

"Luke and I spent the last four hours telling them," he complained. "Now it's put us another day behind with the building and the forecast is predicting it won't be long before we get snow. Don't tell Sammy Jo about this or Luke will have your head."

"I won't," she promised. Seeing the surprise on Sammy Jo's face after listening to her say she thought Luke might be getting cold feet would be worth the wait. "But what does this have to do with my animal shelter?"

"The last thing I need is for the game wardens to think we're raising bobcats for our guests to come and shoot," her father said, furrowing his brows. "Now that Bree has posted Jace's endorsement for our ranch online, the phone's been ringing off the hook and our cabins our booked. We've got dozens of hunters coming in the day after tomorrow."

"More hunters?" Delaney exclaimed.

She had to admit that this time her father was right. With more hunters in the area it would be harder to conceal her animal shelter, and if one of the hunters happened to poke his head inside and saw what was inside, well, she'd hate think about what could happen.

She also hated having to take the cubs back to the wildlife rescue clinic and having to face Carol, Mary Ann, and Ben.

She lay down on her bed while trying to get Meghan to take an afternoon nap, and tears sprung to her eyes. She was a *terrible* public relations representative. Instead of getting good publicity, she'd only managed to bring on bad. Then she fell in love with Jace, which was something she'd promised herself she wouldn't do. And now that she'd finally got the endorsement to make her family happy, more hunters were coming to the ranch to threaten more of the animals she loved. She was *not* happy about that, and her wildlife rescue group wouldn't be either.

She pulled a pillow over her head and wished more than anything she could just stay there, but Meghan lifted up a corner and peeked under at her. "Are you playing hide-and-go-seek?"

"I don't know what I'm doing," Delaney confessed.

Meghan smiled. "I found you. Now it's your turn. You need to find me."

Delaney pulled off the pillow and sighed. She couldn't hide. She had a daughter to support, a daughter who was depending on her to take care of her as much as she depended on her to play. Her hand reached for the bear claw necklace her grandmother had given her for courage. She knew she couldn't live her whole life within her comfort zone, especially when she lived on a ranch with people who fished, hunted, and ate meat. But lately she'd been forced to live completely outside it and she didn't know how much more she could take.

She also thought of the time she'd wasted on Steve. He'd said he didn't want to be trapped with a wife and child, and implied she wasn't good enough, that he wanted someone *better* to spend the rest of his life with. What if she wasn't good enough to hold Jace's attention long term? Was everything she was doing for nothing? Would she never have *her* happy ending?

After Meghan drifted off to sleep for a nap, Delaney went to Jace's cabin and confessed about hiding the cubs, told him how Gavin had once shot a deer she'd just healed, and what her father had told her about finding the antelope.

Jace admitted he'd been feeling a little discouraged, too. "I really screwed up," he said, his voice low. "Eli Knowles gave me a talking-to after we straightened things out with Luke and your dad. He said I could have ruined their covert operation by exposing their cover. Eli reminded me that an undercover agent's job is to infiltrate and gain information, but to let the sheriff and other officials make the arrests so the agent's identity is never discovered. Luckily your family has vowed not to tell anyone so they can continue their search for the true poachers."

Delaney nodded. "Luke said he's posting more Private Property signs along our borders, letting people know they can't hunt in this area without permission."

"I'm not sure that will help. Eli told me it's hard to convict poachers. He said if there's no evidence on paper, they must be caught in the act either by an eyewitness or on video. Preferably both."

"We can use my cameras," Delaney offered. "I have a good pocket camera you can keep in your coat pocket and take with you wherever you go."

Jace drew her into his arms for a warm bear hug and then pulled back to give her a soft kiss. "Do you want me to go with you to drop off the bobcat cubs at the clinic?"

"Considering how my friends reacted the last time they saw you, I'd say that's *not* a good idea," Delaney said, and headed toward the door. "This is something I have to do on my own."

Delaney drove to Fox Creek in her father's pickup and entered the animal rescue clinic with the bobcat cubs in a small wire cage. After she explained why she was there she found the cubs weren't the only ones who could pounce.

"How could you let Jace Aldridge stay at your ranch?" Ben demanded.

"Is that the reason you left us short-handed," Mary Ann asked, wearing an incredulous expression on her face. "To spend time with *him*? A rotten rodeo hunter?"

"He is *not* rotten," Delaney said defensively.

Carol eyed the cage with the bobcats. "Not only are you giving up your values, but now you're giving up the cubs, too?"

"They are no longer safe at my ranch," Delaney pleaded, begging her to understand. "I'll come into the clinic like I used to, and help take care of them. I'll take photos of the new animals who have arrived to post online and try to find homes for them. I'll even speak at your rally."

"Your services are no longer needed here," Carol informed her. Mary Ann and Ben nodded their agreement.

They didn't want her here? Delaney's eyes pricked with hot tears and she fought to hold them back for the second time that day. Her heart tightened painfully in her chest. How could they give her the cold shoulder? They were her friends. How could they be so *judgmental*?

"What about the cubs?" she asked, her voice shaking.

"We'll take the cubs to the wildlife conservation center over in Helena so they can grow up in a natural habitat," Carol told her.

The conservation center, with its large outdoor facility, had Delaney's full approval and at least part of her heartache lifted, knowing the bobcats would be well cared for. But as she took one last look at the three people she left behind, she walked out of the building wondering, like her daughter, who *was* a friend?

She wasn't sure she knew anymore.

THAT EVENING, RIGHT before dinner, Jace kept his eye on Rio's front leg as he, Delaney, and Meghan led him across the field to see the other horses.

"He likes Fireball," Delaney said, smiling as their two horses sniffed one another.

"Rio likes Party Marty, too," Meghan said, pointing to the miniature pony who trotted up beside them, then ran to Grandma's side to follow her to the house.

A deep neigh came from the trail connecting the other properties and both Rio and Fireball stood at attention, their ears perked forward. Jace turned his head to see who was coming and spotted Zach Tanner riding toward them. He sat upon a black quarter horse that was taller than most and flaunted an extra thick black mane and tail.

"Isn't he a beauty?" Zach asked, his eyes on Delaney.

She stepped forward and brushed her hand down the side of the horse's neck in greeting. "He is," she agreed. "Is he yours?"

"Bought him today," Zach said, and then as if just realizing they weren't alone, he lifted his gaze and said, "Hi, Jace."

"What about me?" Meghan demanded. "You didn't say hi to me."

"You didn't give me a chance," Zach said, which Jace didn't think was true. "How are you?"

"You didn't say my *name*," Meghan complained.

"He has other things on his mind," Jace soothed, scooping the child up onto his shoulders. "Like his new horse."

"He runs twice as fast as my other one," Zach told Delaney, sliding out of the saddle to stand beside her. *Too close* beside her. "That's why he's named Jet. Of course, it's possible he could be named for his color, jet black, too. Would you like to ride him?"

For a moment Delaney looked excited, as if she was going to accept the offer. Then she glanced back at him and told Zach, "Maybe another time. I need to watch Meghan."

"Looks like Jace is watching Meghan there just fine," Zach coaxed.

Delaney shook her head and smiled. "Another time."

Jace held Meghan's ankles so she wouldn't wiggle around on his shoulders so much and heard her ask above his head, "Who are the flowers for?"

Jace stared at the flowers in Zach's hands. He'd been wondering the same thing, although he had a sinking feeling he already knew.

"They are for your mother, of course," Zach said, directing his words toward Meghan while handing the flowers to Delaney.

Del thanked him, but didn't blush like she did when *he* flirted with her.

"You didn't bring any flowers for *me*?" Meghan asked, as if shocked by Zach's lack of disrespect.

"Next time," he promised. "Hey, Jace, did you know Del presses wildflowers and uses them to create her own greeting cards?"

"I do now. Thanks for the tip."

He wasn't a fool. He knew Zach was purposely trying to come between him and Del. He guessed she realized it, too, because she abruptly stepped away from Zach and his horse and came to stand back by him.

"Bet your horse doesn't have a toy," Meghan challenged in her cute little high-pitched voice, clearly still miffed Zach wasn't paying her any attention. She held out the plastic toy horse Jace had given her in front of his face to show Zach.

Jace's cousin shook his head. "No, Jet doesn't have a toy that looks like him."

"Didn't think so," Meghan taunted, and held her toy out again. "This is Rio, just like the real Rio. He's a star."

"Meghan!" Del said, color rising to her cheeks. "You shouldn't talk to people like that. You must be *nice*."

"Sorry," Meghan called out, but Jace was certain she didn't mean it.

Zach glanced at the toy Rio in Meghan's hands and then the real Rio, with his hurt leg, and grinned as if he didn't think either one could compare to Jet. "My horse doesn't need a toy," he said with a smirk. "Or titles. He's the real deal, magnificent exactly as he is."

Jace thought Zach was referring to himself, instead of his horse, and didn't like the way he'd been talking either, but gave him a friendly wave as he remounted his horse and rode away. Then Jace remembered Eli's warning at breakfast that he should consider every angle.

What if the incident with the tranquilized deer in the cabin wasn't related to the poachers at all? What if whoever put the deer in there *did* want it to cause a fight between him and Delaney? How far would Zach go to get rid of him so he could win Del's attention?

BREE, DELANEY, AND Luke spent a large portion of the next day cleaning up the mess the panic-stricken, neck-bleeding deer had caused in Cabin 26. The three women who had rented the place had salvaged what they could of their belongings and left the rest for Del to gather up and put into a garbage can. But the extra work didn't bother her. It helped keep her mind off the fact that, as of today, the hunters were allowed to use guns. Already several shots had echoed between the rolling hills and she'd winced each time, praying the targeted animal had managed to escape.

Bree knelt on her hands and knees using a rag to scrub the bloodstains off the wood floor. "This is never going to come up," she complained. "And we need this cabin ready for our new guests tomorrow."

"Clean what you can and I'll use my sander to get rid of the rest," Luke said, then tore down the last piece of the broken paneling separating the bedroom and kitchen. "I'll have this wall fixed before the new guests arrive, too."

Delaney glanced at her watch, realized it was midafternoon, and frowned. "Where are those twins? They promised they'd be here to help clean."

"I saw them a few minutes ago when I drove the gator down to the supply shed to get a new sheet of plywood," Luke said, picking up a hammer and a couple nails. "They were fiddling with their cameras and taking pictures of the people next door at Woolly Outfitters."

Delaney tossed the last bit of broken debris into the trash can and frowned. "I'm going after them before they get themselves into trouble. We don't want our new neighbors to accuse us of spying."

Both Bree and Luke agreed that was a good idea. Frustrated by the twins' lack of focus, Delaney went out the door, but halfway to the property line she was already having second thoughts. Like maybe Bree should have been the one to come talk to them and not her.

Then she spotted the twins, hiding in the brush, each with a camera around their neck, except they weren't looking through the lens. In fact, they weren't taking pictures at all. Nora held a remote control, and Nadine was pointing toward something hovering in the air, a small black object with four tiny propellers like a mini helicopter, barely perceptible through the shadow of the trees.

Delaney moved closer, stared at the UFO, and instead of scolding the twins, she asked, "What is it?"

Both twins jumped, then turned, waved her forward, and placed their fingers to their lips, indicating for her to keep quiet.

"It's a drone," Nora whispered. "With a video camera attached giving us supersharp clarity and a range of up to five hundred feet."

"We combined last month's paychecks to buy it," Nadine said, her face full of excitement.

"But why are you using it to spy on our neighbors?" Delaney asked, glancing around them to make sure no one had noticed them.

"We're not spying on Mr. Woolly," Nora told her. "We're—"

"Filming the new cute guys who came to the ranch with their father," Nadine explained. "We wanted to catch them in action. They took their guns to go hunting, but instead of going up the trail, they crossed over to Woolly's property with Jace."

Delaney gasped. "What's Jace doing over there?"

"Take a look," Nora said, holding the remote control at an angle so Delaney could see.

She leaned her head toward the small two-by-three-inch video screen in the middle of the handheld device to view exactly what the video camera on the drone flying above was recording and saw Jace and the three undercover agents staying at their ranch speaking to Isaac Woolly and another couple in front of the mobile trailer the outfitter had brought in.

"Does this thing have audio?" Delaney asked, wondering what the group on the screen could possibly be talking about.

Both twins gave her a regretful shake of their heads.

"Can we zoom in?"

This time the twins smiled. "Oh, yes," Nora whispered, turning one of the dials on the controller. "Watch this."

The group's faces enlarged and focused in on the two young men, Clint and Clay. One was speaking, the other smiling, and both the twins happily sighed as they gazed at the male images on the screen.

"Let me see the others," Delaney said, squeezing her way in between Nora's and Nadine's shoulders. "Quick!"

"Okay," Nora agreed, her tone showing her reluctance to view anything but the boys.

The view shifted and showed Jace was the one now talking. Then Nora scrolled over to the man next to him and Isaac Woolly's white bearded face came onto the screen.

"Keep going," Delaney encouraged.

The next images were those of the couple standing beside Mr. Woolly, and as soon as Delaney saw them, she fell back and let out a small yelp.

Both Nora and Nadine put their fingers to their lips again to tell her to hush and Delaney cupped her mouth with her hand. Then drawing toward the screen again, she stared at the couple who had racked up so much trouble for her family over the last few months.

"It's the Randalls," she whispered, her pulse racing as she considered what she should do.

"Who are they?" the twins asked in unison.

"Our previous ranch managers," Delaney informed them, her head spinning. "The ones who embezzled our money and want to steal away our ranch."

Delaney ran toward the house and nearly collided with Bree, who came running from the opposite direction.

"The PI called," Bree said, her voice breathless. "The Randalls have been spotted in Fox Creek."

"I know," Del told her, and pointed toward the property line. "I just saw them next door."

It took both of them, Luke, and Ryan Tanner to hold their father back and prevent him from charging next door.

"The sheriff and his men are on their way," Bree scolded. "They'll be here in just a few minutes. We need to let the authorities handle this."

"Susan and Wade Randall have some nerve showing up here," Jed growled, stomping his foot. "I want to talk to them."

"After they're arrested I don't think they'll be allowed to speak to anyone," Luke said, keeping guard by the front door of the main house in case their father tried to run out.

"But at least we'll have peace of mind knowing that they are finally caught," Delaney added.

"That's right," Grandma added. "We must always look on the bright side."

A knock sounded on the door and everyone in the room glanced at one another as Luke moved aside to open it.

"Sheriff McKinley," Delaney's ma called out the moment he stepped over the threshold. "Did you catch them?"

Because he didn't answer right away, Delaney held her breath, and when he shook his head, her stomach squeezed tight. "But I saw them. How could they escape?"

"We searched the premises," the sheriff informed them. "But the Randalls were gone before we arrived. Isaac Woolly said he knew them by a different name and had no idea there was a warrant out for their arrest."

Jace walked through the door next and Delaney ran toward him. "You were there," she gushed. "What did the couple with Isaac Woolly say to you?"

He looked at her as if bewildered, and after the sheriff and Delaney's family filled him in on what was happening, Jace said, "The couple wanted to know if Woolly was interested in forming a partnership with another outfitter."

"What was Woolly's answer?" Delaney's father demanded.

Jace gave him a solemn look. "He said he'd think on it."

Chapter Twelve

WITHIN THE PRIVACY of his cabin, Jace took Delaney into his arms, and tried to allay her fears. "A week has passed and no one's seen the Randalls, not even Isaac Woolly."

"I don't think Isaac would tell anyone even if he did," Delaney said, her voice rising as high as her ma's in a near hysterical panic. "And if they work together and put our ranch out of business, we'll have nowhere to go. I won't have any way of supporting myself or Meghan, and I have no idea what we'll do!"

"You weren't this upset yesterday," he said, pulling back with a frown.

"Yesterday I thought I might still have a chance of getting child support from my ex," Delaney told him. "But I talked to the lawyer and he said that Steve quit his job so the courts can't demand his boss dock his pay."

Jace scowled, his bitterness for her ex growing stronger. "How will he live?"

"Steve has moved in with his new girlfriend and apparently her family has a lot of money," Delaney said, her voice cracking. "He doesn't need to work. They've also switched over his bank accounts, his cars, and everything he owns into her name so none of it can be taken by the courts and given to me to help support Meghan."

"He's a jerk," Jace said, looking her straight in the eye, "but I don't want you to worry. I'm not going to let anyone put your family's ranch out of business. We're going to catch these poachers, the sheriff's going to catch the Randalls, and your family is going to be just fine."

She swallowed hard and gazed up at him with terrified eyes. "What if we're not?"

He pressed a kiss to her lips and then grinned. "If not, then I guess you'll have to marry me."

"Marry *you*?"

"Is that such a terrible idea?" he asked, alarmed by her shocked reaction. He'd said it to tease her, but the thought of marrying Delaney and becoming Meghan's father ignited true desire. He'd never felt such a profound connection with anyone like he did with the two of them before. He'd do anything to protect them, anything to make them happy.

"Are—are you proposing?" she asked, her eyes wide and her mouth dropping open.

"Just think about it," he said, kissing her lips again. "We don't have to make any decisions right now."

"No," she agreed. "We don't. But thank you for offering. And, of course, you're right. My family will be fine. We'll persevere, we always do. Everything will be fine."

Although he'd managed to smooth things over with Delaney, things were *not* fine with his own family. As soon as he and Delaney walked out of the "dead service zone" on their way up to the main house for lunch, his cell phone buzzed with a series of messages telling him he'd missed six calls—four from his sister, two from his mom.

"My mother's received two anonymous threatening letters telling her to drop from the governor's race," he confided to Delaney. "She may have got a third. We believe they are from the poachers who don't want her to increase the amount of game wardens in our state so they continue to make their money without being caught."

"Isn't that her?" Delaney asked, pointing to the two women walking toward them with Bree.

It was. And from the tense, drawn expressions on each of their faces, they weren't here for a friendly visit. His gaze dropped to the suitcases in their hands. "Mom, Nat, what are you doing here?"

"We booked a cabin," Natalie said, giving Bree and Delaney a wary glance as if unsure how much to say in front of them.

"Bree," Del exclaimed. "Why didn't you tell me they were coming?"

"I didn't know," Bree said, equally surprised.

"I booked the cabin under my pen name," Natalie explained. "Natalie Brooks."

Delaney gasped, then she shot Jace a quick glance and

stared openmouthed at his sister. "*You're* Natalie Brooks? The author of *The Power of Positive Relationships*?"

Natalie nodded, and Delaney gazed at her as if star-struck. "I love your books. I have three of them on my nightstand beside my bed right now. You have no idea how much I appreciate what you said about how others should be treated and how to stand up for yourself."

"I'm excited to meet you, too," Natalie said, flashing her a smile. "I've heard so much about you. But right now . . ." Her voice trailed off and when she looked at him there was real concern in her eyes.

"Jace," his mother said, handing him her suitcase. "We didn't know where else to go."

"What happened?" he asked, bracing himself for the news that could have driven his mother from her own house. He watched his mother and sister give Del and Bree a hesitant look and he added, "You can talk in front of them."

"Someone knocked out the security guard," Natalie said, her voice grave. "Then they broke into the house and came upstairs to where we were sleeping."

"When I woke there was a dead rat next to my pillow," his mom said, cringing as she relived the memory. "We're not safe there, Jace."

He thought of the poachers leaving dead carcasses around the Collins property and the fact someone had tranquilized and placed a deer into Cabin 26. Not to mention the possibility these poachers may even be living on the properties next door.

Jace swallowed hard. "I'm not sure you're safe here either."

THE FOLLOWING DAY, Delaney and Jace saddled two horses and took the main trail all the way up the rise toward the silver mine where her grandfather used to work. Grandma had wanted to go to the mine herself to get the mineral water she used to make her lotions, arguing she'd been up there hundreds of times. But the family didn't think it was safe. Not with poachers and the Randalls in the area. Armed with a rifle, Jace had volunteered to go for her and Delaney agreed to show him the way.

"I think Grandma was hoping the sheriff would offer to bring her to the mine," Delaney mused. "Like a date."

"Speaking of dates," Jace said, bringing his mount closer to her and Fireball. "You never responded to the text I sent with our photo."

"Do you want this to count as a date?" she asked, giving him a smile.

"I'll take whatever I can get," he said, and let out a chuckle. "Especially since you won't marry me."

"You weren't serious," she said, laughing as she swatted his arm with her hand.

"Maybe I should have my sister ask for me," he teased. "From the way you were fawning all over her, I doubt you'd say no to her."

Delaney turned Fireball around the next bend and said, "I was not *fawning*."

"You looked at her as if she were a superstar," Jace continued.

"She is," Delaney exclaimed.

Jace's eyes sparkled, as if amused. "And I'm not?"

"Everyone in your family is a superstar. Your mother

is running for governor, and I can't *believe* she's actually renting one of our cabins! Ma almost had a heart attack when she found out. We haven't had many high ranking officials at our ranch before. Then there's your sister, a *real* author." She ran her tongue over her lower lip and then smiled at him. "Then there's you."

"What about me?" he prompted.

She laughed. "You're a rodeo star."

"And?" he pressed.

"Handsome," she added.

"You *are* honest."

She playfully swatted his arm again. "And you've got yourself a bit of an ego."

He puffed out his chest like Gavin had done when crowing about his business. "What else?"

"You're mine?"

Grinning, he leaned over and gave her a kiss on the cheek. "Now *that's* what I like to hear."

Delaney hadn't had this much fun since . . . well, she couldn't remember. She'd overheard Ryan and Bree flirt with each other, and had been witness to many of Sammy Jo's crazy attempts to win over Luke, but she'd never had someone she could comfortably talk to like this. When Jace spoke to her, it was as if he *adored* her. It wasn't just his words, but the tone in which he said them, the depth of emotion in his eyes when he looked at her. He *did* adore her, she was sure of it, and he adored Meghan, too.

"If I'm yours, then why won't you marry me?" Jace teased again.

"Maybe I will marry again someday," Delaney said, turning serious. "After a long, long, very long engagement."

"Geez," Jace said, as if disappointed. "And here I was hoping I could get you to fly to Las Vegas and tie the knot overnight."

"Been there, done that." Delaney smiled and shook her head. "It didn't work out. Like I said, he wasn't even a friend."

The steady clip-clop of her horse's feet upon the fresh-scented earth soothed her soul, and the rhythm rocked her back and forth in a soft, lulling motion. As they walked on, her thoughts turned to the scene in the gazebo she'd witnessed in early August.

"The Hamilton wedding this summer brought in over a hundred guests," she said softly. "They had extravagant decorations, beautiful bridesmaids' gowns, a delicious wedding cake. But it was what the bride said to the groom at the altar that really got to me. She said, 'Today I'm the luckiest gal in the whole world, because I get to marry my *best* friend and there's no one else I'd rather be with than you.' It was the most beautiful moment. Then she cried because she was so happy, and I—I cried with her, because I never had that. If I ever marry again . . . I want to be able to say those words. I want to be *that* happy."

"Happy enough to cry?" Jace asked gently.

"Yes," she repeated, and with a deep longing in her heart and a smile she nodded. "Happy enough to cry."

The entrance to the silver mine came into view, resembling the mouth of a cave in the side of the hill.

"There's the mine." Delaney pointed. "The natural underground spring where my grandma gets the mineral water to make her lotions is inside."

"How do we get in?" Jace asked, studying the structure.

"It was boarded up about fifty years ago after it closed down," Delaney said with a nod, then gave him a mischievous smile. "But that hasn't stopped the local kids from going in there to kiss, or my grandma from getting her mineral water. There's a few loose boards that move aside so we can enter."

Jace helped her hitch the horses to a nearby tree. As they walked toward the mine entrance, Delaney stopped up short. "Someone's been here," she said, pointing to the smoldering campfire in a ring of rocks.

"Del," Jace said, his tone issuing a warning. "This could be where your embezzling ranch managers are hiding out."

The truth was the campfire could have been made by anyone. Which is exactly what the sheriff told them after he'd gone up to the mine to check it out. Still, Delaney had hoped that maybe they'd stumbled on a clue. They hadn't passed anyone on the way up to the mine and on the way back the only person she and Jace met was Gavin McKinley.

"Sure you don't want me to take you out on one of my hunts?" Gavin had asked as he stepped aside on the trail to let them pass.

"Not interested," Jace said, and gave him a half grin. "In fact, I'd love some extra cash to buy the Collinses new posters to advertise their ranch. Are you interested in buying my guns?"

Gavin shook his head. "Nah. I'm going to keep hoping you'll change your mind, Jace. Let me know if you need anything." As if she were an afterthought, Gavin tipped his hat toward her and added, "You, too, Delaney. Have a good day."

"Would you really sell your guns?" she'd asked when they were alone.

Jace hesitated. "I'd sell them if I only used them to hunt. But guns are also used for protection."

That's what her father and brother had told her a million times. But she thought the sound from the sticks of homemade dynamite her grandma used to blow stubborn roots out of her garden worked just as effectively to scare off wild animals as a few bullets shot into the air. The explosions were small and concentrated to only a few square feet to ensure both human and animal safety. And as a bonus, the smoke the dynamite left behind kept predators away long after the blast.

Just like they had the night before. Just before midnight, a few howls had come from the open field behind the cow pasture and Luke had gone out there to toss a few of Grandma's sticks of homemade dynamite in their direction, thinking it was a pack of coyotes.

Grandma said that Grandpa Collins had learned to make the explosive sticks while working at the mine, which led Delaney to think about Jace and his marriage proposals. She tried to imagine what it would be like to work with Jace on a daily basis and see him every day the rest of her life. What new things could they teach each other? What memories could they create?

Jace's kisses could be just as explosive to her senses as one of those sticks of dynamite, and she feared just as devastating if he ever stopped. Hopefully, he would never stop. Jace said he wanted to buy a house in the area, and if he did, who knew where the days ahead would lead them?

Later that night, after Meghan was tucked into bed, Delaney slipped back down the stairs and out the door to see if she could get one more of those heart-racing kisses, but Jace wasn't in his cabin. She found him standing by the stable speaking to Ryan, who sat upon his black horse with the white blaze across its blue eyes, aptly named the Blue-Eyed Bandit.

"Jace, I sure could use your help," Ryan said, swinging his rifle into ready position.

Alarmed, Delaney hurried toward them. "What's going on?"

A howl came from the back field and Ryan said, "Wolves."

Wolves? There hadn't been many sightings in recent years but the packs were reportedly located in all of southwestern Montana.

"They're closing in on the animals in the back pastures," Jace said, opening a stall and leading out the horse he'd borrowed for the trail ride. Grabbing a bridle off the rack, he slipped it over the chestnut horse's nose. "They're probably attracted to the scent of the carcasses the poachers have been leaving around back there."

"We found another one today," Ryan said with a nod.

"Should I go get Luke?" Delaney asked, bringing Jace the saddle.

"He's out on a date with Sammy Jo," Ryan said in a rush. "Bree's in town with your parents, and I called my brothers but it's going to take them a few minutes to get here."

"Where's Meghan?" Jace asked with concern.

"She's asleep," Delaney said, her breath catching in her chest as she heard another howl. "Grandma's in the house with her and promised to check on her while I'm gone. I can go with you."

"We'll round up the cows and bring them into the arena," Ryan said, spinning his horse around. "You bring in the rest of the horses. And lock the stable."

She nodded and glanced up at Jace as he climbed into the saddle and collected his reins. "Be careful?"

He grinned. "Have a kiss waiting when I return home."

She watched the two cowboys ride off, and smiled at his words, thinking how nice it would be to hear him say that as he went off to work each day. Then she hurried to the horse pasture a few yards away and brought the outside horses into the stable two at a time.

JACE SQUINTED THROUGH the darkness, trying to identify the cows ahead. It would have been easier if the moon was as bright as the night he'd shared the stable rooftop with Delaney, but tonight thick clouds had moved in. It didn't help that the two dozen cows the Collinses owned were Black Angus. A couple low moos came from the shifting shapes to his right.

"Go left and I'll come around the other way," Ryan called.

Jace held the reins in his left hand and his gun in his other, ready to fire in case he saw a threat. He let out a sharp whistle and rode around the backsides of two cows, driving them closer to the others. Then he cut off a few more who wanted to run the opposite direction. Rounding another on the outside edge of the herd, he realized the cows in this section were mewing louder than the others and were huddled closer together. *Whew!* That would make their job easier. Now all they had to do was move them.

He called out to Ryan, then prepared to cut back and forth behind the herd to guide them toward the arena, when he heard a growl. His horse sidestepped to the right, tossed its head, and let out a shrill neigh. Then the animal tensed beneath him and pranced back and forth as Jace fought for control. Unfortunately, his gun slipped from his hand in the process and fell to the ground. At least Ryan still had his.

More growls, a bark, a snap, and a series of vicious snarls erupted as Ryan drew close. The smell of blood filled Jace's nostrils, and he realized they'd interrupted the wolves during their dinner. Taking a flashlight from his pocket, he flicked it on, and drew in a sharp breath. A fresh bull elk carcass, minus its antlers, lay on the ground before them. A pack of six wolves stood around it, some tearing into its flesh, the others, including a large alpha, baring their teeth and staring directly at him. The gray wolf closest to him lunged forward and Jace pressed his knee against the side of his horse to steer his mount away.

Ryan fired a shot into the air, which should have scared them off, but the wolves didn't budge. They lowered themselves closer to the body of the elk and appeared even more agitated. More shots, this time coming from the direction of the trail, echoed across the field and a series of hooves thundered toward them. Ryan called out to his brothers and Jace spun in a tight circle to give his trembling, snorting horse a chance to calm down.

He continued to shine the flashlight to alert the Tanners to the wolves' location and Zach, with his fast new horse, Jet, was the first on the scene. Dean and Josh circled around, startling the wolves from the other side, and let off a few more shots with their guns. A few of the wolves scattered, but the alpha snapped at the legs of Zach's horse. Jet let out a terrified neigh, and threw Zach out of the saddle . . . right at the alpha wolf's feet.

Jace's heart stopped for half a millisecond as the wolf bunched its muscles, ready to pounce. Then giving his horse a kick to spring forward, he leaned to the right, slid out of the saddle like he did when bulldoggin', and dropped down over Zach to shield him. Without actually meaning to, his flashlight also struck the end of the wolf's nose.

The wolf yelped and shrunk back, then as the other Tanner brothers circled around and continued to fire off shots, the alpha ran off to rejoin the rest of his pack.

Jace rolled off his cousin and for a moment lay on the ground, staring up at the sky, allowing his heart rate to return to normal. For a moment, Zach didn't move either, then he sat up, scratched his head, and said, "Whoa."

That was an understatement. Jace rolled over and found his gun on the ground a few feet away.

Dismounting, Ryan, Dean, and Josh ran toward them, and Ryan shouted, "Zach, you okay? It happened so fast I couldn't get a clear shot of that beast."

"I'm fine," Zach said, and in the glow from the flashlight, which Jace still held in his hand, he gave him a rueful grin. "Thanks to our fine, bulldoggin' cousin."

Jace shrugged. "We're lucky I didn't get my foot caught in the stirrup this time."

Ryan gave Jace a hand and pulled him to his feet. Dean and Josh did the same for Zach, and for a moment the four of them just stood there. With visions of sharp teeth hovering inches from his face, Jace drew in a deep breath, glad no one had been bit, especially *him*.

Stepping forward, Zach stretched out his hand, and said, "Thanks, Jace. I mean it."

Jace accepted the handshake and then Ryan chuckled and stretched out his own hand. "I owe him one, too. Sorry for the cold reception when you first arrived."

"No problem." Jace grinned as his cousins all gave him a friendly slap on the shoulder. "If it were me, I would've wanted to protect my family, too."

"We *are* family, Jace," Dean said, his face serious. "From now on, we protect each other."

The following morning over breakfast Jace told his

mother and sister about the carcass the poachers had left, and how it drew in the wolves. He didn't mention his close encounter with the largest one, but did warn them not to go anywhere on the Collins property alone.

"Well, then, my protective brother," Natalie teased, "can you escort us safely back to our cabin?"

At his request, his mother and sister had been given the cabin closest to his. He'd wavered back and forth as to whether they should be given one closer to the main house or to him. He worried over their safety, but in the end, it was his bad cell phone service that made up his mind. If they stayed in the cabin next door, all they had to do to get his attention was yell.

"I love hearing the sound of the river rush by the side of our cabin when we sleep," his mother said, and sighed. "This is such a peaceful place. It's hard to believe the Collinses have had as much trouble as they say they've had or that there could actually be poachers nearby."

"They're here," Jace assured her, leading them past the row of cabins. "And if they are the same poachers who have been sending you the threats, then *you* shouldn't be."

"I'll only stay a few days until my house is fixed. I'm having a new security system installed," she said, holding her head high. "And there's only another five and half weeks until the election. After that, I'll go after these poachers with every available resource available to me as governor to put them behind bars where they belong."

"Jace, who's that?" Natalie asked.

She'd stopped walking and both Jace and his mother turned back to look at her. She gave a slight nod across the field and, following her gaze, Jace saw she was referring to the man on the main trail alongside the Collinses' east border.

"That's Isaac Woolly, head of Woolly Outfitters," he told her. "His property is the next one over."

"Why is he *staring* at us?" Natalie demanded, her voice shaking.

Jace glanced back at Woolly. The man didn't move. He stood ramrod straight as he faced them head-on, and he *was* staring.

Concerned for his mother's safety, Jace's pulse quickened. "I think he knows who you are."

Chapter Thirteen

"WE'VE GOT A lead on another outfitter not far from here," Eli said as he slung a backpack into his truck. He nodded toward Clint and Clay. "The boys and I are going to check it out."

Jace frowned. "But what about Gavin McKinley and Isaac Woolly?"

Eli put a hand on his shoulder. "We haven't found anything."

"Not yet," Jace said, "but we know there are poachers in the area. They're killing animals for their antlers and horns and dumping the bodies everywhere."

"Not everywhere," Eli corrected. "Most of the carcasses have all been found on the Collins property."

"Because they want the Collinses to take the blame," Jace said, balling his fists at his side. "Or *me*."

"Possibly both," Eli said with a nod. "Your endorsement won't mean much if the bad guys can tarnish your name by claiming *you're* a poacher. They'll kill two birds with one stone—use you to bring down your mother's campaign and bring down the Collins ranch in the process."

Jace frowned. "Which is why you should stay here."

"We'll be back on Monday," Eli told him. "This new lead may blow this case wide open. In the meantime, keep a watch on the neighbors and let me know if you see or hear anything."

Jace didn't have a good feeling about this. He'd already convinced his mother and sister to go back to Bozeman and check into a hotel for the weekend. They'd left right after lunch. But he still needed to catch the poachers in action.

Delaney had been taking the wasteful deaths of the animals exceptionally hard. Each one was a reminder that not all things always worked out the way they should. Sometimes lives were lost, mistakes were made, and dreams went unfulfilled, proving they lived in a broken world where justice did *not* always prevail.

His mother had learned about the poachers from listening to his friend Bucky talk about his father's work as a game warden. Then when Eli became an undercover agent to track down these heartless poachers, his mother vowed to make this one of her main focus areas when she became governor. Jace had listened to her campaign speeches, but now that Delaney had come into his life mirroring his mother's passion and he'd seen what the poachers did firsthand, he hoped with all his heart that his mother won the governor's seat.

Sometimes all it took was one person to take a stand to change *everything*. And he hoped for all their sakes that his mother's influence could make a difference.

Meghan took his hand and led him toward the kitchen. "Grandma has something for you. It looks like a present."

"She isn't going to give me more hand cream, is she?" he joked.

"No, silly," Meghan said with a laugh. "It's bigger. I hope I get big presents for my birthday."

She still had a couple months to go, but he smiled at her, and asked, "What do you want?"

He expected her to say a pony or a puppy, but Meghan looked at him and smiled, "A bug house."

"You want to catch bugs?" he asked, surprised.

"No," she said, shaking her adorable blond pigtails. "I want to *save* them."

The child pointed toward a bristly black caterpillar with a reddish-orange band around its middle crawling on the ground, and pulled him back so he wouldn't step on it.

"If they stay here people will step on them," Meghan explained, her blue eyes looking up at him in earnest. "But if I put them in my bug house and take them to the field, they will be safe."

He laughed. "I see you have a great future ahead of you in wildlife conservation."

"What's that?" she asked, crinkling her nose.

"It means you are a lot like your mother," he said, his chest tight from the overwhelming affection he had developed for them in so short a time. "And that is a very beautiful, wonderful, incredible thing."

"Okay, Cowboy Jace," Meghan said, squeezing his hand as she looked up at him and laughed again.

He briefly thought of his own life and wondered what career *he* would choose if he decided not to continue with rodeo. If he couldn't "save the world," was it possible he could find a way to at least make a difference in his little neck of the woods?

When he entered the kitchen, Jace discovered Meghan had been wrong. Ruth Collins didn't have a present for him to open, but a package for him to *deliver*.

"These were shipped to the wrong house," she explained, pointing to the fifty-pound bags of dicalcium phosphate.

"It's my fault for accepting the delivery," Delaney said, lifting up the attached tag. "I saw they were some kind of minerals and didn't look at the name on the address label. I thought Grandma had ordered them to make more of her mineral lotions."

"Which is ridiculous because you know I always make small batches to ensure they are fresh," Ruth scolded softly. "What would I do with three fifty-pound bags of minerals? Open my own lotion factory?"

"You could use them to make salt licks," Jace said, and caught Delaney's eye. "Whose name is on the address label?"

"Isaac Woolly." Her mouth fell open as she realized what he was thinking. "Do you think he's making salt licks to attract the animals onto his property to boost his outfitting business?"

Ruth furrowed her brows. "That would be illegal, wouldn't it?"

"It sure would," Jace said, and lifted the first bag of mineral supplement into his arms. "He could be caught for poaching."

REFUSING TO STAY behind, Delaney asked her grandma to watch Meghan, then grabbed her camera and jumped into the truck with Jace to go with him to deliver the minerals to Woolly.

The outfitter appeared surprised to see them and his brows raised even higher when he saw what they had for him. "Sorry to trouble you," Isaac said, taking the bags Jace unloaded. "Some of the delivery trucks don't realize there's a new resident on this road."

"No problem at all," Jace said, scanning the grounds. He nodded to a few other bags leaning against the mobile unit. "Is that rock salt?"

Delaney sucked in her breath, then pressed her lips together. Rock salt was another key ingredient to make salt licks.

Isaac stroked his white woolly beard and said, "Yeah, with snow in the forecast I figure I better stock up for winter. We'll need to deice the roads to get our trucks in and out."

"And the minerals?" Jace asked, distracting Isaac

while Delaney raised her camera to her eye and snapped a few pictures. "What do you plan to do with them?"

"Figure I'd mix it into the horses' feed," Isaac said, gesturing toward his outdoor pasture filled with trail horses.

"I usually give Rio supplements designed *specifically* for horses," Jace said, arching his brow.

Isaac shrugged. "Everyone has their own beliefs and ways of doing things."

Delaney gave the man a direct look and said, "That's for sure."

She'd zoomed her lens in on the bags' labels, but what she really needed was a picture of a salt lick. She focused the lens across the field to a patch of trees, but didn't see anything. "Beautiful piece of land you have here," she said, lowering her camera. "I always wondered what it would be like to own this piece over here one day."

Isaac chuckled, and he glanced over the border toward her family's house. "I'm sure the feeling is mutual. We always want what we can't have, eh?"

"What do you think of Gavin McKinley's outfitting operation?" Delaney asked, hoping she appeared curious and not too inquisitive.

Isaac scrunched his face like Meghan did sometimes and shrugged. "I'm not worried about him."

"Aren't you worried about him putting you out of business?" Delaney pressed. "He told me the day you moved in that this area can support only one outfitter."

"He did, did he?" Isaac asked, drawing back to give her a good look. "Are *you* worried?"

"Not at all," she lied, lifting her chin.

"Well, then, neither am I," Isaac said, and gave them each a nod. "May the best outfitter win."

Delaney hesitated, and bit her lip. "That's what *he* said."

Jace took her arm as they returned to her house and murmured in her ear, "He didn't ask about my mother or sister at all. Don't you think he would have wanted to know what they were doing here?"

"Maybe he already knows," Delaney suggested.

"I hope he knows they left," Jace said, spinning her around and taking her into his arms. "You didn't book anyone else into their cabin, did you?"

"No. Bree thought it best to leave their cabin empty."

They didn't want anyone breaking in and giving their new guests a scare. *Or worse.* At this point they needed to avoid lawsuits and bad publicity as much as possible.

"Any luck with the camera?" Jace asked, brushing a stray hair back away from her face.

"No," she said, her gaze drifting toward his mouth, eager for one of their daily kisses. "I should have known he wouldn't have his salt licks out in the open."

"From the way you're looking at me, maybe *we* shouldn't be out in the open," Jace teased.

Delaney smiled. "Maybe you're *right*."

"Bold words," Jace teased again.

She shook her head and laughed. *"Honest."*

Bree ran into the hall and placed one hand on each of their arms to keep herself from bowling them over. "Jace! Delaney! Come quick. We have news."

Delaney glanced at Jace. "Later?"

Jace nodded. "That's a promise."

Then, hand in hand, they followed Bree into the living room. When they arrived, Delaney's father was pacing back and forth, his face contorted in a dark scowl, and she wondered who would be the target for his wrath this time. With dread already pouring over her, slowing her steps, she prayed it wouldn't be her.

"It's the Randalls," Bree informed them, and as she glanced around the assembled family, Delaney realized it was the first time they'd also included Jace.

"Have they been seen?" Ma asked. "Did the sheriff find out where they've been hiding?"

"No," Bree said, and cast a worried look toward her father. "I had a call from Doug Kelly, our private investigator. He says Isaac Woolly is Susan Randall's *cousin*."

Jace sat up straight in his seat. "*What?*"

"Well, that just figures, doesn't it?" Delaney's father demanded. "Seems the Randalls have *everyone* in their back pocket, all willing to go against us."

"You haven't exactly made a lot of friends over the years," Luke reminded him. "You could at least *try* to be a little friendlier to the townspeople."

"I'm plenty friendly," their father growled.

Delaney shared a look with Bree and Luke, confirming they, too, thought his words were contrary to the truth.

"Who else is in on their scheme to run us off the ranch this time?" their father barked.

"Isaac Woolly has a daughter named Alicia Stevens Woolly," Bree said, checking her notes.

"Alicia?" Delaney asked, glancing over at Jace. "There's a woman named Alicia working for Gavin McKinley."

"If she's Isaac's daughter, why wouldn't she be working for her father?" Ma asked, confused.

"Maybe she is," Jace offered.

"Gavin McKinley and Isaac Woolly could be working together," Delaney exclaimed.

"With the Randalls directing their steps, of course," her father added. "They know how to manage, all right. Instead of managing our ranch, they've managed to hire all the right people to put us out of business."

"We can't go making snap judgments and pointing fingers without proof," Grandma scolded.

"No, we can't," Delaney said, backing her grandma, and quoted, " 'You can't blame the most obvious fox in the henhouse,' right, Grandma?"

"That's right, sweet pea," her grandma nodded proudly.

Bree said she'd talked to the sheriff, but Delaney suspected there wasn't one person in her family who expected the lawman to do anything. Except Grandma, who still looked at him through rose-colored glasses and thought he was as handsome as her movie hero, Clint Eastwood.

"I could take the sheriff some cookies," Grandma said, smiling. "And urge him to look into the Randalls and Woollys a little closer."

"Yes, Grandma, that's a great idea," Bree agreed.

But from the set look of determination on her sister's face, Delaney could tell Bree had formulated another

plan. And from their similar expressions, it appeared
Luke, their father, and Jace were busy thinking up plans,
too.

It would be easy for Delaney to sit back and see what
ideas the rest of her family came up with like she'd always
done. But after the phone call from her lawyer that morning concerning her ex, she knew she couldn't hide in the
shadows any longer and wait for others to make decisions
for her.

She'd enact her own plan to expose those poachers
and she'd do it *tonight*.

JACE SPENT THE remainder of the afternoon in town
making sure the hotel room his mother and sister
checked into had adequate security. His mother settled
into her new accommodations and acted as if the incident at the ranch with Woolly had been an insignificant
consequence. She trusted the authorities would expose
the poachers and couldn't wait to get back on the phone
with her political supporters and campaign managers.
Natalie still shuddered at the way Woolly had stared. As-
suring he'd let them know if there was anything else to
report, Jace drove back to Collins Country Cabins eager
to spend the evening with Delaney.

He entered the main house looking for her, but Loretta said, "She asked if I'd watch Meghan and slipped
out of the house right after dinner."

Jace asked around but no one else had seen her. His
imagination played havoc with his emotions as the hour

drew later and still Delaney had not returned. Where could she be? Sunset was around seven-thirty and soon it would be dark. What if she came across one of the poachers or a pack of wolves? After grabbing his gun from his cabin, he caught up with the Walford twins on his way down to the stable.

"Have you seen Delaney?" he asked, his heart beating a mite too fast.

"She borrowed our drone," Nora said, narrowing her gaze. "But I told her it didn't have night vision capability and—"

"We saw her go across the trail toward Mr. Woolly's property," Nadine finished.

Jace's heart slammed into his chest. "She went over there—alone?"

The twins nodded and Nora called after him as he took off in Woolly's direction. What was Delaney *thinking* going over there without him? She should have waited for him to get back. Maybe she had been afraid she'd lose the light. Still not an excuse. No, he'd seen the look in her eye when Bree told them the news from the PI. Delaney had been planning this even then. Which meant she hadn't wanted to involve him. The question was . . . *why?*

He found someone had forged through an overgrown path into the back half of Woolly's property. Following the series of soft scuff marks from a boot and a couple broken twigs along the brush, he tucked his gun under his arm and kept himself in a half crouch to prevent himself from being seen. The path wound around the horse pasture and came up about a hundred yards from the back end of the mobile unit Isaac used as a registration office. A larger field lay to the left, partially wooded, and Jace thought he could make out a figure crouched low behind a bush. A black cap covered the top of a small head, but when it lifted above the top of the field grass again, Jace could see a few tufts of blond hair sticking out beneath the rim. *Delaney.*

He made his way toward her and saw she held the black controller of the drone in her hands. Glancing up higher, he spotted the drone itself hovering in the air, a small red light blinking to show the camera on the device was recording. Letting his gaze drop to the field below, he drew in a sharp breath. *Salt licks. Dozens of them.*

A small herd of deer had stepped from the wooded patch on the other side of Del and walked up to lap at the salt and mineral mixture set out to attract them. A larger buck appeared behind them, and a hunter in an orange cap, one of Woolly's men, raised a rifle and took aim.

Geez. Delaney was going to capture the poacher in action. This might be exactly the kind of proof they needed to shut Woolly's outfitting business down. He held his breath, waiting for the poacher to take the shot and keeping his eye on Delaney at the same time. The blast pierced the air like a rocket, but instead of dropping the deer, the bullet dropped the drone.

The hunter ran forward, chasing the deer off in different directions, and picked up the shattered remains of the drone in his hand. Turning his head, the guy then scanned the area and pointed in Delaney's direction.

"She's over there," he called, and in a matter of minutes five more men entered the field behind the first hunter.

Jace leaped forward and said, "Delaney, run!"

Her head jerked his way, and rising from her position, she ran toward him, only glancing once toward the hunters, still a few hundred feet out, who were closing in. Jace stretched out his hand, intending to grab her as soon as he could so he could get her safely off the poacher's property and back to her own ranch.

Then all at once a deer bounded past her, one of the does, and flew past him as well. And there was another animal, a large dark beast chasing after the deer, tearing the brush apart as it bounded forward, claws exposed, with its mouth open in a snarl showing a jaw full of sharp teeth.

Bear!

Jace barely had time to raise his gun before the bear rose up on its hind legs behind Delaney. She stumbled to the right, not even realizing the beast was there, and fear, unlike he'd ever known, shot through him the same time the bullet shot through his rifle. He wasn't sure if the noise he heard was a growl from the bear as it went down or the sound of his own gun, but a second later, Delaney fell against his chest, knocking him backward onto the ground.

Lifting her head, Delaney glanced over her shoulder and let out a shrill cry, but the bear didn't move. "I didn't see it coming," she whispered.

He nodded, and held her tight, unable to push any words over his tongue until he drew in another couple of deep breaths. "Delaney, you could have been killed."

"You protected me," she said, her face reflecting the horror of what could have happened had he not.

"Sometimes it's necessary to take a life to save one," he said, his body tense as he awaited her reaction. She wasn't going to hate him for saving her life, was she?

The bushes rustled and a loud clicking sound froze them both in place. "Oh, Jace," a low voice chided as Isaac Woolly stepped toward them. "I'm not sure who's going to be more disappointed—your mother or your sweet dear Delaney. You don't happen to have a tag to legally shoot bear, do you?"

Jace sprung up to a sitting position, pulling Del up with him, and stared at the camera in Woolly's hand. "I fired in self-defense."

"I suppose you could offer the public that argument once the media gets wind of this," Isaac taunted, "but I got just as good a shot as you did. Except instead of a bear, my video footage is going to kill your mother's career."

"We'll tell the media the truth," Del said, defending him.

"By then, it'll be too late, won't it, Jace? We all know how the media likes to embellish a good story and I think it's safe to say they'll have a *field day* with this one. I can already see the headline: *Jace Aldridge Arrested for Poaching.* "

"You can't do that," Delaney said, shaking her head.

Isaac grinned, revealing a mouth full of crooked teeth. "I'm afraid once the press finds out Collins Country Cabins lodges poachers, your reputation won't fare much better."

"Leave them out of this," Jace warned.

"The sheriff's already on his way. I had one of my guys make the call," Isaac told them, and sneered. "Now I'd suggest you get yourselves off my property before I have you arrested for trespassing as well."

THE TEARS FELL before they reached the main trail. Delaney couldn't control them and the torrent was so fierce it was almost useless to even try to brush them away.

Darkness closed in more heavily second by second, and Jace drew her into the stable where the soft golden lights illuminated the aisle between the stalls. "Delaney," Jace soothed, drawing her into his arms. "Everything's going to be all right. We'll figure it out. *Together.*"

Delaney pulled out of his warm embrace and stepped away from him, her heart breaking as she shook her head.

Jace's eyes widened. "You know if I didn't shoot the bear, he could have torn you apart."

She glanced up at the ceiling and squeezed her eyes shut, unable to face him. Unable to suppress the nausea burning her insides raw. Gathering her courage, she looked into his handsome face, those beautiful green eyes, memorizing every facet, and swallowed hard.

"It's not the bear."

"Then what's wrong?" he asked, his gaze boring into her. "Are you afraid I'll be arrested?"

"It doesn't matter if you are or not," Delaney whispered. "You heard what Isaac said, your reputation will be in ruins after the video is released to the public."

"I expect there will be an investigation," Jace admitted. "But we can fight this."

"I—I can't," Delaney said, and winced. "I . . . just *can't*. My lawyer called this morning. He says Steve's going after full custody of Meghan."

"What?" Jace stared at her as if in disbelief. "I thought he didn't care anything about her."

"He *doesn't*." Fighting back another onslaught of tears, she added, "But he figures if he takes Meghan, he won't have to pay me."

"He can try but he'll never win," Jace told her. "You said he isn't even working."

"He just got hired as head clerk for a prominent lawyer's office. The top lawyer in the firm is his new rich girlfriend's *father*," she said, her chest tightening as she thought of all the money and emotional stress a court battle was going to cost her.

"I don't care who your ex has on his side," Jace said, his expression fierce. "There's no way he's ever going to take Meghan. He'd have to prove you are an unfit mother."

"Which he can do once the newspapers are flooded with news I'm dating a *'poacher,'*" she exclaimed, trembling. "The trouble our ranch has had over the past summer is bad enough, but if they use *you* against me, too—I'm sorry, Jace, but I can't take that risk. I'm *scared*. And I'm going to have to ask you to leave."

The Adam's apple in his throat bobbed up and down and Jace's face pulled tight as if fighting back his own tears like she'd seen him do that first day at the rodeo. He didn't cry, although his eyes were glassy. True cowboys never did. But she could see by the torment on his face, and the conflicting emotions he was going through, that he thought her fears were justified. She watched him swallow again and her stomach squeezed tight, knowing he was feeling the same way she did. Surely in the days ahead she'd cry enough for the both of them.

"I never wanted to hurt you," he said, his voice hoarse.

She nodded. "I know."

"I love you."

Dear God, how will I ever get through this? Her throat tight, she couldn't speak, but stepped forward and threw her arms around him. His big, strong arms came around her at the same time and he pulled her so tight against his chest she could hardly breathe, nor did she want to. She only wanted to stay safely tucked in Jace's embrace and never let go.

He pressed a warm, moist kiss to the top of her forehead, then stepped back and gave her one last long look, during which a thousand things they'd never had time to say passed between them. Then as Delaney's breath caught on a sob, he turned and slowly walked out the door.

Chapter Fourteen

JACE STOOD IN the middle of the wide swath of fenced-in
dirt the Collinses had designated as a parking lot to stay
within range of the satellite strength he needed to call his
mother on his cell phone.

"I'm sorry," he said after he'd explained what had happened over at Woolly Outfitters. "He caught me and now
we need to prepare ourselves for the worst."

"I don't blame you, Jace," his mother said after sniff-
ing into the phone. "This isn't your fault, it's mine. Isaac
Woolly is after *me*. There's no doubt my campaign's going
to suffer from the rumors that are bound to swirl. But it's
too early to think it's going to knock me out of the race.
We've dealt with bad publicity before."

"Like when the animal activists blamed me for hurt-
ing Rio at the rodeo?" That had been his fault, too, and it
was possible the media could remind the public of that
fiasco all over again, along with their new poaching story.

"Actually, I was thinking of the time I was invited to a debate in front of the state capital building. I stepped forward to shake my opponent's hand but somehow ended up tripping him and he fell down the steps. His face was a bloody mess and the newspapers claimed I did it on purpose. They called me '*Un*-Grace-*ful* Aldridge' after that." She sighed. "It took a long time to turn my image around. But I did it, Jace. And we'll do it this time, too."

"But perhaps not in time for the election," he said, feeling lower than he ever had in his life. His mother had spent her entire life working to get to this point. And now he'd gone and blown it. Just like he'd blown it with Delaney.

"There will be other elections," his mother said softly. "We can't always win. Sometimes we have to take a loss."

He thought of their reputations, their careers, their monetary income derived from their fame. "Mom," he warned. "We could lose everything."

"Not everything," she countered. "We've still got each other and that's the important thing. How's Delaney? How's she handling this?"

Jace glanced up at the empty roof of the stable, then the sky, with no moonlight yet visible, and he remembered the intense hug they'd shared right before he'd left.

"I've lost her," he murmured into the phone. "I might have lost her for good."

Delaney hadn't said anything when he told her he loved her, but he knew she loved him, too. He could see it in her eyes, hear it in her voice, and feel it within her tight, desperate hold. He wasn't one to give in to defeat.

When he lost a round at bulldoggin', he'd pick himself up again, brush himself off, and plan to do better the next time around. But he wouldn't do anything to put Delaney's court case in jeopardy either.

He planned to talk to her lawyer to discuss possible solutions, but in the meantime, he feared she was right. It was in her best interest, and Meghan's, if they stayed away from him.

Before he left Collins Country Cabins, Jace decided he'd pay Gavin McKinley another visit.

"Jace," Gavin greeted, showing him in. "Didn't expect to see you again after you turned down my offer *twice*."

"I don't think you'll want to partner with me once the newspapers label me a poacher," Jace told him. "I shot a bear to protect Delaney and Woolly caught the whole thing on video. Of course the media will take that shot, along with my reputation of being an 'avid hunter,' and twist the whole thing around. You can't whip me up a fake bear tag to put on my hunting license before all this comes out, can you?"

Gavin's eyes widened. "If I did, the authorities would think I'm leading one of those confounded poaching rings that they're trying to find."

"What if you talked to Woolly and put in a good word for me?" Jace suggested. "You might be able to get him to shelve the video. I could pay you both. In fact, I'd pay *a lot* to have that video in my hands."

"What makes you think Woolly and I are friends?" Gavin demanded.

"The fact his daughter works for you?"

Gavin scowled. *"What?"*

"I could be mistaken," Jace said, then arched his brow. "What's Alicia's last name?"

Gavin hesitated. "Alicia Stevens."

Jace looked him in the eye and corrected, "Alicia Stevens *Woolly*."

The large man did a double take and began to pace the room. "How do you know this?"

"A private investigator found it on her birth certificate."

Gavin sucked in his breath and gave him an incredulous stare. "Woolly sent over a *spy*. The bearded gorilla must want to know how he can bring me down!"

Jace had hoped he could get Gavin to admit the two had been working together to set him up and bring down the Collinses, but it was clear Gavin had *not* known about Alicia.

"Thanks for telling me," Gavin said, putting a hand on Jace's shoulder. "A guy's got to know what he's up against."

"I know what you mean," Jace said with a nod, wishing he knew what kind of trouble that video would release. He glanced down the hall to Gavin's extra guest rooms. "Mind if I stay here tonight? I'm not exactly welcome at the Collinses' anymore."

Gavin shook his head and stepped back. "I'm sorry, Jace, but I've got a reputation to protect. If what you say is true, the reporters are going to be all over you by first light and I can't have anyone accused of being a poacher staying here."

After returning to the Collinses', Jace loaded Rio into

the trailer and headed toward the Tanners. He'd called first to make sure it was okay, in case they didn't want him either, and was told they had plenty of room for both him and his horse. Maybe if he'd known them better, he would have stayed with them from the beginning. But if he had, he never would have gotten to know Delaney. And despite how things worked out, he wouldn't give up the time they'd shared together for the world.

Ryan helped him settle Rio into a stall, then Jace made his way up to the Tanners' single-story house where his aunt Lora greeted him with compassionate tears and a warm, welcoming hug.

"Get a good night's sleep," she told him. "And in the morning everything will look better."

He'd often scoffed when he heard those same words from his own mother over the years. But occasionally she was right. Hopefully this was one of those times.

DELANEY DIDN'T SLEEP. She couldn't stop thinking of Jace, the intensity of his gaze, the depth of emotion behind his words. His smooth, baritone voice saying, "*I love you*," reverberated inside her head, bouncing back at her from different angles and leaving her exhausted.

Meghan didn't sleep either. The night before she'd looked out the window and seen Jace load Rio into the trailer and drive away. "He didn't say goodbye," her daughter had pouted. "When is Cowboy Jace coming back?"

"I don't think he *is* coming back," Delaney told her.

Meghan burst into tears and threw her plastic replica of Rio on the floor, but later she'd picked it up again and took the toy horse to bed with her. Then she'd tossed and turned, tangled the sheets, got up three times for a cup of water, and five more times to use the bathroom. Delaney kissed her on the forehead and assured her little girl they'd be fine. But her words sounded hollow. And as she thought of the way Meghan had bonded with Jace, her inadequacies as a single mom flew up to haunt her and scared her into thinking having one parent wasn't enough.

Tossing on her old overalls, and throwing her hair up into a ponytail, Delaney trudged down the stairs with her camera to take her siblings' engagement photos.

"Are you sure you're okay with this?" Bree asked, startled by her appearance. "We can do this another time if you aren't up for it."

"Sweetie, I'm so sorry," Sammy Jo said, her voice so apologetic Delaney didn't even take offense to being called "sweetie."

"I'm fine," Delaney said, lifting her chin. She tried to think of a positive quote her grandma would use in this situation but couldn't think of any. "Let's do it now before it snows."

However, as she looked through the lens at the couples in front of the gazebo, she *wasn't* fine. Ryan, dressed in his cowboy best, held a firm, possessive hand around Bree's waist, and her stylish sister, wearing a slim, flouncy dress she'd designed herself, looked up at him like he was Prince Charming himself. Next to them stood Delaney's brother, Luke, sporting his new short hairstyle, with his loving gaze on Sammy Jo, who had finally won the heart of the love of her life.

They reminded her of the way Jace held her and looked at her, and how she'd hoped to one day marry someone she could call not only her "husband" but also her "*best friend*," like the Hamilton bride had done this summer, in this very gazebo.

She'd never had engagement photos, never had wedding photos, and now that Jace had left and taken her heart with him, she didn't know if she ever would. She was always talking about giving everyone a chance, but she hadn't been willing to give Jace a chance. It was her own fault he'd left. The truth was, she was too afraid to stand up to her ex-husband. Too afraid of losing Meghan. Too afraid she might not have "*what it takes*" to live the life she'd always dreamed about but was too afraid to pursue.

Before the photo shoot, while waiting for the men to arrive, she'd walked down the path and taken a peek into Jace's cabin, wondering if he'd left anything behind.

He did—across the middle of the bed lay his gun.

After only snapping a few pictures, her eyes flooded with tears so she couldn't see. "I'm sorry," she said, pulling the camera away and wiping her face. "A bug must have flown right into my eye."

"Yeah, I heard Meghan say she wanted a bug catcher," Luke drawled. "Except a box of tissues might work better on a day like today."

Sammy Jo frowned. "Don't tease her like that, Luke. Can't you see her heart is broken?"

"I *am* sorry it didn't work out for you, Del," Luke said seriously.

By "it" he referred, of course, to her relationship with Jace, whatever *that* was anyway. They hadn't gone on a single regular real date like most couples did when trying to get to know each other. No, instead they'd snapped stupid photos, shot wayward arrows, and perched on peaked rooftops together. What kind of couple did that? She should have known it wouldn't work out.

But they'd also talked . . . and hugged . . . and kissed long into the night. A sob lodged in her chest, choking her. Fresh tears sprang into her eyes.

"Another bug?" Luke teased, and Sammy Jo jabbed him in the ribs.

Brushing her eyes again, Delaney smiled at her brother's attempt to cheer her up. "Yeah, these bugs seem to be flying at me in droves today."

"Let's reschedule," Bree said, coming over to wrap an arm around her.

Delaney nodded. "Jace left and I don't even know where he is."

"He stayed the night at our house," Ryan said, giving her a sympathetic look. "And if it's any consolation, I think he had to swat away a bug or two."

"True cowboys don't cry," she said, shaking her head.

Ryan held her gaze. "I think this one did."

Delaney walked across the yard and opened the door to the ranch office, intending to head straight up to her room, but the two girls sitting behind the desk staring at the computer caught her attention.

"What are you looking at?" she asked, pausing in front of them.

Neither of the twins would look at her. Or speak to her, which was a first.

"I'm sorry about your drone," Delaney said, coming around the desk to stand beside them. "I'll buy you a new one."

How she would manage that, she didn't know. The drone the twins had used their savings to buy had cost hundreds of dollars. How could she pay for a drone on top of her lawyer fees?

Still the twins didn't respond, and Delaney dropped her head in closer. "Is that a video you took with the drone?"

This time Nora shrugged. "It's the *only* video we were able to upload before you took the drone and managed to get it destroyed."

The images on the screen featured the two cute young men who had come to the ranch and posed as Eli Knowles's sons.

"Can you at least help us zoom in on this video so we can get a closer look?" Nadine pleaded.

"Of course," Delaney said, glad she could appease them in some way. "I'm good at video editing and Photoshop. Wait—" Pointing to the screen, she frowned, then reached over and pushed a few buttons on the keyboard to get the video to rewind.

"What are you doing?" Nora cried.

Nadine gasped. "You aren't going to ruin this, too?"

Delaney replayed the last section and pointed once

again to the background. In the distance, behind Clint and Clay, who were facing the camera and couldn't see what was going on behind them, there was a hunter who took a shot and killed a deer—a deer who had been nibbling at a salt lick.

"Was this taken on Woolly's property?" she asked, unable to believe their luck at catching the scene, no matter how gruesome it was.

Nora shook her head. "No, this was filmed in front of Fox Creek Outfitters."

"Are you sure?" Delaney asked, thinking they must be mistaken.

"See the sign on his building right there in the far corner?" Nadine asked.

Delaney sunk into a chair beside them. "Oh my gosh, you're right."

Obviously Gavin McKinley *did* run a poaching operation after all. He and Woolly could even be partners, along with the Randalls, like they'd suspected.

"Can I borrow this video?" she asked excitedly.

Both twins scowled and said, "No!"

However, they did allow her to make a couple copies on CD. If the poachers were determined to ruin Jace's reputation with their video, then she'd ruin theirs with the one in her hands. At least *some* justice would be served.

Not wasting another moment, Delaney grabbed the keys to her father's truck and drove into town, the poaching proof tucked securely under her arm.

She'd expected Sheriff McKinley to be shocked to

learn that Gavin was participating in illegal activity, but from the strange, calm expression on the lawman's face, she had a chilling notion he already knew.

"Is *this* the only copy of the video?" he asked, his hand already taking the CD away from her.

"Yes," she lied, glancing toward the door. "I trust you'll do what needs to be done?"

He nodded, but she didn't think the sheriff intended to do anything but protect his son.

Which meant she needed to take the second copy of the video to someone higher up in the government. Walking down the block, she pulled out her cell phone and called Jace's mother. If anyone could do something it was her.

"My mother's not here," Natalie said on the other end of the phone. "She went into the hospital late last night after hearing Jace may be accused of poaching. The stress of what might happen to her son and her campaign was too much for her to handle."

This situation was becoming more than Delaney could handle. What was she to do?

A loudspeaker broadcasted that the rally for animal rights was about to begin. A fairly large crowd had gathered in front of a stage at the end of the street. Her friends would be at that rally. She could give the video to them and they could place it into the hands of the proper authorities.

She found Carol directing a man to raise the projector they would be using so it would be properly centered on the ten-foot screen behind her.

"Carol," she said, tugging on her sleeve. "I need to talk to you."

"Not now, Delaney," she said, pulling away from her. "This is not a good time."

"This is the *perfect* time," Delaney pleaded, glancing again at the screen. "Please, it's urgent."

Carol turned on her, her expression livid. "Look," she said, her hands on her hips. "If you've got something to say, go ahead, be my guest."

Carol pointed at the stage, and Mary Ann and Ben, who had undoubtedly overheard, stopped adjusting the microphone for a moment and looked up to see what she would do.

Delaney glanced over the crowd and the nauseous dread she'd experienced so many times before filled her stomach and rose higher, tightening her chest. Her heart rate went into overdrive. The back of her throat closed and her tongue grew dry. Suddenly dizzy, she thought she might even faint.

Then she spotted the officials in attendance on the other side of the platform who wore uniforms with the official Department of Fish, Wildlife, and Parks' yellow patch on the sleeve of their shirts. And in the middle of the patch, staring right at her, was the head of a *bear*.

Her hand flew up to her neck to reach for the bear claw necklace her grandmother had given her, but it wasn't there. She'd lost it, probably in Woolly's field the day Jace had shot the bear behind her and saved her life. Her gaze swung back toward the stage and her grandmother's words floated back to her. *"True courage comes from within."*

Was her grandmother right? The week before she'd found another rabbit by the cabins, except this one was dead. There were no signs of an injury, but sometimes they could die simply from the stress of smelling or hearing a predator nearby. She didn't want to be like that rabbit. She didn't want these poachers to win because she was too afraid to take a stand.

Climbing the stairs, she walked out on stage where scores of eyes fixed upon her. Then taking the microphone in her hand, she said, "Poaching is not a problem we can leave to someone else to solve. The solution starts with us, working together as a team to protect our state's wildlife. It starts with you . . . and *me*." Handing a CD to Mary Ann to give to the man behind the table with the laptop and computerized projector, she said, "I have something to show you."

The rally to support stricter disciplinary action against poaching turned out to be a huge success. After viewing the video, the state officials promised they'd take immediate action against Fox Creek Outfitters. Carol, Mary Ann, and Ben apologized, commended her speech, and asked her to come back to their local wildlife rescue clinic. Delaney smiled and told them she'd let them know, *after* she talked to Jace.

She returned home and picked up her phone to call him as she walked through the front door, but hesitated in midstep when she saw the look on her mother's face.

"Grandma's missing!" Ma exclaimed.

Delaney stared at her. "What do you mean 'missing'?"

"She wasn't here to cook lunch and I was about to call the cook and beg her to come back, but Bree said the woman got a job cooking at Woolly's and now its midafternoon and time to prepare dinner and your grandma still isn't here."

Sammy Jo and Bree burst through the door behind her and Bree said, "She's not in the stable, the sheds, or any of the cabins. We already searched the entire house. I don't know where she could be."

"Do you think she walked up to the silver mine?" Sammy Jo asked breathlessly.

Delaney shook her head. "I saw Party Marty standing at the end of the driveway. He follows Grandma wherever she goes, which means he's waiting for her to come home."

"She left by car?" Ma demanded. "Who could have picked her up?"

"I heard her mention she had a hot date," Nora said as she and her sister passed through toward the kitchen.

Delaney froze. "A hot date with the sheriff?"

Their worries increased tenfold when she told them about the video and how the sheriff had acted when she'd brought him the CD, then a hundredfold when Delaney went down the driveway to coax Party Marty back to the house and got a call on her cell phone.

"We have your grandma," said a muffled male voice Delaney didn't recognize. "She says the deed to the ranch is in the top drawer of her bedroom dresser. Bring it up to the silver mine by four p.m. if you don't want to see her get hurt. No police. And, Delaney? We want you to come alone."

Racing back to the house, she shouted, "Grandma's been *kidnapped*!"

With her voice shaking almost as much as her legs, Delaney told them what the caller had said. Her ma's face went white. Bree's mouth fell open. Sammy Jo clutched Luke's arm and his eyes narrowed as he clenched his fist. But her father's reaction was the most alarming.

The blood vessels in his face and neck stood out as his tan complexion turned first to red, then into a shade of deep purple. The vein in his neck pulsated with what Delaney could only assume was rage, and he bellowed, "They took my *ma*?"

"Whoever kidnapped her will never get away with it," Bree assured him. "The moment they take Grandma into the courthouse to make the transfer of the deed legal, we can have them arrested."

"It's got to be the Randalls," her father stormed. "They've wanted to steal our ranch away from us since the very beginning. They probably tricked your grandma into *thinking* she was being picked up by the sheriff."

"Unless the sheriff is in on it," Delaney warned.

"He's been a lawman for over thirty years," Ma argued. "He'll be retiring soon. He'd never do anything to jeopardize his pension or—or put himself in *prison*."

"Poachers make more money than he could ever hope to get from his pension," Delaney informed her. "And Gavin is his son, who might be working with Woolly and the Randalls."

"Well, we can't call him," Luke warned, "or trust anyone in his department."

Bree looked at Delaney, and said, "Can we call Jace's mom? Maybe she could help us notify the FBI or other authorities?"

"I'll try," she promised, punching in the number on her phone. "But earlier this afternoon, she was in the hospital." A few minutes later, she shook her head. "The hospital says Grace was released and I can't get through to her or Natalie on their cell phones."

All of the sudden the lights went out and the room darkened. "The landline is dead," Sammy Jo reported, returning from the other room. "And we have no power. The snow is starting to fall pretty heavy and communication is going to be sketchy all across the county."

"One of us will have to drive the truck into town to contact the authorities," Luke said, and glanced at Sammy Jo. "Think you can make it through?"

She took the keys from his hand and nodded. "I'll get help," Sammy Jo promised.

"They won't kill her," Bree said, her voice hard, as if trying to make herself believe what she was saying were true. "If they did, the ranch would go straight to us."

"She doesn't have a will on file," her father choked out. "She wanted to transfer the title of the ranch into all our names and take care of all her legal business at the same time but didn't have a chance. If something were to happen to her, anyone could stake a claim on the property and the courts would decide who takes control."

"Do you think the Randalls have people working for them in the court system?" Ma asked.

"Anything's possible," Delaney's father growled. "But we aren't going to let it get that far. We're going up there."

"Jed!" Ma exclaimed. "Don't you think we should wait and let the authorities handle this?"

"The people holding my mother are people we *know*," he said, his expression resolute. "We live off this land and fix what needs fixing day after day, year after year, all without outside help. So—no. I am *not* going to sit back and twiddle my thumbs hoping the authorities make it in time."

Bree agreed. "It's going to take at least an hour for any outside officers or the FBI to get to the mine, even if they take a chopper. We have to go up there and keep watch until they arrive."

"The caller said he wanted *me* to bring the deed to the silver mine," Delaney reminded them. "Why me?"

Luke arched his brow and gave her a sympathetic look. "You're the only one in this family who they know will not shoot."

I'm the weakest link. The least threat. "They want me to come alone."

"Well, there's no chance of that happening," her father said, grabbing the rifles from the gun cabinet in the living room. He tossed one to Bree and another to Luke. "There's no way we're going to waste another minute standing around talking about it either—it's almost four o'clock."

THE MINUTE JACE opened the door, Delaney shoved his gun into his hands. "We need your help," she pleaded. "Grandma's been kidnapped."

She quickly filled him and the rest of the Tanner household in on the details, then added, "Ma's back at the house watching Meghan. Bree, Luke, and my dad are gathering the hunters. Sammy Jo drove into town to alert the authorities, but it's snowing and the roads are bad. We're—we're not sure they're going to make it in time."

"They might not," Jace said, taking her arm. "But we *will*."

Grabbing their own rifles, the Tanner brothers and Jace's uncle, Bo, promised to help and together they followed Delaney up the rest of the trail toward the old abandoned silver mine. The snow fell heavy and thick and Jace had to grab hold of Delaney's arm more than once to keep her from slipping even though she wore heavy boots. She might have had more balance if she weren't carrying her bow and a quiver of arrows over her shoulder.

"What made you decide to bring the bow?" he asked, steadying her once again. "Are you planning to shoot the kidnappers with an *arrow*?"

"No," she assured him. "I have a different plan."

"Be careful. You said that the state officials from Fish and Wildlife are going to shut Gavin's outfitting business down, but he might not know it yet," Jace warned. "I'm sure he and the others think they can get away with this and have his father cover for him, which makes Gavin dangerous."

Delaney cast him a sidelong look. "I didn't see any newspaper stories about *you* yet either."

"Doesn't mean it's not going to happen." He didn't want to get either of their hopes up. "It's only been a day."

Jed Collins waved them to a stop in the last cluster of trees before the mine. "Luke is leading the hunters over the rise and around the other side. The Tanners, Bree, and I are spreading out on this side and creeping up as close as we can to see if we can spot your grandma."

"We won't go in and confront them unless they threaten her, right?" Jace asked.

Jed let out a low grunt. "That's the plan."

"What about me?" Delaney demanded.

"You're unarmed and staying back here."

She held up her bow. "I am *not* unarmed."

Her father gave her a skeptical look, then turned toward him. "Jace, you stay with her."

"She's not going anywhere without me," he promised, then watched as the groups slowly circled the mine like a pack of wolves.

Delaney nodded toward an outcropping of rock a few feet away. "C'mon," she said, her earnest expression pulling him along as much as her hand. "Let's move closer."

Except closer didn't mean stopping behind the rocks. A moment later, she took off toward another grouping, then another, and he had no choice but to follow her and hope neither one of them were either seen or heard.

"There's my grandma," Delaney choked out in a whisper as they crouched behind an old rusted piece of mining equipment with a large pulley and metal base. "And there's the sheriff. We thought maybe the Randalls had tricked Grandma into only *thinking* she had a date with him, but he's here. I can't believe he could betray her like this." Glancing at her watch, she added, "There's only five minutes left before it's four o'clock."

"Your father said you are *not* going out there to face them," he reminded her. "They said they'd handle it if they have to."

"If they go in with a bunch of guns, someone's going to get hurt," she argued.

Gavin McKinley walked into view and spoke to Isaac Woolly and the Randalls, who stood by the sheriff. Each of them held a pistol but it was the sheriff who kept his gun on Ruth Collins. They'd tied a rope around her hands, another around her feet, and placed a gag around her mouth, but she stood erect, so at least she wasn't sitting in the snow. Sadly, she wore dress slacks and a stylish black winter coat and matching fuzzy hat, as if she'd dressed to go someplace special.

"It's time," Gavin said, marching toward Ruth. "The weather's taken a turn for the worse and the Collinses aren't going to show."

"Wait a minute," the sheriff said, holding out his hand. "We're not really going to shoot her?"

"Yeah, we *are*," Gavin said with a half snarl as he narrowed his gaze.

Jace swallowed hard. He believed the man *would*. Glancing around for a sign of the Tanners or the rest of the Collinses, he didn't see any movement and wondered where they were. Didn't they see what was happening here?

Jace cast a glance at Delaney and did a double take. He'd been so preoccupied looking for the others he didn't see what Delaney had been doing beside *him*. She'd placed the tip of an arrow through the deed, loaded it onto her bow, and prepared to shoot. Then she let go of the string and with a sharp *twang* the arrow flew into the air with the attached paper and stuck up straight in the ground five feet in front of the group of kidnappers.

"Good shot," he murmured, and Delaney flashed him a quick smile.

Gavin glanced around, his gun at the ready, then motioned toward the rusted mining wheel in front of them. "It came from over there."

A jolt of adrenaline shot up his spine and he realized Delaney had just given away their location. "We've got to get out of here," he whispered, pulling her arm.

She nodded and together they scrambled back the way they had come. But when they dove behind the original outcropping of rocks, two rifle tips snapped to attention in front of them. For a heart-stopping second, he thought their lives were over.

A guy Jace recognized as one of Gavin's men said, "Drop the gun."

Not seeing he had another option, Jace complied, even though it left him and Del dangerously defenseless. With an inward groan, he realized that when she said she had a plan, he should have insisted she share it with him.

GAVIN MCKINLEY'S MAN kept a tight grip on Delaney's arm and pulled her forward toward the outfitter himself. She'd dropped her bow when Jace dropped his gun, and wished she'd thought to wear a boot knife, but she hadn't thought things through before she left her house that day.

Obviously she hadn't thought things through when she shot the deed to the kidnappers on the end of her arrow either. Now she'd placed them in danger, for she feared that anyone who could kill an animal just for the value of its horns wouldn't care about people either.

She glanced over at Jace as he was pushed forward by another of Gavin's men.

"You were told to come alone," Gavin complained, eyeing Jace by her side. "Although I guess none of us believed you would."

"Her father must be here somewhere," Wade Randall warned. "There's no stopping that old coot. He never listens to anyone but himself."

"Hurry," Susan hissed. "We need to have the old woman sign the paper and get out of here."

"Wade Randall!" Delaney heard her father's voice bellow as he stepped out from behind the sheriff's truck and joined them, unarmed.

Susan smirked. "What are you calling him for? This was *my* idea."

"Actually, it was *mine*," Gavin said, keeping his gun leveled at Delaney's father. "I'm the one who came up with the idea to drive away your business to make you sell. You see, I need that river, Jed, and all those nice cabins of yours to expand my outfitting business."

"You?" her father sputtered. "But the Randalls hired the others who sabotaged us all summer long."

Gavin nodded. "And I hired *them*."

Delaney's father looked at her, his face full of concern. "Are you okay?"

She nodded, then Gavin ordered, "Hands in the air, Jed."

Her father raised his hands and Gavin motioned for him to join her and Jace. Unfortunately, they were separated from her grandma, who stood on the other side of the group.

"Let Delaney and her grandma go free," her father barked. "You have what you want."

"Not yet, we don't," Isaac Woolly said. Pulling the arrow Delaney had shot out of the ground, he removed the deed, and placed it on the large overturned mining cart beside them. "Who has a pen?"

"I do," Susan said as Wade untied Delaney's grandma's hands and feet and brought her over to sign the document.

"Don't forget to have her write a letter to go along with it," Gavin instructed. "One that says she's decided to sell the designated land to the named buyer because her family is greedy and they want to force her to divide her ranch between them."

"If anyone is greedy, it's you," Delaney's father barked, coming forward. Two of Gavin's men held him back.

Delaney's heart pounded as she watched her grandma take the pen the Randalls handed her and sign the paper. Her grandma's hands were shaking. Usually it was her grandma who was the tough, strong one, but Delaney had seen Grandma glance her direction, and her father's, and knew the old woman wasn't afraid for herself. Her grandma was afraid for *them*.

"I'll sign next," Susan said, grabbing the pen. Except the writing implement slipped out of her hands and fell on the ground.

As she scrambled to pick it up, her husband yelled, "Susan, we can't waste any more time!"

"The pen is *slippery*," Susan said, fumbling it again. "There's some kind of cream on it."

Grandma's hand cream? Delaney watched her grandma smirk, then step back away from them.

Wade lunged for the pen, but it slipped out of his fingers, too. Isaac reached out to catch it, but Gavin snatched the pen in midair and clenched his hand to keep it secure. "You won't be needing to sign after all," Gavin told them. "The deed is mine."

"That wasn't the deal," Susan exclaimed. "The Collins ranch was supposed to go to *us*. You've set us up to take the fall again and again, while you kept your hands clean."

"And you set *me* up, by bringing in your cousin Woolly here, to be our new partner, and sending over his daughter to spy on me and my operations," Gavin sneered, waving three more of his men in from the edges of the field. "You should have known better than to try to double-cross me by bringing in a rival poacher."

"We're taking over," Isaac said, trying to rip the deed from Gavin's hands. "Alicia's meeting with a couple of game wardens to turn you in. You and your father."

"Over my dead body," Gavin growled.

"That is the plan," Isaac said, waving his hand. A group of six men came forward, their guns on Gavin, the startled sheriff, and Gavin's two men. "After we kill Aldridge and the Collinses, the authorities will find your dead bodies here and think there was a shootout."

Gavin scoffed. "You're deluded. Ballistics will nail you to the scene. But you're right, we do have to kill the others."

Kill them? Delaney sucked in her breath and glanced at Jace. This was *not* the end she had in mind for them. Her stomach squeezed tight and her legs trembled from more than the cold. Jace stepped closer and took her hand, intertwining his fingers with hers. From the tight, rebellious expression on his face, Delaney knew he would do everything in his power to protect her, no matter the cost. And that scared her even more.

"After we take Ruth into town to make the deed transfer official, I will be the only outfitter in the area," Isaac continued, "with Susan and Wade as silent partners, running the management behind the scenes."

As two more of Woolly's men closed in, Delaney suddenly realized why Luke, Ryan, the Tanners and the hunters, and everyone else in her group hadn't moved forward. Both Gavin and Isaac had men out in the field, keeping watch. She and Jace had somehow slipped past them because they'd come up from the south. But now that both outfitter groups had moved in for what looked to be a rival poacher war, she could see her brother's head pop up to take a quick look, then wave his arm in some kind of signal.

Jace had also taken the opportunity the argument gave them to drop his head in close to her ear and say, "Get ready to run."

Run? How was she supposed to do that? The two guards who had pulled them from hiding still had guns trained on them. Did Jace know Luke's plan? Her brother was ex-military and great at leading recon missions, although he rarely included her in them.

Something flew through the air and a second later the boarded opening of the silver mine exploded, sending bits of wood flying out everywhere and blanketing the area with smoke. Mingled with the falling snow, it was practically a whiteout.

Jace's strong hand pulled her back and he tucked her into his side as they ran toward the trees. Shots rang out behind them, and shouts erupted in almost every direction. The only voice she could clearly recognize was from her father, who called out, "I've got Grandma!"

Seconds later she and Jace ran into Bree, and together they moved farther back, running as fast as they could.

"We've got them surrounded," Bree said, her voice coming out in shallow gasps.

"Did you hear the shots?" Delaney asked, her voice filled with panic. "I couldn't see if anyone was hit, could you?"

Bree shook her head. "We'll find out soon enough."

Dozens of armed, uniformed men ran up the trail toward them. A few stopped to ask questions while others charged on ahead toward the mine. Sirens wailed in the distance. The road to the mine that the vehicles used was located opposite them, sandwiching the poachers and blocking off both paths of escape. Their only other option would be on foot through the trees, but Delaney didn't think they'd get far.

After they were a safe distance, Jace spun her around and cupped both sides of her face in his hands and kissed her with an intensity that she had only dreamed about.

"I never want to lose you," he said, his voice low. "Please tell me I'm not going to lose you."

Delaney's heart flipped over in her chest and she assured him, "If I can face down a group of rifle-bearing poachers who want to kill me, I suppose I can stand up to my ex-husband in court."

Jace broke into a grin and wrapped her in a warm, bear hug. Then after sharing a profound look of relief that the ordeal was over, she snuggled against him, and they walked the rest of the way back to the ranch.

Chapter Fifteen

THE COLLINSES' DINING hall transformed into a refugee camp of sorts that night with uniformed officials questioning each person and making sure they hadn't suffered any injuries. A couple of the hunters had some scrapes and cuts that Delaney helped the other medics bandage.

Jace watched her, admiring her nursing skill, and wished he had a few cuts she could attend to so he could capture a few moments alone with her. But he'd been luckier than most. The only one who sustained any real injury had been Delaney's father, who twisted his ankle.

"At least it isn't broken again," his wife had told him. "A couple days on crutches isn't going to kill you."

Jed shook his head and chuckled. "No, it won't. But losing the ranch to those Randalls would have." He narrowed his gaze and turned toward Delaney. "You were awful quick to hand over that deed."

"Grandma's life was in danger," Del said defensively,

then smiled. "Besides, the deed was a fake. I printed it off the computer while you were searching for the real one."

"A fake?" Jed chuckled and slapped his knee, then shouted to Bree and Luke, "Did you hear that?"

Delaney's siblings shot him a grin, then gathered closer as Eli Knowles and his two "sons" walked in the door.

"What's the news?" Grandma demanded, lifting her white bushy brows. "Did you catch them?"

Eli took off his hat and nodded. "Yes, ma'am. Gavin McKinley, his father, Isaac Woolly, the Randalls, and all their accomplices are accounted for. Not only do they face enormous fines for poaching, but they've been arrested for kidnapping, extortion, and aggravated assault."

An audible sigh circled the room and relief washed over Jace as he thought about his mother. She'd be happy about that. Hopefully this would put an end to the threats.

"What about Alicia?" he asked.

Eli chuckled. "She was quite helpful. Alicia gave us photocopies of paperwork incriminating Gavin McKinley and his father for taking guests on hunts without the proper licenses and tags. He's also been selling antlers and animal parts on the black market for thousands of dollars. What she didn't know was that the cook Isaac Woolly had hired turned in evidence against her and her father. She was arrested, too."

"Are you talking about the cook who used to work for *us*?" Delaney's ma asked, shooting Ruth a sideways look. "The one Grandma *fired*?"

"Yes," Eli confirmed, and he, too, looked at Ruth. "It's

a pity that after helping you she's now out of a job. Both Fox Creek Outfitters and Woolly Outfitters have been closed down."

Grandma pressed her lips together in a tight line, then relented. "I guess I *could* use a little help in the kitchen."

Jace grinned. It appeared the Collinses had their own undercover agent and didn't even know it.

"Gavin admitted to tranquilizing the deer and placing it in the cabin," Eli informed them, "but it was Isaac who put the carcasses around the property." Turning toward him, Eli added, "Jace, we also now know for sure it was Isaac who sent those letters to your mother. He and Gavin were part of a larger poaching ring covering different parts of the state. Looks like your mother's going to get her wish to see those rings brought down. It should boost her campaign ahead in the rankings."

"Not when the video Gavin gave the media shows up and I'm featured shooting a bear on the front page of the newspapers," Jace said, glancing at Delaney.

Eli reached into his jacket and pulled out a disc. "You mean *this* video?"

Jace stared at him, then swallowed hard. "What about the memory chip in his camera?"

Eli reached into another pocket and held it up. Delaney crossed the room and took the camera chip into her hands. "Are there no more copies?"

"The cook assured me there wasn't," Eli said, and grinning, he slapped a hand on Jace's shoulder. "I've got you covered, son."

Jace looked up, clasped Eli's hand, and nodded his

thanks, so overcome with emotion that he couldn't speak. No reporters would be knocking at his door, no camera flashes would be flaring in his face, and no one would be able to twist the truth or blacken his name. He looked at Delaney, who smiled at him through tears.

Happy tears.

DELANEY PICKED UP the pen in the county assessor's office in Bozeman and signed her name on the quick claim deed beside the signatures of her parents, Grandma, Bree, and Luke.

"Now it's official," Grandma cackled in her gravelly voice, a smile on her face. "We each legally own one-sixth of Collins Country Cabins."

"And we're the *only* guest ranch in the area offering accommodations and recreational activities," Bree added. "We're already booking cabins for spring."

"Who knows?" Delaney teased. "We may have to expand."

Luke grinned. "I could build a few more cabins."

"Jed," Ma said with a frown. "Are you all right?"

He rubbed the corner of his eye and nodded. "Yeah," he said, and glanced around at them all. "I just can't stop thinking that the trouble we've had this summer was all my fault. I never wanted to drive you three kids away from your home in the first place. Then I hired Susan and Wade Randall, and because I'm so good at offending people, they had no trouble finding others to turn against us. *I'm* the reason we almost lost the ranch."

Her father paused and Delaney caught her breath as his gaze fell on her. "I know you think I blame you for your failed marriage, but I was the one who made you feel like you had to go prove yourself. I was the reason you felt you had to marry that creep instead of coming home."

"No," Delaney said, shaking her head. "That was my mistake. My choice. No one can take responsibility for that except me."

"Although it's good to admit your faults," Grandma said, pinching his cheek as if he were still just a boy, "there's no sense having a pity party over the past."

Delaney nodded. "We need to look forward to the future, right, Grandma?"

"That's right, sweet pea," Grandma said, lifting her chin.

"I don't show it very well, not very well at all," Delaney's father said, his eyes glistening as his gaze circled to each of them. "But I love you. And I'm proud of you for stepping up and helping your old man out."

"That's what family does," Bree said, smiling, and a tear ran down her cheek.

Luke cleared his throat, as if he'd had something lodged, and asked, "Hey, Del, did Meghan get that bug catcher yet?"

"Not yet," she said, wiping her own eyes, and teased, "You'll just have to use tissues."

JACE JUMPED OUT of his truck and hurried around the other side to open the door for his mother. She hesitated before getting out and stared at the single-story house surrounded by vast acres of fields for both hay and cattle. Of course, the last of the hay had been harvested and the ground lay white from the six-inch layer of snow that had fallen the night before.

Taking her hand so she wouldn't slip, he said, "C'mon, Mom. It's going to be all right."

She nodded, but looked as if she didn't believe him. Her wide eyes stared at the house as if it were haunted. But clutching her purse, she raised her chin, like he'd seen her do before giving one of her campaign speeches, and climbed out of the truck, her confidence intact. Or at least so it seemed on the outside.

Natalie slid over from the middle of the truck seat and got out behind her. "The Tanners didn't do too bad," she said, gazing over the outlying stables, and various sheds.

"They are hard workers," Jace assured her. "Oh, and Nat—they like to tease."

"I'm sure I can handle it," she said, smiling. "After all, I'm used to *your* teasing."

"Yeah, but there's *four* of them," he said with a grin.

"Teasing would be better than giving us the cold shoulder," their mother muttered.

Jace nodded, thinking of his first meet with Ryan and Zach. "You've got that right."

There was still a lot he had to learn about his new cousins, but since the wolf attack the week before they'd made him feel as if he were a fifth brother. He hoped they accepted his sister as one of their own, too.

The front door opened, and Aunt Lora stepped out on

the square concrete landing. For a moment she and Jace's mother just stared at each other. Then Lora gave them a smile and motioned them inside.

Jace entered first, glanced over his cousins' attire, and raised his brows. "Suits? Were we supposed to dress up?"

"The only reason I'm wearing this," Ryan said, pointing his thumbs toward his dress shirt, vest, and blazer, "is because Delaney's retaking engagement photos."

"Me, too," said Ryan's son, Cody, showing off his new dress shoes.

Dean glanced down at his similar attire and said, "We didn't want Ryan to make the rest of us look like slobs."

"Yeah," Josh said with a smirk. "We wanted to make a good first impression."

"Especially since we didn't do so well the last time," Zach said with a nod. Coming closer he added, "I didn't mean to be a jerk around you and Delaney either. I know she doesn't think I'm the guy for her. I was just looking out for her. I didn't want her to get hurt, you know?"

"I'll take care of her," Jace assured him, and Zach grinned.

Then Jace's mother and Natalie walked into the kitchen and the Tanner brothers went silent. Their eyes were all on Natalie, but they just . . . *stared* at her. Oh, no. *Not* good. Natalie dropped her gaze and her skin paled three shades whiter, contrasting all the more with her dark wavy hair, making her look like Snow White. Hurrying to her side, Jace looped his arm through hers and introduced her to Aunt Lora and Uncle Bo, then his cousins, from oldest to youngest, Dean, Ryan, Josh, and Zach.

Jace was afraid from their reactions that they weren't going to accept her into the family after all. But seconds later, they were all talking at once and vying for their new cousin's attention.

Figuring she was in good hands, Jace walked back to his mother, who was making polite small talk with his aunt and uncle. As if his presence gave her extra courage, his mother opened her purse and retrieved an envelope in which he knew she'd placed a check.

"I should have given this to you a long time ago," his mother told Lora. "I'm so sorry. Your brother, Trent, he was a good man. He would have wanted you to have it—no matter how late."

Aunt Lora glanced at her husband, then reached out and took the envelope. "Thanks, Grace."

"Thank *you*," his mother said, nodding toward Natalie as she and her followers rejoined them. "For welcoming us into your home."

Aunt Lora caught Jace's eye, then turned back toward his mother and smiled. "Not just into our home, but into our *family*. Are the three of you free for Thanksgiving?"

Jace hesitated. "I'd love to, but I'll have to check with Delaney first."

"No need," Aunt Lora assured him. "It's already been decided that this year the Collinses and the Tanners are eating turkey together. And other dishes, of course," she added quickly. "For those who don't eat meat."

Jace accepted, and glanced at his watch. He couldn't wait to get back to Delaney. They hadn't had much time to speak while being interviewed and writing statements for the authorities the night before, and there was still so much he had to tell her.

He also needed to make amends with Meghan, who he'd heard was mad at him.

DELANEY DITCHED THE overalls and put on a dress over warm leggings, then pulled out the rubber band that held her ponytail and let her hair drop loosely about her shoulders. Jace had told her she didn't need to dress up for him, but she'd discovered over the last few weeks that she kind of liked it.

Dashing down the stairs, she ran into Sammy Jo, who took her hands and spun her around in a little dance. "Luke showed me the cabin he's building for us to live in after we're married," she said excitedly. "He said he got the idea when he heard that Ryan and Bree are going to move into the extra cabin on the edge of the Tanner property after they marry."

"I guess Meghan and I will be the only ones living in the main house with the old folks," Delaney teased.

Sammy Jo gave her a mischievous look, then nodded toward Jace as he walked in the door. "Maybe not."

Delaney swallowed hard as the stocky, dark-haired cowboy whose image continuously graced the cover of every regional western themed magazine smiled, his eyes on her—yes, definitely *her*—as he drew near.

She broke away from Sammy Jo to go to him, but the twins intercepted him first.

"Look what the papers printed about you," Nora said,

thrusting the newspaper into his hands. "They're calling you—"

"A *'True Country Hero,'*" Nadine announced. "For saving Delaney from that ferocious bear and then going up to the mine to fight those poachers."

"I didn't do much fighting," Jace said, narrowing his gaze as he read the headlines.

"You know the media prints whatever they like," Delaney teased. "But I do think the title 'True Country Hero' suits you."

"I'm sorry the sheriff didn't turn out to be the hero Grandma hoped he was," Bree said as the rest of the family filtered into the kitchen.

"That's all right," Grandma assured her. "I was married to my true hero for many long years—your grandpa. And I still have my Clint Eastwood movies."

Bree handed them all one of the new trifold brochures she'd printed up to advertise the ranch. "I put Jace's endorsement on the inside flap," she said, pointing.

Delaney read, "'Collins Country Cabins is the best dude ranch I've ever had the pleasure of staying at,' says rodeo champion, Jace Aldridge. 'In addition to their award winning menu, this rustic, western retreat offers comfort, beautiful landscapes, and as many thrilling activities as your heart can handle.'"

"*This is terrible!*" Nora squealed.

Nadine followed her sister's gaze and shrieked. "Oh, *no!*"

"What's the matter?" Bree demanded. "Is there a misprint?"

"We were supposed to be cover models," Nora exclaimed. "But this photo has us—"

"Working in the kitchen wearing aprons, and bandanas over our hair!" Nadine finished.

Bree frowned. "What's wrong with that?"

"We'll never attract cute guys that way," the twins chorused together.

Delaney laughed. "You mean like the undercover agents working for Fish and Wildlife? Clint and Clay?"

"They were undercover agents?" Nora squealed.

"How cool is that?" Nadine said, and laughed. "And *we* were spying on *them*!"

"I got a call from *True Montana Magazine* this morning," Delaney announced. "They saw all the articles in the newspaper about the arrests and the poachers' plot to put us out of business, and they want to feature our ranch in their next issue, using my photos. Jace's sister, Natalie, offered to help me write the accompanying story that tells the public what *really* happened."

"That will give us even more publicity," Bree said, her face lighting up. "Who knows? Maybe Natalie could even write a book about it."

"And have it turned into a movie," Nora said, and her mouth fell open. "Do you know what that means?"

"We could be movie stars!" Nadine said excitedly, slapping her sister a high five.

Delaney bundled Meghan up in her coat, hat, mittens, and boots and took her hand as they walked across the first snow of the season to Isaac Woolly's property with the rest of her family. Jace had some kind of surprise over there he wanted to show her, but she didn't know what it was. Apparently her father *did* or he never would have insisted on joining them on his crutches.

Jace had gone on ahead, and when they arrived, Delaney saw him standing outside the Woolly Outfitter mobile unit. His eyes sparkled with excitement as he awaited her reaction, but she didn't see anything until he pointed up toward the banner hung across the roof.

Delaney's Animal Rescue.

"Jace, I don't understand. What does this mean?" she asked, coming closer.

"I'll explain in a minute," he promised, and knelt down toward Meghan, who looked up at him with a scowl on her face. Pulling out the hand he'd hidden behind his back, he handed her a little mesh covered cage with a latched door in front. "This is for you."

Meghan frowned. "But it's not my birthday."

"We can't wait," he told her. "The bugs will all be gone by then. And now that it snowed, we need to save as many as we can."

Delaney watched, amused, as her daughter took the bug catcher, gave him a glimmer of a smile, then pouted, "You left and didn't say goodbye to me."

"That's because it hurt too much," he said, gathering her onto his knee. "I don't ever want to say goodbye to you, Megs."

Meghan giggled. "I like when you call me Megs."

"I like *you*," he told her. "And from now on you'll be able to see me every day."

"Okay, Cowboy Jace," Meghan said, and hugged him around the neck.

Jace looked up and taking Delaney's hand, he said, "I found out Isaac was only leasing the land, and after the news hit this morning, the owner was willing to sell it to me on the spot."

Delaney's mouth fell open. "You bought it?" She glanced at the sign again and gasped. "You're giving me my own animal shelter? What will you do with the rest of the land?"

"Well, you see," Jace said, and the corners of his mouth lifted into another grin. "I talked to your father and we decided, with all the publicity, Collins Country Cabins is going to need to expand. I'm going to be a partner and help organize activities when I'm not working my other job."

"You mean rodeo?" she asked, unable to believe this turn of events.

He shook his head. "No, I'm going to apply to be a game warden."

"Are you serious?" She glanced from Jace to her father and he gave her a nod to confirm the news. Bree, Luke, Sammy Jo, and her ma all stood watching her reaction and Delaney realized she was the center of attention. She laughed and told Jace, "If you're a partner, then I guess that makes you part of the family."

"Not quite. But there's something else that would."

Lifting Meghan off his knee, Jace stood and took both her hands in his. "I called your lawyer and he said that

Steve is willing to relinquish parental rights if we marry and I adopt Meghan. That way he won't have to pay child support."

Delaney stared at him, not sure she understood what he just said. "Wh-what?" she stammered.

"You'll never have to worry about him again," Jace assured her. "Of course, I realize you might not be ready for a real marriage, so if you agree, we can continue to be friends, or date if you want to. I know you said you'd never marry again unless it was with someone you could call your best friend, so I promise you," he said, his voice hoarse, "I'm going to do everything I can to be the greatest best friend you ever had."

Tears filled her eyes as she looked at the wonderful man before her who had taken every step he could think of to make her and Meghan feel special and keep them safe. "You already are, Jace," she choked out, her heart in her voice. "You already are."

He hesitated. "Does that mean—?"

"Yes."

Jace grinned. "Is that a *direct* answer?"

Returning a smile, she nodded. "Yes. Yes, I will marry you."

"What? No redirection or sidestepping?" he teased.

She shook her head and laughed and Jace drew her into his arms. "I love you, Del."

"I love you, too," she said, and Jace gave her a heart-stopping look that flooded her with warmth, made her dizzy, and caught her breath all at the same time.

He captured her mouth in a tender kiss, then pulled

back and announced to the rest of her family. "We'll have to marry right away. Does next week work for all of you?"

Delaney glanced at Bree and Sammy Jo, who looked on with identical ear-to-ear grins. "Will you two be *my* bridesmaids?"

They both nodded their heads vigorously and shouted in unison, "Yes! Of course!"

Then as Jace drew his head toward her again, Delaney heard her mother say, "She's only known him four weeks!"

"An intense four weeks," Luke defended.

Her father chuckled. "Better than knowing him just one day."

Jace smiled, his mouth just inches from her face. "I want us to know each other for an entire lifetime."

"Me, too," she said, closing her eyes.

Then his lips touched hers, and Delaney melted against him, and kissed him back, dreaming of the wedding, their future together, and all the other possibilities that could now be theirs—as she, her handsome hero, and Meghan all lived *happily* . . . ever . . . after.

Keep reading to check out Darlene Panzera's
second Montana Hearts romance,

MONTANA HEARTS: SWEET TALKIN' COWBOY

*Darlene Panzera continues her
heartwarming western series
with a roughed-up cowboy, the feisty girl next door,
and the deal that brings them together.*

If it wasn't for an injury to his leg, Luke Collins would
be riding rodeo broncos all day, every day. Until he heals,
he's determined to help his family's guest ranch bring in
money any way he can. But when a cranky neighbor gets
in the way of his goal, Luke turns to the only person he
knows can help: the gorgeous, rodeo-barrel-racing spitfire next door.

It's no secret: Sammy Jo's father is a pain in the neck.
But if anyone can persuade him, it's her. So when Luke
asks for help, Sammy Jo is more than willing to make a
deal with the handsome cowboy. The cost? He's gotta get
back up on that horse—with Sammy Jo's help, of course.

As teamwork reveals a deeper connection, Luke finds
himself falling for the beautiful girl next door. But to win
her heart? He'll just have to do whatever it takes.

An Excerpt from

MONTANA HEARTS: SWEET TALKIN' COWBOY

A LOUD SCUFFLE sounded from within the cabin, followed by a thud, as if something had bumped against the interior wall. Luke Collins stopped his trek down the dirt path in front to listen and wondered who or what was inside. The two unfinished cabins at the end of the row on his family's guest ranch were *supposed* to be empty.

He glanced down at his two-and-a-half-year-old niece and tightened his hold on her small hand.

"Onkle Uke, what's that?"

"What's *what*?" Luke asked, keeping his tone light to hide his alarm.

Another thud creaked the woodwork beside them.

"*That*," Meghan said, her blue eyes wide.

Luke's gut tightened as he noticed the front door had been left ajar. "Could be a squirrel," he told her. Then he remembered the other creature they'd found in a cabin the month before and forced a smile. "Or a skunk."

"Pee-yew!" Meghan said, scrunching up her nose.

Luke nodded. "Yes, skunks smell pee-yew. Stand back while I check and see."

The first of the two unfinished cabins had been framed, roofed, and sheeted with plywood; nearly complete. He stepped onto the wooden porch and adjusting his weight to his good foot, pushed the door in with the tip of his cane. Although he'd never dreamed he'd be using an old-man stick while still in his twenties, the cane *did* come in handy from time to time and provided him with a ready weapon—if ever he should need one.

The hinges on the door were new and didn't screech like some of the older cabins when opened. Luke waited a second to see if anything would run out. Nothing did, but another bump sounded on the inside wall, letting him know something was in there.

Something a whole lot larger than the creatures he'd mentioned to his niece.

A shot of adrenaline coursed through his veins and glancing over his shoulder, he told Meghan, "Go over to the garden and stay with your great-grandma for a moment."

He watched until the toddler had joined the eighty-year-old white haired woman a safe distance away. The day before, a few of the guests at Collins Country Cabins had reported seeing two men in black ski masks looking through their window while they were undressing. What if the peeping toms were holing up in *this* unfinished cabin?

Luke pressed himself against the outside wall and strained his ears to listen, but all was silent. Then, despite the limp from his left leg, he used the stealth he'd maintained from his past military training to move inside.

His first glance around the rough interior revealed a man's jacket lying on the floor. The savory scent of pepperoni pizza permeated the air. He heard a soft murmur of voices and spun toward his right, his cane raised high, ready to strike. And standing not ten feet away from him there was indeed a man . . . with his arms around his older sister.

Bree jumped away from her fiancé, Ryan Tanner, with a start. "Luke! What are you doing here?"

"My job," he said, shooting them each a grin as he lowered the cane. "Which is more than I can say for the two of you, unless you've added kissing to your list of ranch duties."

Ryan chuckled and wrapped an arm around Bree's shoulders. "Absolutely. No cowboy can work at peak performance without a few stolen kisses."

"If you say so," Luke said, unconvinced.

"I worked all morning on the finances and future bookings," Bree informed him. "And Ryan doesn't have to lead the mini round-up until tonight."

Meghan peeked her blond, double-pony-tailed head through the doorway. "No pee-yew?"

"No skunk," Luke assured her. "Just Aunt Bree and Cowboy Ryan."

"Looks like Delaney has *you* working hard," Bree teased, referring to their younger sister. "She's got you baby-sitting?"

Luke picked Meghan up with one arm and lifted her

onto his shoulders. "Del's getting ready to take a few guests on a trail ride, and Ma, Dad, and Grandma plan to take a trip into town, so Meghan's gonna watch me work. I need to finish siding this cabin and continue framing the next."

Bree gave him an earnest look. "We need the cabins finished before the Hamilton wedding in August."

"Don't I know it." His family was depending on his carpentry skills to get the job done and reminded him at every turn.

Luke couldn't blame them. As co-owners of Collins Country Cabins, they each needed the large amount of money the wedding with its 100-person guest list would bring in. Especially after their previous ranch managers fled at the beginning of the summer season with most of their cash. Their father had trusted Sue and Wade Randall, but when a fall from his horse landed him in the hospital, the couple used the opportunity to embezzle as much as they could.

"When are you going to start planning your own wedding?" Luke asked, trying to take the focus off himself.

Bree glanced at Ryan and smiled. "Sammy Jo agreed to help me plan an engagement party set for the end of next month, but the actual wedding won't be for another year."

Ryan nodded. "I tried to convince her to marry me *now*, but she says she needs time to plan out all the details."

"I just want it to be perfect," Bree said, her cheeks coloring. "And I'm hoping the Hamilton wedding will give me some good ideas. You know, I thought we could decorate all the guest cabins with white garlands and . . ."

Bree's voice trailed off and Luke watched her gaze drift toward his cane. "Of course I'll do all the decorating. I don't expect *you* to have to get up on a ladder, Luke. In fact, why don't you let Ryan and I help you right now?"

Luke stiffened. "Nope. I've got this. No offense, Bree, but you don't know the first thing about construction."

"Well, then, why don't you let *me* watch Meghan," she persisted, "so she doesn't get in your way and—"

"Trip me?" Luke frowned. "No, I promised little Meggie that she and I would spend the afternoon together."

Bree pursed her lips and her gaze drifted toward his cane again. "But it would be easier if—"

He shook his head. "The days are longer now that it's the tail-end of June. I'll get it done," he promised.

Without anyone taking pity on me.

He knew his sister didn't mean to look at him like that, but he and his siblings hadn't seen each other for close to a year before they returned to Fox Creek to help out on their family's Montana guest ranch six weeks before. And up till then, he'd kept his injury to himself.

They still weren't used to the idea he needed a cane to get around, but then again, neither was he. The sooner he got the money for the knee surgery, the better, except . . . he cringed every time he thought of being knocked out for the procedure.

Greg Quinn, one of his friends in the army, survived a horrendous helicopter crash only to die twenty-four hours later due to complications from the meds used to put him to sleep prior to surgery to remove a damaged kidney.

Luke swung Meghan off his shoulders and in one

swift move, set her back on her feet. "Like I said, I've got it handled."

"Okay, then," Bree said, her voice still hesitant. A second later she smiled. "If you *do* need help, you know where you can find us."

"Yes, I do." Luke glanced down at his niece. "We'll leave them be and work on the other cabin," he told the blond-haired cutie. "The other one's more fun anyway."

Back outside, Meghan giggled as she ran toward the open slatted two-by-fours framing up the walls of the cabin next door. "You can't catch me!"

Luke hobbled along with the help of his cane to chase after the child, but his mind remained back with Ryan and Bree.

He was happy for them. He was. They'd all grown up together and Ryan Tanner was a good man. With *money*. His family owned the Triple T cattle ranch, largest in Fox Creek, maybe largest in all of Gallatin County.

But only six weeks had passed since their father had been injured in a fall from his horse and Luke, Bree, and Delaney had come home. Only six weeks since their grandmother offered them each part of the ranch profits if they agreed to stay. Six weeks since Bree and Ryan had reunited after years of being apart—long enough for Ryan to have a seven-year-old son.

And now, as of last night, they were engaged. How crazy was that?

There was no way *he'd* ever get engaged to someone after so little time together. At least they were planning to wait a year before going through with the actual wedding. Bree said she needed time to plan but he hoped it also gave her enough time to make sure she was doing the right thing.

Of course, he had to admit she and Ryan seemed meant for each other. He glanced down at his leg. Maybe after he saved enough money and had the surgery he needed to carry his weight, he'd consider dating again. But not before then. Not until he was whole. The *last* thing he needed was for a country cowgirl to remind him with every soulful glance that he was damaged goods.

And not the hair-raising, high-flying, bronco-bustin' cowboy he used to be.

SAMMY JO MACPHERSON raised the brim of her straw hat to get a better look at the pair in front of her.

"You can't catch me," Meghan giggled again, her small body running easily through the open slats between the two-by-fours.

Luke grinned. "Oh, you don't think so?"

Meghan shook her head, making her pony-tails swing back and forth. "Noooo."

Luke pretended he couldn't find an opening big enough for him to squeeze through the beams like she had, which made Meghan laugh so hard she almost fell down backward. Then he went through the opening for the door and she squealed and ran through the vertical beams framing the future bathroom.

Sammy Jo smiled, the longing in her heart doubling at the sight of them. Luke would make a good father someday. A man tough enough to jump onto the back of a wild bronc, but tender enough to give in to the whims of a toddler.

"Can I play too?" Sammy Jo asked, her breath catching in her chest.

Luke turned his head, and when their gazes locked, the muscle along the side of his jaw jumped. "*Sammy Jo.* Aren't you a little old to play games?"

"Not if you're the one I'm playing with," she teased.

He gave her a puzzled look as if trying to figure her out. Then his expression relaxed and the corners of his mouth lifted into a welcoming grin. She smiled at him in return. She couldn't wait to spend the afternoon with him. Her cheeks warmed and her insides were already dancing around in anticipation.

Luke arched a brow. "Does your father know you're over here consorting with the enemy again?"

She laughed. "I'm a rebel. You know I don't have anything to do with my father's silly feud with your parents."

Luke glanced at his niece. "What do you say, Meghan? Should we let Sammy Jo play?"

Meghan looked at her and giggled. "You can't catch me."

"Oh yes I can, you little munchkin," Sammy Jo called out and chased her through the open framework.

"Not if I catch her first," Luke countered, and dropping his cane, he leaned down and scooped the little girl up in his arms as she ran past.

"Aaaah!" Meghan squealed with delight. "Onkle Uke got me!"

"Lucky girl," Sammy Jo said, coming to a halt beside them.

Luke held her gaze for a fraction of a second, then released the squirming toddler and glanced at the cane which lay on the floorboards between them.

Before he could ask, or do it himself, Sammy Jo bent down and retrieved the unique wood-carved stick he'd brought back with him from the Florida Keys. No doubt he'd fashioned it himself from a piece of driftwood.

"Here," she said, handing the cane back to him.

He hesitated, then reached out and took it. "Thanks."

"No problem."

But obviously, it was a problem for him. His smile disappeared and his expression sobered. And she was sure something other than the cane had passed between them. Something . . . cold.

"Do you want to talk about it?" she asked, placing a hand on his arm.

He pulled away. "Nothing to talk about."

"You know, there's a rehabilitation horse at the kids camp where I work on weekends. They said I could bring him over and let you give him a try."

"I can't ride," he said, shooting her a sharp look.

"You could," she argued. "The horse lays down for easy mounting."

She followed his gaze across the yard to the staging area where Delaney was helping some of the inexperienced greenhorn guests mount up for a trail ride.

"No," he said, shaking his head. "I don't need special assistance."

"The horse is a real sweetheart. There's nothing to fear."

"I'm not afraid," Luke said, almost cutting her off. "I'm fine the way I am."

Sammy Jo found that hard to believe. Especially coming from *him*. Luke had been one of the best riders on the rodeo circuit before he left for the military. And over the last several weeks she'd seen the way he'd encouraged his sister Bree to get back up in the saddle again. She'd seen the envy in his eyes when he watched Ryan and the guests going on the mini roundups ride out through the gate. And she'd seen the way he sat for hours in the stable, polishing the tack of his favorite horse.

He *must* want to ride again. All he needed was something to spur him into action.

A flurry of pounding hooves sped toward them, and Sammy Jo spun around and jumped when a runaway horse brushed its shoulder against the outside beam of the cabin they stood in. Her gaze fell upon the rider. A woman of medium build clung to the animal's back like a spider atop its prey. Except the woman didn't have any control. And Sammy Jo feared she'd soon be the real victim, not the horse.

"Help!" the woman cried. "He won't slow down!"

"Pull back on the reins!" Delaney shouted from across the yard, but both horse and rider disappeared out of sight.

Sammy Jo squeezed through the open-slatted woodwork and stepped onto the dirt path that stretched before the cabins lining the river. *Someone* had to go after the pair before the Collins' guest, who'd somehow managed to spook the horse, fell off and got hurt.

She glanced at Delaney, who still held the reins of two other horses tacked up for the group trail ride. Then she glanced toward Luke. For one intense moment, their gazes locked and then, in the next instant, she knew.

It wouldn't be him.

About the Author

DARLENE PANZERA WRITES sweet, fun-loving romance and is a member of the Romance Writers of America's Greater Seattle chapter. Her career launched when her novella "The Bet" was picked by Avon Books and *New York Times* bestselling author Debbie Macomber to be published within Debbie's own novel, *Family Affair*. Darlene says, "I love writing stories that help inspire people to laugh, value relationships, and pursue their dreams."

Born and raised in New Jersey, Darlene is now a resident of the Pacific Northwest, where she lives with her husband and three children. When not writing she enjoys spending time with her family and her two horses, and loves camping, hiking, photography, and lazy days at the lake.

Join her on Facebook or at www.darlenepanzera.com.

Discover great authors, exclusive offers, and more at hc.com.

Give in to your Impulses . . .
Continue reading for excerpts from
our newest Avon Impulse books.
Available now wherever ebooks are sold.

YOU'RE STILL THE ONE
RIBBON RIDGE BOOK SIX
by Darcy Burke

THE DEBUTANTE IS MINE
A SEASON'S ORIGINAL NOVEL
by Vivienne Lorret

ONE DANGEROUS DESIRE
AN ACCIDENTAL HEIRS NOVEL
by Christy Carlyle

An Excerpt from

YOU'RE STILL THE ONE
Ribbon Ridge Book Six
By Darcy Burke

College sweethearts Bex and Hayden were
once the perfect couple but is five years
enough time to heal broken hearts . . . and
give them a second chance at first love?

Ribbon Ridge, July

Hayden Archer drove into the parking lot at The Alex. The *paved* parking lot. He hadn't been home since Christmas, and things looked vastly different, including the paved lot instead of the dirt he'd been used to. The project to renovate the old monastery into a hotel and restaurant was nearly complete, and his siblings had done an amazing job in his absence.

He stepped out of his car, which he'd rented at the airport when his flight had arrived that afternoon. Someone would've picked him up, of course. If they'd known he was coming.

He smiled to himself in the summer twilight, looking forward to seeing his brothers' surprise when he burst in on Dylan Westcott's bachelor party. Hayden glanced around but didn't see anyone. They'd all be at the underground pub that Dylan had conceived and designed. It was fitting that its inaugural use would be to celebrate his upcoming wedding to their sister Sara.

Hayden could hardly wait to see the place, along with the rest of the property. But he figured that tour would have to wait until tomorrow. Tonight was for celebrating. And shocking the hell out of his family.

He made his way to the pub and immediately fell in love with what they'd done. He'd seen pictures, but being here in person gave everything a scale that was impossible to feel from half a world away.

They'd dug out the earth around the entrance to the pub and installed a round door, making it look distinctly hobbit-like. He wondered how much of that design had come from his brother Evan, and was certain Kyle's fiancée, Maggie, the groundskeeper of the entire place, had tufted the grass just so and ensured the wildflowers surrounding the entry looked as if they'd been there forever. A weathered, wooden sign hung over the door, reading: Archetype.

As he moved closer, he heard the sounds of revelry and smiled again. Then he put his hand on the wrought-iron door handle and pushed.

The noise was even louder inside, and it was nearly as dim as it had been outside. There were recessed lights in the wooden beams across the ceiling and sconces set at intervals around the space, all set to a mellow, cozy mood.

Hayden recognized most of the twenty or so people here. A few tables had been pushed together, and a handful of guys were playing some obnoxiously terrible card game while others were gathered at the bar. Kyle, one of his three brothers—the chef with the surfer good looks—stood behind it pouring drinks.

Hayden made his way to the bar, amused that no one had noticed him enter. "Beer me."

Kyle grabbed a pint glass. "Sure. What were you drinking?" He looked up and blinked. "Shit. Hayden. Am I drunk?" He glanced around before settling back on Hayden.

"Probably. Longbow if you've got it."

Kyle came sprinting around the bar and clasped him in a tight hug. He pulled back, grinning. "Look what the cat dragged in," he bellowed.

The noise faded then stopped completely. Liam, his eldest brother, or at least the first of the sextuplets born, stood up from the table, his blue-gray gaze intense. "Hayden, what the hell?" Like Kyle, his expression was one of confusion followed by joy.

"Hayden?" Evan, his remaining brother—the quiet one—leaned back on his stool at the other end of the bar. Like the others, he registered surprise, though in a far more subdued way.

"Hayden!" This exclamation came from the table near Liam and was from Hayden's best friend, Cameron Westcott. He was also the groom's half-brother.

The groom himself stood up from where he sat next to Evan. "What an awesome surprise." Dylan grinned as he hugged Hayden, and for the next several minutes he was overwhelmed with hugs and claps on the back and so much smiling that his cheeks ached.

"Why didn't you tell us you were coming?" Liam asked, once things had settled down.

Kyle had gone back behind the bar and was now pulling Hayden's beer from the tap. "Do Mom and Dad know you're here?"

Hayden looked at Liam. "Because I wanted to surprise

everyone." Then he looked at Kyle. "And no, Mom and Dad don't know." Hayden took his glass from Kyle and immediately sipped the beer, closing his eyes as the distinct wheat flavor his father had crafted brought him fully and completely home.

Kyle leaned on the bar. "Mom is going to be beside herself." He slapped the bar top. "Now this is a party!"

An Excerpt from

THE DEBUTANTE IS MINE
A Season's Original Novel
By Vivienne Lorret

USA Today bestselling author Vivienne Lorret
launches a new historical romance series featuring
the Season's Original—a coveted title awarded
by the ton's elite to one lucky debutante . . .

The Season Standard—the Daily Chronicle of Consequence.

Lilah read no farther than the heading of the newspaper in her hand before she lost her nerve.

"I cannot look," she said, thrusting the *Standard* to her cousin. "After last night's ball, I shouldn't be surprised if the first headline read, 'Miss Lilah Appleton: Most Unmarriageable Maiden in England.' And beneath it, 'Last Bachelor in Known World Weds Septuagenarian Spinster as Better Alternative.'"

Lilah's exhale crystallized in the cold air, forming a cloud of disappointment. It drifted off the park path, dissipating much like the hopes and dreams she'd had for her first two Seasons.

Walking beside her, Juliet, Lady Granworth, laughed, her blue eyes shining with amusement. Even on this dull, gray morning, she emitted a certain brightness and luster from within. Beneath a lavender bonnet, her features and complexion were flawless, her hair a mass of golden silk. And if she weren't so incredibly kind, Lilah might be forced to hate her as a matter of principle, on behalf of plain women throughout London.

"You possess a rather peculiar talent for worry, Cousin," Juliet said, skimming the five-column page.

The notion pleased Lilah. "Do you think so?"

After twenty-three years of instruction, Mother often told her that she wasn't a very good worrier. Or perhaps it was more that her anxieties were misdirected. This, Lilah supposed, was where her *talent* emerged. She was able to imagine the most absurd disasters, the more unlikely the better. There was something of a relief in the ludicrous. After all, if she could imagine a truly terrible event, then she could deal with anything less dramatic. Or so she hoped.

Yet all the worrying in the world would not alter one irrefutable fact—Lilah needed to find a husband this Season or else her life would be over.

"Indeed, I do," Juliet said with a nod, folding the page before tucking it away. "However, there was nothing here worth your worry or even noteworthy at all."

Unfortunately, Lilah knew what that meant.

"Not a single mention?" At the shake of her cousin's head, Lilah felt a sense of déjà vu and disappointment wash over her. This third and final Season was beginning on the same foot as the first two had. She would almost prefer to have been named most unmarriageable. At least she would have known that someone had noticed her.

Abruptly, Juliet's expression softened, and she placed a gentle hand on Lilah's shoulder. "You needn't worry. Zinnia and I will come up with the perfect plan."

As of yet, none of their plans had yielded a result.

Over Christmas, they had attended a party at the Duke of Vale's castle. Most of those in attendance had been unmarried young women, which had given nearly everyone the hope of marrying the duke. Even Lilah had hoped as much—at first. Yet when the duke had been unable to remember her name, she'd abruptly abandoned that foolishness. And a good thing too, because he'd married her dearest friend, Ivy, instead.

The duke had developed a *Marriage Formula*—a mathematical equation that would pair one person with another according to the resulting answer. Then, using his own formula, the duke had found his match—Ivy. As luck would have it, both Ivy and Vale had fallen deeply in love as well. Now, if only Lilah could find her own match.

"I have been considering Vale's *Marriage Formula*. All I would need to do is fill out a card." At least, that was how Lilah thought it worked. "Yet with Vale and Ivy still on their honeymoon, I do not know if they will return in time."

Then again, there was always the possibility that the equation would produce no match for her either.

Juliet's steps slowed. "Even though I couldn't be more pleased for Ivy, I'm not certain that I want to put your future happiness in the hands of an equation."

Lilah didn't need *happiness*. In fact, her requirements for marriage and a husband had greatly diminished in the past two years. She'd gone from wanting a handsome husband in the prime of his life, to settling for a gentleman of any age who wasn't terribly disfigured. She would like him to be kind to her as well, but she would accept any man who didn't bellow and rant about perfection, as her father had done.

"A pleasant conversation with someone who shares my interests would be nice, not necessarily happiness, or even love, for that matter," Lilah said, thinking of the alternative. "All I truly need is not to be forced into marriage with Cousin Winthrop."

An Excerpt from

ONE DANGEROUS DESIRE
An Accidental Heirs Novel
By Christy Carlyle

Rex Leighton dominates the boardroom by day
and prowls the ballroom at night. Searching for
the perfect bride to usher him into the aristocracy,
he abandoned the idea of love the last time he
saw the delicious May Sedgwick. But when he's
roped into a marriage bet, Rex is willing to go
all in. There's just one problem—he's competing
against the only woman he's ever loved.

The duke strode into the sitting room first, stopping and gesturing toward the American.

"My dear, you must help me convince Mr. Leighton to join us next week. And see here, sir, we can even supply a fellow countrywoman to encourage you. Miss Sedgwick, may I present Mr. Rex Leighton."

The duke was speaking, making introductions. The minuscule part of May's mind still capable of processing words and considering polite etiquette told her to curtsy or extend her hand, but she couldn't manage any of it.

A man she'd relegated to her dreams had crashed in and collided with her Thursday afternoon. Impossibly, *he* stood before her. The man she kept confined in her heart and mind. The same man, and yet so changed. He looked nothing like the poor shop clerk she'd pined for, impossibly yearned for year after year until she'd almost forgotten how to yearn for anything else. The eyes were the same mercurial brew of gold and azure, and all the angles of his face still aligned with irritating perfection, set off by a divot in the center of his chin.

That gleaming dark hair she'd once sifted through her fingers shone like rich mahogany in the afternoon light.

But his gaze was remote, impassive, as if a pane of murky glass separated them. She was the one stuck on a curio cabinet shelf, and he was coolly examining her from the other side. His clothes were those of a prosperous gentleman, not the outdated and oft-mended single suit owned by Reginald Cross. Worst was the arrogant tilt of his chin. The Reg of her memories had only ever looked at her with admiration and pleasure, what she imagined in her silly youthful way was love. No one had ever made her feel as important with a single glance.

He wasn't the same man. Couldn't be. The duke called him Leighton, not Cross. A striking resemblance. Nothing more.

May reminded herself to breathe and stepped forward to be introduced to the polished gentleman who could not be the shop boy who'd broken her heart in New York City.

Mr. Leighton took two steps forward, and her momentary grasp on composure faltered. *Reg.* His scent, the firm line of his mouth, the large, elegant hand extended toward her—they belonged to Reginald Cross. Smarter, wealthier, older, and with an abundance of confidence his younger self lacked, but still a man she'd once known. The only man she'd ever loved.

Emily touched her arm, urging May to accept his offered hand. She obeyed and moved toward him, sliding her fingers against his until their palms met. Warm. How could a memory be so warm? But he wasn't a memory. He was real. Alive. He was in London, had been for goodness knew how long, and she was meeting him in her dearest friend's sitting room. By complete and utter chance.

"A pleasure to meet you, Miss Sedgwick."

Same deep-toned voice. Same ability to raise shivers across her skin. Even when there was something silvery and practiced in his timbre, even while he still wore that placid mask.

"How do you . . ." The rest wouldn't come. May knew the words she was expected to say. Felt the gazes of Emily and her father. Sensed their discomfort at her odd behavior.

His hand tightened around hers and the glass between them shattered. He blinked, a quick fan of sable lashes, and then those unique eyes of his saw her. Not as a stranger to whom he was being introduced, but as the woman he'd held and kissed. The woman to whom he'd broken every promise he'd ever made. She detected his recognition in the tremor of his lush lower lip, felt it through the heat of his skin, read it in his blue-gold gaze that flitted from her mouth to her eyes and over each aspect of her face.

"May." He breathed the word quietly, intimately, just for her to hear, as if a duke and his daughter weren't standing nearby.

Grief, too long repressed, welled up like floodwaters, fierce and fast and just as unstoppable.

May wrenched her hand from his with a burning friction of skin against skin. When she spun around, Emily's face whirled past, a blur of confusion and concern. Moving, walking away from him, felt good. Like victory. Like strength. Like she would finally get to choose the conclusion to their tale. She needed it to end and had never gotten the satisfaction of a proper parting. She would explain her rudeness to Emily later, but for now she needed to find the mettle to keep going, to leave him as he'd left her.